ALSO BY MILTON HATOUM

The Tree of the Seventh Heaven

THE BROTHERS

THE
BROTHERS

Milton Hatoum

Translated by

John Gledson

FARRAR, STRAUS AND GIROUX

NEW YORK

Farrar, Straus and Giroux

19 Union Square West, New York 10003

Copyright © 2000 by Milton Hatoum

Translation copyright © 2002 by John Gledson

All rights reserved

Distributed in Canada by Douglas & McIntyre Ltd.

Originally published in 2000 by Companhia das Letras, São Paulo, as Dois irmãos

English translation published in 2002 by Bloomsbury, Great Britain

Published in the United States by Farrar, Straus and Giroux

First American edition, 2002

Library of Congress Cataloging-in-Publication Data

Hatoum, Milton, 1952–

[Dois irmãos. English]

The brothers / Milton Hatoum ; translated from the Portuguese by John Gledson.

p.   cm.

ISBN 0-374-14118-5 (alk. paper)

I. Gledson, John, 1945–   II. Title.

PQ9698.18.A86 D6513 2002

869.3'42—dc21

2002017054

Designed by Abby Kagan

www.fsgbooks.com

1   3   5   7   9   10   8   6   4   2

The author is grateful to the Fundação Vitae for the award
of a literature scholarship in 1988.

FOR RUTH

The house was sold with all its memories
all its furniture all its nightmares
all the sins committed, or just about to be;
the house was sold with the sound of its doors banging
with its windy corridors its view of the world its
imponderables.

CARLOS DRUMMOND DE ANDRADE

THE BROTHERS

Zana had to leave everything: the Manaus Harbor area, with its sloping street shaded by ancient mango trees, a place almost as vibrant as Biblos, the small town in Lebanon where she had spent her childhood; she recalled it out loud as she wandered through the dusty rooms, losing herself finally in the garden. There the crown of the old rubber tree shaded the palms and the orchard, which had been cultivated for more than half a century.

Near the veranda, the odors of the white lilies and her younger son mingled together. Then she would sit on the ground, praying to herself and weeping, longing for Omar to return. Before she abandoned the house, Zana saw the shadows of her father and her husband, in the nightmare of her final nights there; she felt both their presences in the room where they had slept. In the daytime I heard her repeating words from the nightmare: "They're here somewhere, my father and Halim have come to visit me . . . they're in this house"; and woe betide anyone who doubted her with a word, a gesture, or a look. She imagined the gray sofa in the room where Halim would put his hookah down to come and give her a hug, and remembered her father's voice chatting with the boatmen and fishermen in Manaus Harbor. There on the veranda she remembered her younger son's red hammock, the smell of him, the body she herself would undress in the hammock where he finished up after his nights on the town. "I know he'll come back one day," Zana said to me without looking at me, maybe not even aware of my presence; her once beautiful face was now somber and despondent. I heard the same phrase, like a muttered prayer, on the day she disappeared from the deserted house. I looked for her all over the place and only found her at nightfall, stretched out on leaves and dried-up palm fronds; the cast on her arm was dirty and splashed with bird droppings, her face puffy, her skirt and petticoats wet with urine.

I didn't see her die; I didn't want to see her die. But I heard that some days before her death, laid out on the hospital bed, she lifted her head up and asked in Arabic, so that only her daughter and her friend, herself nearly a hundred, could understand—and so that she wouldn't give herself away: "Have my sons made their peace with each other yet?" She repeated the question with all the strength left in her, the courage an anguished mother finds when death is near.

No one answered. Then Zana's smooth, almost unfurrowed face vanished; she merely turned her face to one side, searching for the only tiny window in the gray wall, where a patch of evening sky was gradually going dark.

1

When Yaqub returned from Lebanon in 1945, his father went to Rio de Janeiro to fetch him. The quay at Mauá Square, close to the center of the city, was teeming with the relatives of officers and men of the Brazilian Expeditionary Force, coming back from Italy. Brazilian flags decorated the balconies and verandas of the apartments, rockets were bursting in the sky, and wherever Halim looked, there were signs of victory. He caught sight of his son on the gangway of a ship that had just come in from Marseilles. He was no longer a boy, but a young man who had spent five of his eighteen years in southern Lebanon. His bearing was still the same: his quick, firm steps gave him a poise and stiffness unthinkable in the other, younger son.

Yaqub had grown by a good few inches. As he came down to the quay, his father compared the physique of the son just arrived with the image he'd built up in the years of separation. Yaqub was carrying a threadbare gray canvas bag, and under his green cap his large eyes were wide open, taking in the shouts and tears of the soldiers of the Brazilian Expeditionary Force.

Halim waved with both hands, but his son took a while to recognize this man in a white suit, a little shorter than he was. He had almost forgotten his father's face, his eyes, in fact everything about him. Apprehensively, Halim came up to the lad, the two exchanged glances, and then the son asked "Baba?" First came four kisses on the cheek and a long, drawn-out embrace, then the greeting in Arabic. They left the quay arm in arm and went to Cinelândia. The son recounted his journey, and his father complained of the hard times in Manaus—the poverty and hunger of the war years. In Cinelândia they sat at a café table, and amid the surrounding hubbub Yaqub opened his bag and took out a parcel; his father saw moldy bread and a box of dried figs. Was that all he'd brought from Lebanon? No letters? No presents? No, there was nothing more in the bag, no clothes, no presents, nothing! Yaqub explained in Arabic that his uncle, his father's brother, hadn't wanted him to go back to Brazil.

He stopped. Halim lowered his head, thought of mentioning the other son, and hesitated. He said: "Your mother . . ." and stopped in his turn. He saw Yaqub's tense face; then his son got up, looking harassed, and let his trousers down to piss against the bar wall, right in the middle of Cinelândia. He pissed for a long time, and was now relaxed, quite indifferent to the loud laughter of the people passing by. Halim managed to shout, "No, you shouldn't . . ." but his son either didn't understand or pretended not to.

He had to swallow his shame. That wasn't the only time: there were others, with Yaqub and the other son, Omar, the younger, the twin who had been born a few minutes later. What bothered Halim was the twins' separation, "Because you never know how they're going to react later . . ." He never stopped thinking about his sons meeting again, and how they would get on after so long apart. Since the day he left, Zana never stopped saying: "My son will come back a hillbilly, a shepherd, a *ra'i*. He'll forget Portuguese and he'll never set foot in a school; there isn't one in your family's village."

It happened a year before the Second World War, after the twins' thirteenth birthday. Halim wanted to send the two of them to southern Lebanon. Zana resisted, and managed to persuade her husband to send Yaqub on his own. For years Omar was treated as an only child, the only boy.

In the center of Rio, Halim bought clothes and a pair of shoes for Yaqub. On the journey back to Manaus he gave him a long sermon on manners: you shouldn't piss in the street, wolf your food, or spit on the floor. Yaqub said, "Yes, Baba," with his head bowed, vomiting whenever the twin-engine plane shook, his eyes deep set in his pale face, and a look of panic every time they took off or landed on the six stops between Rio de Janeiro and Manaus.

Zana had been waiting at the airport for them since early evening. She parked the green Land Rover, went up to the veranda, and stood looking east. When she saw the silvery twin-engine coming up to the head of the runway, she ran downstairs, crossed the arrivals lounge, bribed an employee, walked proudly to the plane, went up the steps, and burst into the cabin. A bouquet of heliconias she had brought fell to the floor as she embraced her pale, frightened son. She said, "My darling, my dearest, light of my life," and again, in tears, "Why did you take so long? What have they done to you?" kissing him on the face, neck, and head in front of the incredulous gaze of the crew and passengers, until Halim said, "That's enough! Now let's get off, Yaqub's done nothing but throw up, next thing we'd have had his guts all over the floor." But she wouldn't stop caressing him, and got down from the plane holding onto her son; down the stairs she went and into the arrivals hall, radiant, full of herself, as if she had finally gotten part of her life back: the twin who had gone away through Halim's whim or obstinacy. What was more, for some incomprehensible reason she had let it happen, whether out of passion or sheer folly, a blind, uncontrollable devotion, or all those things rolled together; either she didn't know what to call it, or didn't want to know.

Now he was back: as handsome and tall as the other son, the younger one. They had the same angular face, the same big chestnut eyes and black, wavy hair; they were exactly the same height. After he laughed Yaqub let out a sigh, just like his brother. Distance had not removed certain tics and common mannerisms, but Yaqub had forgotten certain words in Portuguese. He didn't say much, only uttering monosyllables or short phrases; when he could, he kept quiet—sometimes, when he should have said something.

Zana saw straightaway. She saw her son smile, sigh, and avoid words, as if surrounded by a paralyzing silence.

On the road home from the airport Yaqub recognized a part of his Manaus childhood; with a jolt, he saw the brightly painted boats moored along the creeks where he and his brother and father had rowed their straw-roofed canoe. Yaqub looked at his father and only managed to stammer out some jumbled noises.

"What's happened?" asked Zana. "Have they ripped your tongue out?"

"*La*, no, Mama," he said; he couldn't take his eyes off this scene from a childhood that had come to such a sudden, untimely end.

The boats, and the children running back and forth across the beach when the river dried up; trips to the Careiro on the other side of the river Negro, when they would come back with baskets full of fruit and fish. He and his brother would run into the house, chasing through the back garden, hunting lizards with a slingshot. When it rained, the two of them climbed into the rubber tree at the back of the house, and Omar climbed higher. He was more adventurous, and made fun of his brother, who swayed back and forth in the middle of the tree, hidden in the leaves, holding onto the thickest branch, shaking with fear and afraid of losing his balance. He could hear Omar's voice: "I can see everything from here, come on, come up." Yaqub didn't move, didn't even look up; gingerly, he got down and waited for his brother: he didn't want to be told off on his own. He had hated being scolded by Zana when they had run outside on mornings of torrential rain, and Omar, with only his shorts on, covered in mud, plunged into the creek near the prison. They could see the prisoners' hands and their silhouettes, and he listened to his brother jeering and swearing, with no idea of who he was insulting: whether it was the prisoners, or the kids helping their mothers, aunties, or grandmothers get the clothes off the lines tied to the stilts of the shacks built out over the mud.

No, he certainly hadn't the energy to follow his brother—nor the courage. He was angry with himself and with Omar when he saw his brother's arm around the neck of a boy from the slum at the back of the house. He felt angry at his own powerlessness, and shook with fear and cowardice when he saw Omar challenge three or four stocky youngsters, taking their punches and giving as good as he got, swearing furiously. Yaqub hid, but he couldn't help admire Omar's courage. He wanted to fight like Omar, feel his own face swollen too, the taste of blood in his mouth, the stinging of his grazed lip, and the bruises on his head and face; he wanted to run barefoot, unafraid of the hot road surface scorched by the afternoon sun, or jump up and grab the kite's string or its tail, as it sailed upwards in slow circles. Omar crouched down and leapt up, twirled in the air like an acrobat, fell on his feet, and let out a war whoop, showing off his scratched hands. Yaqub flinched when he saw his brother's hands full of blood, cut by the mixture of wax and ground glass on the kite string meant for cutting the strings of rivals.

Yaqub was no acrobat; he didn't smear his hands with wax, but he did have a good time at the Carnival balls at Sultana Benemou's house; Omar went to the adults' party and stayed up all night with the merrymakers. Yaqub was thirteen, and it was as if his childhood had come to an end at that last ball at the Benemous' mansion. That night he'd not even dreamed that two months later he would be separated from his parents, his country, and this landscape that now breathed new life into his face as he sat in the front seat of the Land Rover.

The young people's ball had started before nightfall. At ten o'clock, the grown-ups in their fancy dress came into the room singing, dancing, and shooing the youngsters out. Yaqub wanted to stay till midnight, because a fair-haired niece of the Reinoso family, a fine tall girl, was going to stay too and dance into the early hours of Ash Wednesday. It was Lívia's first night at the grown-ups' party, and the first time Yaqub had seen her with lipstick on, lids shaded with black eyeliner, her braids scattered with sequins that made her tanned arms flicker with light. He wanted to stay to dance, hold her, and feel he was almost an adult too. He was just summoning the courage to go up to Lívia when Zana's voice ordered: "Take your sister home. You can come back later." He did as he was told. He took Rânia to her room, waited till she was asleep, and raced back to the Benemous' house. The room was bursting with revelers; amid all the colors and masks he saw the shining braids and painted lips, then went weak at the knees when he saw a face and hair just like his own, right next to the face he admired.

Lívia and his brother were dancing in one corner of the room. They were silently entwined, with a rhythm all their own that had nothing to do with Carnival. Whenever revelers bumped into them, their two faces met; then their laughter did suit the occasion. Yaqub glowered. He hadn't the courage to go up and speak to her. He hated the dance. "I hated all the music they played, I hated the masks, I hated it all," Yaqub said to Domingas on Ash Wednesday afternoon. He didn't sleep a wink. He pretended to be dozing when his brother came into the room at daybreak, as Carnival tunes and drunken shouts filled the Manaus air. With his eyes closed, he could smell the

perfume squirted by the revelers, and the sweat, the two bodies
wrapped around each other, and he sensed his brother sitting on the
floor looking at him. Yaqub lay there quiet, apprehensive, defeated.
He saw his brother go slowly out of the room, his hair and shirt covered with confetti and streamers, and a contented smile on his face.

It was his last Carnival party, the last morning he saw his brother
coming in from a spectacular night out. He didn't understand why
Zana never reproached Omar, and he didn't understand why it was
he, not his brother, who went to Lebanon two months later.

Now the Land Rover was going around Nossa Senhora dos
Remédios Square, getting near the house, and he didn't want to
remember the day he had left. He had gone alone, in the care of a
family of friends who were going to Lebanon. Yes, why him and not
Omar, he wondered, staring at the mango trees and *oitizeiros* over-
hanging the street, and those huge clouds, motionless, as if painted
on a blue background, taking in the smell of the childhood street,
the gardens, the humid heat of the Amazon, the sight of the neighbors leaning out of their windows, his mother caressing his neck,
her gentle voice saying: "We're home, love . . ."

Zana got out of the jeep and looked in vain for Omar. Rânia was on
the veranda, beautifully dressed and perfumed.

"Is he here? Has my brother come yet?" She ran to the door, and
there saw a timid young man, taller than his father, holding his battered canvas bag and now looking at her for the first time as a young
woman, not the skinny little girl he had embraced on the Manaus
Harbor quay. He didn't know what to say: he dropped the bag and
opened his arms to enfold her slim body, lengthened by her dignified
pose; her slightly upturned chin gave her an air of self-confidence,
perhaps a little distant or standoffish. Rânia was hypnotized by her
brother's presence: an almost perfect replica of the other, without
being him. She observed him, trying to find something that would

differentiate him from Omar. She looked at him closely, very closely, from several angles; she saw that the greatest difference was his silence. However, she heard her brother asking, "Where's Domingas?" in a mature voice, and saw him walk to the garden and embrace the woman there waiting for him. They went into the little room where Domingas and Yaqub had once played. He saw the drawings he had done as a child up on the wall—the houses, the buildings, the colorful bridges—and he saw the pencil for his first writing exercises and the yellowed notebook that Domingas had kept, and now handed to him as if she was his mother, not the maid.

Yaqub lingered in the garden, then paid a visit to every room, familiarizing himself again with the furniture and objects there; he was overcome as he went into his bedroom. On the wall he saw a photograph: himself and his brother sitting on a tree trunk over a creek. Both of them were laughing: Omar, mockingly, his arms stretched upwards; Yaqub, his laughter checked and his hands grasping the trunk, looking apprehensively into the dark waters. When was that photo from? It had been taken a little before or maybe a little after the last Carnival party in the Benemous' mansion. In the background of the picture, at the edge of the creek, were the neighbors, whose faces seemed to be as blurred in the photo as they were in Yaqub's memory. On the writing desk he saw another photograph: his brother sitting on a bicycle, his cap cocked on one side, with shiny boots, and a watch on his wrist. Yaqub went closer and scrutinized the photograph to see his brother's features, his brother's look, and got a shock when he heard a voice: "Omar will be coming in at nightfall, he's promised to have dinner with us."

It was Zana's voice; she had followed in Yaqub's footsteps and wanted to show him the sheet and pillowcases where she had embroidered his name. As soon as she knew when he was coming back, Zana repeated every day: "My boy is going to sleep with my words, my lettering." She said this in Omar's presence; jealously, he would ask: "When's he coming back? Why has he stayed in Lebanon so long?" Zana didn't answer him, perhaps because she too was unable to explain why Yaqub had spent so many years far from her side.

She had furnished Yaqub's room with a rocking chair, a mahogany wardrobe, and a bookcase with the eighteen volumes of an encyclopedia Halim had bought from a retired magistrate. A vase of caladiums decorated one corner of the room, near the open window overlooking the street.

Leaning on the sill, Yaqub watched the passersby going up the street towards Remédios Square. He could see carts, one or two cars, peddlers sounding their metal triangles; on the sidewalk, there were chairs in semicircles in readiness for conversation at nightfall; on the windowsills, candle stubs would later provide light in the darkened city. This had been the way during the war years: Manaus in the dark, and its inhabitants elbowing one another in front of the butchers and grocery stores, fighting over a piece of meat, a packet of rice, beans, salt, or coffee. Electricity was rationed, and an egg was worth its weight in gold. Zana and Domingas got up early each morning, and the maid waited for the coal man while her mistress went to the Adolpho Lisboa Market; then the two of them did the ironing, prepared dough, and cooked. When he was lucky, Halim managed to buy the canned meat and wheat flour the American planes brought to Amazonia. Sometimes he would get food in exchange for unsold cloth: frayed madras or plain cotton cloth, soiled lace, and suchlike.

Around the table they talked about these things: the war years, the wretched encampments in the suburbs of Manaus, where former rubber tappers flooded in. Yaqub, silent, listened attentively, drumming his fingers on the wood, nodding in agreement, happy to be able to understand the words, the sentences, the stories told by his mother and father, with now and then an observation from Rânia.

Yaqub understood. The words of the language, its syntax, its lilt, everything seemed to come back. He ate, drank, and listened, on the alert; he was immersed in this reconciliation with his family, but short of certain Portuguese words. He missed them when the neighbors came to see him. Yaqub was kissed by Sultana, by Talib and his two daughters, by Estelita Reinoso. Someone said he was more standoffish than his brother. Zana disagreed: "Not at all, they're the same, they're twins, they've got the same body and the same heart." He smiled, and this time his hesitation before speaking the half-forgotten language and the fear of saying something stupid were heaven-sent. He unwrapped the presents, saw the smart clothes, the leather belt, the wallet with his initials in silver. He fingered the wallet and slipped it into the pocket of the trousers Halim had bought him in Rio.

"Poor thing! *Ya haram ash-shum!*" said Zana. "They mistreated him in that village."

She looked at her husband.

"I can imagine what he looked like when he got to Rio. Just look at the luggage he brought! A foul-smelling old bag! Isn't it dreadful?"

"Let's change the subject," said Halim. "Bags and old clothes are soon forgotten."

They changed subject and expression: Zana's face lit up when she heard a long whistle—a sign, or token, that the other son had come. He was dressed in white linen trousers and a blue shirt, damp with sweat on his chest and armpits. Omar went over to his mother, opened his arms to her, as if he were the absent son, and she greeted him so effusively that it seemed to negate the homage to Yaqub. They stayed that way, her arms clasped around Omar's neck, absorbed in a complicity that made Yaqub jealous and Halim worried.

"Thanks for the party," he said, his voice tinged with cynicism. "Any food left over for me?"

"Isn't my Omar a tease?" Zana tried to undo what he had said, kissing his eyes. "Yaqub, come here and embrace your brother."

The two looked at each other. Yaqub took the initiative: he got up, gave a forced smile. The scar on his left cheek changed his expression. They didn't embrace. A small tuft of gray hair stuck out from Yaqub's curls, but what really differentiated them was the pale, half-moon scar on Yaqub's face. The two brothers looked at one another. Yaqub took one step forward, and Halim smoothed things over, talking of the exhausting journey, the years of separation; from now on, though, life would improve. Everything improves when wars end.

Talib agreed; Sultana and Estelita proposed a toast to the end of the war, and Yaqub's return. Neither joined in: the tinkling glasses and the restrained euphoria had no effect on the twins. Yaqub merely held out his right hand and greeted his brother. They barely spoke, and this was all the more strange in that when they were together, they looked like the same person.

It was Domingas who told me the story of the scar on Yaqub's cheek. She thought an insignificant jealous spat had caused the attack. She always watched the twins' smallest movements, listened to conversations, spying on everyone's privacy. She was able to do this because the family's meals, and the shine on the furniture, were her department.

My story, too, depends on her, on Domingas.

It was a cloudy Saturday, soon after Carnival. The children in the street were getting ready to spend the afternoon in the Reinosos' house, where they were awaiting an itinerant film projectionist. On the last Saturday in each month, Estelita told the mothers in the neighborhood that a film would be shown in her house. It was a real event. The children had lunch early, dressed and perfumed themselves, and went out dreaming of the images they were to see on the white wall of Estelita's basement.

Yaqub and Omar wore linen suits and bow ties; they were exactly alike, with the same haircut and the same scent of essence of Pará sprinkled on their clothes. Domingas, arm in arm with both, also had to spruce herself up to accompany them. Omar tore away, ran on, and was the first to kiss Estelita's cheek and give her a bouquet of flowers. In the drawing room, Zahia and Nahda Talib were chatting with Lívia, a niece of the Reinosos, a big girl with blondish hair; two children from a family that lived in the Seringal Mirim neighborhood were serving *guaraná* and biscuits made with Brazil nuts to the guests. They were awaiting the projectionist, and the minutes dragged by; they couldn't wait to sit face to face with the white basement wall, and see the story, of adventure or romance, that transformed Saturday into the most anxiously anticipated moment of the week. Then heavy, dark clouds began to close in, and Abelardo Reinoso decided to turn the generator on. In the brightness of the room, a battalion of toy soldiers was arranged on the table, and foreign stamps passed from hand to hand, with their tiny pictures of landscapes, faces, and faraway flags. The big girl with the blond hair admired a particularly rare stamp, and her arms brushed against the twins'. She stroked the stamp with her index finger, while the other boys amused themselves with the green battalion, and she seemed attracted to the scent surrounding the twins. Lívia smiled at one, then the other, and this time, said Domingas, it was Omar's turn to get jealous. He made a face, took off his bow tie, unbuttoned his collar, and rolled up his sleeves. Then he snorted, making an effort to be polite. He stammered: "Should we go out in the garden?"; still looking at the stamp, she said: "But it's going to rain, Omar. Just listen to the thunder." Then she took a stamp out of the album and offered it to Yaqub. Omar really hated that, Domingas said; he hated seeing his brother's fingers playing cat's cradle with Lívia's. She was no fool. A forward girl with an artless smile, she attracted the twins along with all the boys in the neighborhood whenever she climbed the mango tree; around the trunk a swarm of boys lifted up their heads and followed the rippling of her red shorts with their eyes. But the ones she really liked were the twins; she looked coyly at both; sometimes, when she was distracted, she would look at Yaqub as if he had something the other didn't. Yaqub was a little shy; did he notice? Omar thought that after the dance at the Benemous' house Lívia would have a bite at the apple, and would be seen with him at the matinees at the Guarany or the Odeon. He had already promised to steal his parents' Land Rover and take her on a trip to the waterfalls at Tarumã. Zana suspected something, and hid the key to the jeep, taking the wind out of his sails. Lívia and Yaqub were holding hands, and Omar had already moved away when the projectionist arrived. In his leather case were the projector and the roll of film. He was tall and unhurried, with a thin face divided in two by an enormous mustache: "Roll up for the big show, kids! See all your dreams come true!"

Stamps, soldiers, and cannons were forgotten. The lively music on the record player was switched off. An old clock struck four times. The rush down the wooden staircase made the house shake, and in no time the basement was alive with shouting, as people fought over the front-row seats. Yaqub kept a place for Lívia, and Omar, with a look, showed his disapproval of this polite move. From the darkness there emerged black-and-white pictures, and the monotonous sound of the projector underlined the afternoon silence. Domingas said goodbye to the Reinosos. The magic of the dark basement lasted some twenty minutes. Then a breakdown in the generator effaced the images, someone opened a window, and the audience saw Lívia's lips pressed to Yaqub's cheek. Next there was a sound of chairs pushed to the ground, the crash of a bottle breaking, and Omar's furious, quick, well-aimed thrust. The silence lasted for some seconds. And then came Lívia's cry of panic as she saw Yaqub's torn cheek. The Reinosos came down the stairs, and Abelardo's voice drowned the hubbub. Omar was panting, leaning against the white wall, with the piece of dark glass in his right hand, and his gleaming eyes fixed on his brother's bloodied face.

Estelita took the victim upstairs and called one of the house-boys: "Go to Zana's house and call Domingas, but don't say what's happened."

The scar was already beginning to grow in Yaqub's body: the scar, the pain, and a feeling he didn't show, and perhaps didn't even understand. They didn't speak to each other again. Zana blamed Halim for the lack of a firm hand in the twins' education. He didn't agree: "It's nothing to do with that; you treat Omar as if he were our only son."

She wept when she saw Yaqub's face, said Domingas. She kissed his right cheek over and over and wept bitterly when she saw the other cheek swollen, with its semicircle of stitches. Sewn with black thread, it looked like a tarantula's leg. Quietly, Yaqub reflected. He avoided speaking to his brother. Did he despise him? Was he silently brooding over his humiliation?

"Scorpion-face," they said at school. "Sickle-cheek." There were lots of nicknames, new ones every morning. He swallowed these insults and never reacted. His parents had to put up with a silent son. They feared Yaqub's revenge, and feared for the worst: violence in the home. That was when Halim decided on the journey and the separation. Distance would be sure to extinguish the hatred, the jealousy, and the act that had given rise to them.

Yaqub left for Lebanon with his father's friends and came back to Manaus five years later—alone. "A hick, a shepherd, a *ra'i*. Just look at the way my son eats!" Zana complained.

She tried to forget the scar, but distance brought Yaqub's face even closer. What letters she wrote!

Dozens? Hundreds, maybe. Five years of words. No replies. The little news she got about Yaqub's life was transmitted by friends or acquaintances coming back from Lebanon. A cousin of Talib's who had visited Halim's family had caught sight of him in the basement of a house. He was alone, reading a book, sitting on the ground, beside a pile of dried figs. The boy tried to speak to him, in Arabic and Portuguese, but Yaqub paid no attention. Zana spent the night putting the blame on Halim, and threatened to go to Lebanon, even with the war on. Then he wrote to his relatives and sent the money for Yaqub's passage.

That was what Domingas told me. However, I also saw a lot of what happened, because I watched this little world from the outside. Yes, from outside, and sometimes from a distance. But I was the observer of this game, and I was present at many of the moves, until the final outcome.

In the first months after Yaqub's arrival, Zana tried her best to give both sons equal attention. Rânia meant much more than I did, but even so, less than the twins. For example: I slept in a small room built in the garden, separate from the house. Rânia slept in a small bedroom, but on the first floor. The twins slept in similar rooms, adjacent to one another, with the same furniture; they got the same monthly allowance, the same pocket money, and both of them went to the Salesian college. It was a privilege: it also caused trouble.

The two of them left for school early; anyone who saw them from a distance, walking along together in their uniforms starched by Domingas, would think that the two brothers were reconciled forever. Yaqub, who had lost a few years' schooling in Lebanon, was like a beanpole in a room full of pygmies. Zana was afraid he would piss in the schoolyard, eat with his hands in the refectory, or kill a kid and bring it back home. Nothing like that happened. He was shy, and maybe that was why people thought he was a coward. He was too ashamed to speak: *p*'s turned into *b*'s ("Yes blease, baba!" "What a bity!"); he was an object of mockery from his fellow pupils, and from some of the teachers who thought he was uncouth and strange: like a badly made pot. But he also attracted looks from the girls. One thing he did know how to do was look—straight in the eye, fearlessly, raising his left eyebrow: shy he might be, but you could see the ladies' man. He smiled, and chuckled, beautifully timing it to draw a sigh from the girls congregated in the squares, and at dances in clubs and in the open air. At home, Zana was the first to notice her son's taste for flirting. Domingas, too, fell under the spell of that look. She said: "He's got the dolphin's eye; if you let him, he'll carry everyone off to the bottom of the river." But he didn't carry anyone to the enchanted city. The spell of his eyes left hopes and promises in the air. Zana had to put up with the local girls who laid siege to her son. They sent notes and messages via the manicurist. She read these words of supplication with an almost cruel pleasure, safe in the knowledge that her Yaqub wouldn't succumb to verses copied from the Romantic poets. Shut in his room, he spent whole nights studying Portuguese grammar; over and over again, he repeated words he'd pronounced wrong: *atoníto* instead of *atônito*. Where to put the stress: it was a terrible problem for Yaqub. Slowly he learned, spelling out the words, chanting them, until the fishes, plants, and fruits, all with their indigenous names, no longer stuck in his throat. Even so, he was never exactly chatty. He was the quietest one in the house and the street, reticent as could be. Inside this laconic, tongue-tied twin, a mathematician was taking root. His talent for abstraction, calculation, and working with numbers more than made up for what was missing in his ability to use the language.

"You don't need a tongue for that, just a brain," his father said, proudly. "His brother might be short that way, but Yaqub's got plenty and to spare."

Omar heard those words, and heard them again years later, when Yaqub, in São Paulo, told his family that he'd got into the Polytechnic School (the Bolytechnic, Baba, he wrote, jokingly); he was top of the list. Zana smiled in triumph, as Halim said repeatedly: "Didn't I tell you? Brains, intelligence, that's what Yaqub's got plenty of."

He was a mathematician, and a proud young man, guarded and trusting in no one; the chess player who, on the sixth move, wrapped the game up and whistled like a bird, in an aimless, guttural fashion, with the cornered king already in his sights. He would beat his opponent, emitting this rather irritating whistle, the sure harbinger of checkmate. Days and nights he spent in his room, never going for a plunge in the creeks, not even on Sundays, when the people of Manaus come out in the sun and the city makes its peace with the river Negro. Zana was worried about this hermit, stuck in his cell. Why didn't he go to the dances? "Look at your son, Halim, hidden away in a hole like that. If he goes on that way, he'll get mildewed." His father couldn't understand why he was giving up on his youth, the noisy parties and serenading that echoed through the Amazonian nights.

What nights? Forget it! Proud in his solitude, he despised the Carnival balls, which in the years after the war were even crazier. The parades with their Harlequins and Columbines left from the Praça da Saudade and went down the avenue in a mad frenzy to the Municipal Market; he despised the midwinter festivals with their native *tipiti* dances, the boat races, the parties on board the Italian ships, and the football matches in the Parque Amazonense. He shut himself in his room and lived in his own world, closed off from anyone else. Was he a shepherd, a hillbilly terrified of the city? Maybe, or perhaps something more: he was a tough peasant plotting a brilliant future for himself.

Yaqub, going pale like a chameleon on a damp wall, made up for keeping out of the sun and not exercising his body by honing his ability to calculate and do equations. At school, he was always the first to find the value of z, y, or x. He had his teachers baffled: the most complex equations would be worked out in Yaqub's head; chalk and blackboard were of no use to him.

Omar, on the other hand, went overboard in his youthful escapades; he played truant from his Latin lessons, bribed the po-faced school porters, and went out for the night disguised from head to toe, the complete delinquent. He went around the dance halls of the Maloca dos Barés, the Acapulco, the Sheik Club, the Shangri-la. In the early morning, when the last mists of the night were lifting, he came back home. There was Zana, impassive in her red hammock, a surface serenity on her face; at bottom she was tormented, grieved at having spent another night without her son. Omar could hardly make out her curved shape, suspended on the veranda. He went straight to the bathroom, brought up the night's drinking in one spasm after another, then staggered as he tried to go up the stairs; sometimes he completely fell over, his heavy body bathed in sweat, unconscious of what the night had done. Then, she would get out of her hammock, drag her son's body to the veranda, and wake Domingas up: the two of them then took his clothes off, cleaned him with alcohol, and settled him in his hammock. Omar slept until midday. His face swollen, parched by his hangover, gruffly he would ask for ice-cold water, and off went Domingas with the pitcher. She poured the liquid into his open mouth; first he gargled, then swallowed it like a thirsty jaguar. It got on Halim's nerves; he hated his son's smell, which infected the sacrosanct places where they took their meals. His father prowled around the room, crossing it obliquely and glancing at the red hammock on the veranda.

One day when Omar spent the whole afternoon in his underpants lying in the hammock, his father nudged him, lowered his voice, and said: "Aren't you ashamed of carrying on like this? Do you mean to spend your whole life in that filthy hammock, with a face on you like that?" Halim was getting ready to mete out some exemplary punishment, but Omar's insolence only increased when his father was involved. He wasn't bothered; it was as if he had done nothing wrong, and was free of any guilt. But he did get a black mark: he flunked two years running at school. His father took him to task, using his brother as an example, and Omar, though he kept quiet, seemed to be saying: "Go to hell! They can all go to hell, I'm living my life the way I want to."

That was what he shouted when he was expelled from school. He shouted several times in front of his father, daring him to do anything as he ripped up his blue uniform and taunted him: "I landed one on the math master that teaches your blue-eyed boy, the one who's all brains and nothing else."

Zana and Halim were called in by the headmaster. She went alone, with Domingas, her servile shadow. She let him have it right in the eye. Didn't you know my Omar was ill when he was an infant? He nearly died, Father. Only God knows . . . only his mother and God . . . She was sweating, reveling in her role as the great protective mother. They heard the bell ring six times, and the commotion and shouting of the boarders on their way to the refectory, then silence, and then again her voice, calmer, not so much the innocent victim. How many of the orphans in this school eat at our expense, Father? And what about the Christmas dinners, the charity bazaars, and the clothes we send to the Indian girls in the mission stations?

Domingas was fanning her mistress's body. The headmaster let her give vent to her feelings, looked outside into the warm dusk that was beginning to hide the huge Salesian college. There were goats feeding in the college yard. The orphan children, in uniform, were playing on a seesaw; their bodies, perched in midair, gradually melted into the night. He opened a drawer and gave Zana Omar's school record and a copy of the ruling expelling him. He showed her the medical report on the health of Father Bolislau, the math master. He understood a wounded mother's indignation, and the excessive energy and rashness of some young people, but this time it had been inevitable. It was the only expulsion in the last ten years. Then the headmaster asked about the other son, Yaqub. Would he be staying on?

She stammered, confused; her eyes rested on the seesaw, now empty. The view from the window was going dark; the night came inside the room. She was thinking about her son's penchant for math. The shepherd, the country boy, the genius with numbers, who promised to be the brains of the family. She put the reply off and suddenly got up, half bitter, half optimistic, saying to Domingas a phrase she would repeat later, like a prayer: "Hope and bitterness . . . are alike."

In her old age, which could have been less melancholy, she repeated this several times to Domingas, her faithful slave, and to me, without looking at me, unconcerned whether I was there or not. The truth is that, for Zana, I only existed as an echo of her sons' world.

Omar, after his expulsion, was finally taken on by a school in Manaus where, years later, I was to study. It had a pompous name—the Rui Barbosa Lyceum, named after the "Eagle of The Hague"—but its nickname was much less edifying: The Vandals' Cockpit.

Nowadays, I think the nickname wasn't right, and was just a bit prejudiced. The Lyceum wasn't a completely worthless school; there was an atmosphere of daring that flouted the norm and scared conventional people. The scum of Manaus frequented it, and I was carried along by the mass of half-wits. No one there was *très raisonnable*, in the words of the French master, himself an eccentric, a dandy exiled to the provinces, who recited symbolist poets, and ended up merely aping his own eccentricity. He didn't teach grammar; instead he recited, in his baritone, the illuminations and green snows of the French symbolist he adored the most. Who was going to understand these refulgent images? Everyone succumbed to the enchantment of his voice, and someone, in a flash, would grasp something, feel a spark, and lose his bearings. After the "class," in front of the Café Mocambo, he would intone the praises of Diana, the bronze goddess, elegantly beautiful in the Praça das Acácias. These tributes then passed from the goddess to a girl in uniform, completely Indian, with a coppery complexion, and bursting with desire; the two of them together would slip away from the Mocambo, and disappear into the night, in the unlit city.

This master, Antenor Laval, was the first to welcome the new pupil, just expelled from the Brothers' school. He was delighted, and wanted to know what the reason for this summary expulsion was. Omar didn't hide the true version from anyone: it was the most insubordinate, the vilest act in the whole history of the Salesian missions in Amazonia, he said. He told everyone the story. He told it in front of the pupils in the Vandals' Cockpit, in a loud voice, laughing when he said that the Polish priest who had humiliated him could only eat soup, and would never be able to chew his food again. It had happened in the math teacher's class; Bolislau was a red-faced giant with an athlete's build, always in his black, greasy, sweaty cassock. His sadistic eyes looked for a victim, and fixed on Omar. Bolislau asked a really difficult question, and, when he got no answer, made a mockery of him. Omar got up, went to the blackboard, stood there in front of giant Bolislau, and gave him a punch on the jaw and a kick in the balls: fearsome blows that made poor Bolislau double up like a hunchback and reel around like a falling top. He didn't cry out; he grunted. His pale eyes, wet with tears, bulged out in his ashen face. There was a commotion in the room, and laughter, some nervous, some delighted, before silence fell, and the headmaster came in with his posse of monitors.

Omar had not forgotten the humiliation of a previous punishment: he had had to kneel at the foot of a Brazil-nut tree, from midday until the first star could be seen in the sky. The boarders had taunted him, surrounding the tree and shouting: "What if it rains, eh, tough guy? What if a tree-porcupine falls on your head?" Insults came from every side, while the figure of Bolislau loomed in the victim's sight, twisted and loathsome. It didn't rain, but in the dim evening sky, the first twinkle took a long time to appear. Omar, still buoyed up by his vengeance, said to his mother: "He-man Bolislau saw every star in the sky, Mamma. And there wasn't even any sky. That's a miracle, isn't it? Seeing a constellation without a sky?"

This time, Omar really had gone too far. This episode had shaken his mother's pride: her pride, not her faith. She considered her son's expulsion unjust, but God had so willed it; after all, even God's ministers are fallible. "That Bolislau did something wrong," she muttered. "My son only wanted to prove he's a man . . . what's wrong with that?"

She didn't want to see her son as the aggressor. In the Vandals' Cockpit there were no demands made on the pupils; the masters didn't take roll call; flunking was a real achievement, a privilege attained by very few. Green trousers (any color of green) and a white shirt were the only uniform required. The real scum in the

Cockpit were after a diploma, a stamped, signed piece of paper, with a green-and-yellow border around the top corner.

That was what I was going to get: the diploma from the Vandals' Cockpit, the evidence of my freedom from servitude. Unknown to me, Halim put into my room the schoolbooks that Omar despised, and the many books that Yaqub left behind when he left for São Paulo, in January 1950.

Yaqub's departure was providential for me. Apart from his used books, he left old clothes that would fit me years later: three pairs of trousers, several vests, two shirts with frayed collars, and two worn-out pairs of shoes. When he left for São Paulo, I was about four, but his clothes waited for me to grow up, and gradually fit my body; the trousers were loose and looked like sacks, and the shoes, which would later be a little tight, were pushed onto my feet, partly by sheer determination, and even more out of necessity. Bodies are flexible. Yaqub, however, showed his own inflexibility when he confronted his mother's resistance and informed them, at Christmas 1949, that he was leaving Manaus. He said this point-blank, finally translating into action an idea he had repeatedly turned over in his mind. Nobody had had wind of his plans; he was evasive in his replies, elusive even in small day-to-day things, and indifferent to the devilments of his brother, still running loose in the Vandals' Cockpit.

Yaqub revealed almost nothing about his life in southern Lebanon. Rânia, impatient with her brother's silence and this piece of buried past, needled him with questions. He covered his tracks. He would say, laconically: "I looked after the flock. I was the one responsible for the flock. That's all." When Rânia pushed him, he became sharp, almost intractable; he was no longer his usual open, proud self—perhaps he took on something of the roughness he had cultivated in the village. However, something had happened when he was a shepherd. Maybe Halim knew, but no one, not even Zana, ever got that secret out of him. Nothing: Yaqub let nothing out. He pulled back, withdrawing into his cocoon at the strategic moment. Sometimes, when he emerged, he could be surprising.

One morning in August 1949, the twins' birthday, Omar asked for money and a new bicycle. Halim gave him the bicycle, knowing that his wife secretly filled her son's pockets with coins.

Yaqub refused the money and the bicycle. He asked for a gala uniform for Independence Day. It was his last year at the college, and now he was going to parade with the others, with a sword by his side. He was already smart in mufti, so you can just imagine how he looked in his white uniform with gold buttons, his epaulettes decorated with stars, his leather belt with a silver buckle, his spats and white gloves, and the shining sword he gripped in front of the mirror in the drawing room. His mother, dazzled, didn't know whether she was looking at her son or his image. Perhaps she had eyes for both of them, or rather all three, because from the veranda Omar was looking at the spectacle from his bicycle, a slightly dopey look on his face, and a strange smile, whether of resentment or mockery there was no way of knowing. He took no notice of the parade, or of Independence. Halim preferred to take advantage of the holiday to stay at home in peace. He urged Zana to stay with him and let their son march and parade as much as he liked, but she wanted the thrill of seeing Yaqub in uniform in the middle of the Avenida Eduardo Ribeiro.

The women of the house rushed eagerly to admire the soldier. They were there from the crack of dawn to get a place near to where the bands and regiments passed by. They took straw hats, pineapple juice, and a bag full of *tucuma* nuts. They waited for three hours in the hot September sun. They watched the march-past of the Infantry Battalion, with its armored cars, bazookas, and bayonets, and the soldiers with their jaguar mascots in the scorching sun.

They heard the drumrolls and the music of the brass in a stirring crescendo; the band, as yet invisible, thundered louder and louder, a cadenced roar echoing out in the middle of Manaus. The crowd turned to look at the top of the avenue. Zana was the first to make out a white figure brandishing a gleaming sword. The figure advanced slowly; the rhythmic steps divided the avenue in two. The swordsman was marching in front of the band and the eight platoons, on his own, in the midst of claps and whistles. They threw white lilies and wildflowers at him; he stepped on them without compunction, concentrating on the rhythm of the march, ignoring the blown kisses and the wisecracks coming from the women watching, and not even winking at Rânia. He looked at no one: he paraded by, looking for all the world like the only son he wasn't. Yaqub, the man of few words, let appearances speak for him—appearances and the press; the next day a paper published his photograph, with a few well-chosen lines of praise.

For months, Zana showed off this paragraph about the handsome swordsman she had produced. The sword flashed in the newspaper photograph, though time dulled its metallic glint; but the image of the weapon with its pointed end remained. The complimentary words about her son might as well fade away, for all Zana cared; she already had them by heart.

Yaqub all the time had been thinking about moving to São Paulo. It was Father Bolislau who advised him to go. "Get out of Manaus," the math master had said. "If you stay here, you'll be ruined by the provinces, and eaten alive by your brother."

Bolislau was a good master and an excellent preacher. Zana was bewildered at Yaqub's decision. Halim, on the contrary, encouraged his son to go and live in São Paulo, and even promised him a tiny monthly allowance. Things had improved for him in the postwar years. He sold all kinds of things to the inhabitants of Educandos, one of the most populous areas of Manaus, which had grown a lot with the arrival of the tappers who had gone into the jungle in the wartime boom. At the end of the war, they migrated to Manaus from the farthest reaches of Amazonia, and built shanties on stilts at the edge of the creeks, in gullies, and in any empty space they could find in the city. That was the chaotic way Manaus grew: first come, first served. Halim was a part of it; he sold things before anyone else got in. He didn't make that much money, but he always had one eye on a possible collapse—one day he told me it was a yawning chasm. He didn't fall in, but he wasn't that ambitious. The worst chasm was at home, and there was no way Halim could avoid that.

The parade in his gala uniform had been Yaqub's farewell: a little show put on for the family and the city. In the Salesian college they had a ceremony in his honor. He got two medals and ten minutes of speeches: he was also praised by the Latinists and mathematicians. The Brothers knew that their ex-pupil had a glorious future ahead of him; at that time, both Yaqub and Brazil itself seemed to have a promising future. Omar was not so brilliant; he really was unfathomable for priests and laymen, a lunatic, distant and drunk on the licentious atmosphere of the Vandals' Cockpit and the city itself.

Omar didn't come to his brother's farewell dinner. He arrived early in the morning, at the end of the party, when only family members were left and were making their exhausted goodbyes after their last night with Yaqub. Halim was proud: his son was going to live on his own at the other end of the country, but he was going to need money, he couldn't just go off empty-handed . . . For a moment, Yaqub's voice echoed in the house; already it was a man's voice, full of determination, saying "No, Baba, I won't need anything . . . This time it was me that wanted to go away." Halim embraced his son, and wept as he had on the morning Yaqub had left for Lebanon. Zana still kept on: she would send him a monthly allowance, for he wouldn't have time to work. "Your studies . . ."

she added. "Not a cent," he said, looking at his mother. Then they heard a noise: Omar had dropped his bicycle in the garden and was fixing his hammock. He wasn't drunk; he took some time to get to sleep and woke up several times with the sun burning his head—it got on his nerves to the point of making him punch the ground and the wall. He was forgotten; for once Omar had gone to sleep without the protection of the two women. He only got up after lunch, and refused the cold food. He was watching his mother's movements, while she only had eyes for the other son, the traveler. Halim was still in his room, and Domingas was stuffing bags of manioc flour and slabs of dried *pirarucu* fish into his case. Omar didn't move an inch; he stayed sitting at the table, motionless in front of his untouched plate, looking sideways, furtively at his brother's face. Yaqub's decision hurt him. He, Omar, was going to stay there, he'd be the king of the castle, in the house, the streets, the city, but the other had had the courage to leave. The lionheart, untamed in his childhood, was spent, wounded. "He wanted to leave the room, but he couldn't make it," Domingas told me. He didn't want to see his brother proud and serene, or hear his mother beg Yaqub to send her a letter a week, tell him he wasn't even to think of leaving her with no news, worried sick here in the back of beyond. Rânia kept close to Yaqub, kneeling down to speak words that only he could hear. Domingas didn't take her eyes off him, and years later told me that she was worried about the journey. Not even Zana could stop him leaving.

Domingas's hands anxiously took clothes out of the case, and tried to find space for the dried fish and the flour. Zana was watching over this complicated process, and was just going to interfere when the bell rang insistently; Omar got there first, ran to the front door, and they all heard a confused jumble of words.

"Who is it, Omar?" his mother asked; then there was an argument, the door banged shut, and once more the bell rang.

"Where's Omar got to?" asked Zana. "Domingas, go and see what's happening."

Domingas shut the case and quickly went to the door. Then her voice sounded, loud and insolent: "He's leaving shortly."

The click of high heels echoed down the corridor. Zana glanced, first in mystification, then with contempt, at the woman who came into the room looking around for Yaqub. No one had heard of her since that afternoon when Omar had torn his brother's cheek in the Reinosos' basement. Zana blamed the scar on Yaqub's cheek on the devilish seduction of this big blond girl. "I don't understand how that hefty piece could have bewitched my son." Sometimes she adjusted the wording: "I don't understand how my Yaqub let himself be bewitched by that lizard."

"She looked just the same, except that on that visit Lívia showed part of her breasts and thighs," Domingas told me.

Wide-eyed, Zana scrutinized the rest of Lívia's body; cattily, she asked her: "Has the sweetheart come to take leave of my young gallant?"

Lívia kept clear of her and went out of the room, enticing Yaqub into the garden. They whispered together in giggles, and disappeared into the bushes at the back. They were there the time it took to take dessert, the thick coffee, and a siesta. Zana was uneasy, and made a sign to Domingas, who found them near the fence. They were stretched out in the undergrowth, and Yaqub was caressing the woman's breasts and belly, putting off the final goodbye. Domingas kept quiet, breathing hard; she bent over, moved the leaves, and angrily broke some of the branches of a breadfruit tree. She stared at the scene openmouthed, and retreated, dry in the mouth, desperate for some of that water.

Lívia didn't reappear; she must have gone out by the alley at the back. Yaqub came into the room alone, his neck marked with scratches and love bites, his face still burning with passion.

That was how he left: his clothes crumpled, his face wet, and his hair full of twigs, leaves, and strands of blondish hair. He went quietly, leaving the house where he had lived with frugality and discretion. He had hardly occupied the place, hardly more than a shadow. He left the house with the memory of these two powerful scenes: the parade in his gala uniform and the encounter with the woman he loved.

Omar, gnawed by jealousy, never uttered his brother's name. Zana, desperate with worry, said that a son who leaves home a second time never returns. Halim agreed, but without the worry. He was dreaming of a glorious future for Yaqub, and that was more important than his return and stronger than the separation. Halim's grayish eyes lit up when he talked about it.

I saw those eyes many times, not lit up like that, but not dim either; just tired of the present, and with no future of any kind in their sights.

2

A round 1914, Galib opened the Biblos Restaurant on the ground floor of the house. Lunch was served at eleven, a simple meal, but exotic and delicious. Galib himself, a widower, did the cooking, helped serve, and looked after the garden, covering it with a veil of tulle to protect it from the burning sun. In the Municipal Market, he would choose a fish, a *tucunaré* or a *matrinxã*, stuff it with *farofa* and olives, roast it in a wood-fired oven, and serve it with a sesame sauce. He came into the restaurant with the tray balanced on the palm of his left hand; the other was around his daughter Zana's waist. They went from table to table and Zana offered *guaraná*, sparkling water, or wine. The father talked in Portuguese with the customers: street peddlers, skippers of small boats, river traders, and workers from the Manaus Harbor. From its inception, the Biblos was a meeting point for the Lebanese, Syrian, and Moroccan Jewish immigrants who lived in Nossa Senhora dos

Remédios Square and the streets giving onto it. They spoke Portuguese mixed with Arabic, French, and Spanish. Here, all kinds of voices mingled together, as people passed through and their lives crisscrossed; one thing after another—a shipwreck, black fever in a village on the river Purus, a swindle, a case of incest, distant memories, and burning emotions: a pain still smarting, a passion still smoldering, grief over irreparable loss, or hope that a cheat might eventually pay his debts. They ate, drank, and smoked, drawing out this moment of communion, and putting off the siesta.

The person who recommended the restaurant to the young Halim was Abbas, a friend of his who said he was a poet; he had worked in Acre, by the Bolivian border, and now made a living on the Amazon, traveling between Manaus, Santarém, and Belém. Halim began coming to the Biblos on Saturdays, then started going every morning, partaking of some fish, a stuffed aubergine, or a piece of fried cassava; he would take his flask of arrack from his pocket, drink it, and devour Zana with his eyes. He spent months in this fashion: alone in a corner of the room, excited whenever he saw Galib's daughter, and following this gazelle with his eyes wherever she went. He stared at her, his face tense, waiting for a miracle that didn't happen. He went fishing in the lakes and brought *tucunarés* and slabs of *surubim* for Galib. The owner of the Biblos thanked him, didn't charge for lunch, and Halim was full of enthusiasm about this friendship, which still was not enough to get him nearer Zana.

One day, Abbas saw his friend in Rouaix's, a shop near the Avenida Restaurant, in the center of Manaus. Halim was in the process of buying a French hat from Marie Rouaix, and arranging to pay for it in installments. Abbas got in first and gave his friend a nudge; they left the shop and went to the Café Polar, near the Opera House. They talked. Halim gave vent to his feelings, and Abbas suggested that he give Zana not a hat, but a poem.

"It's cheaper," said the poet, "and there are some words that never go out of fashion."

Abbas wrote a *gazal* of fifteen couplets, in Arabic, which he himself translated into Portuguese. Halim read the rhyming verses over and over: gloom and moon, dawn and wine, day and way. He put the sheets of paper into an envelope and the next day pretended to leave it by accident on the restaurant table. He went a week without showing his face at the Biblos, and when he went back, Galib gave him the envelope back:

"You left it on the table, and we nearly threw it out. Been fishing?"

He didn't answer; he opened the envelope and began to read Abbas's *gazals* in an undertone. Galib listened attentively, but the noise from the customers drowned Halim's voice. Zana wasn't around, and he gave up reading before the end, in discouragement.

"Lovely poems," Galib said admiringly. "A woman would really feel their caress."

Their caress, Halim repeated, as he went out of the Biblos. He reread Abbas's *gazals* in his breaks from work. At six in the morning he was already selling his trinkets in the streets and squares of Manaus, in the tram stations and even on the trams themselves; he only stopped hawking his wares at about eight at night; then he went around by the Café Polar, before going back to his room in the Pension Oriente.

Early one Friday morning, he met Cid Tannus, who paid court to the last Polish and French girls still living in the city, decaying in the wake of the rubber boom. They drank the wine Tannus had bought from French and Italian sailors. Then came Abbas, still sober, but buoyed up by other orders for *gazals*. He slapped Halim on the back: "Well, old pal? What kind of a face is that?" Abbas, faced with the prospect of failure, whispered into his friend's ear: "The *gazals* will have their effect, and patience is a powerful weapon, but a timid man will never win his lady." He asked for two bottles of wine, gave them to Halim, and said: "Tomorrow, Saturday, two bottles of wine and . . . congratulations, old man!"

Finally, Halim decided to act, full of a courage heightened by the wine. Always, in our conversations, he got excited when he recounted the details of his campaign. "Ah . . ." he said to me, "the burning desire, the anguish that overtook me that morning."

Abbas rhymed avid and fervid. What more could Zana want? So, on that Saturday morning, Halim staggered into the Biblos. His eyes focused on the girl in the middle of the room. The widower Galib saw the fire in the visitor's face. He stood stock still, paralyzed, with the fish, openmouthed and eyes bulging, on the tray balanced on his left hand. Knives and forks went silent, and faces turned around towards Halim. The blades of the fan made the only sound in the heavy, warm atmosphere. He took three steps towards Zana, stood up straight, and began to declaim the *gazals*, one by one, in a firm, deep, melodious voice, accompanied by enraptured gestures with his hands. He didn't stop, couldn't stop declaiming; this flood of emotion, this sudden outburst of passion had overwhelmed his shyness. Zana, a girl of fifteen, was stunned, and took shelter by her father. The hum of the fan was drowned by mutterings; someone laughed, a few others followed suit, but the wisecracks didn't change the expression on Halim's face. His gaze was fixed on Zana, and every pore seemed to exude the heady wine of happiness. Shy, but capable of moments of audacity, he himself had no idea how he crossed the room and took hold of Zana's arm, whispered something to her and then moved away, facing her, staring at her, his eyes full of promise, with a hungry, docile look. He stayed that way until the laughter stopped, and a solemn silence underlined the power and meaning of his gaze. No one interrupted him; not a voice was raised. Then he left the Biblos. Two months later he was back, as Zana's husband.

How beautiful Abbas's *gazals* sounded in Halim's voice! He sounded like a Sufi in a trance as he recited each rhyming couplet to me. He looked at the green, damp foliage, and spoke with energy: his voice came from deep within, pronouncing every syllable, celebrating a moment from the past. I didn't understand the words when he spoke in Arabic, but even so I was moved: the sounds were strong, and the words vibrated as he intoned them. I liked to hear his stories. His voice still resounds in my ears, aflame in my memory. At times he forgot himself and spoke in Arabic. I smiled, and gestured my incomprehension: "It's beautiful, but I don't understand what you're saying." He touched his head and mumbled: "It's age; in old age you don't choose the language you speak in. But you can learn a few little words, dear boy."

Intimacy with his sons was something Halim never had. One part of his story, the courage he had shown in life, he never told the twins. He revealed one thing one day, then another much later, in bits, "patches in a quilt." I heard the patches, but the colorful, sturdy quilt itself gradually wore away into shreds.

He suffered, like many other immigrants who had come with nothing more than the clothes on their backs. Drunk with idealism, he believed in ecstatic, passionate love, with every metaphor under the sun—or the moon. He was a late-flowering Romantic, a little out of place and time, indifferent to the power of money, whether honestly or dishonestly come by. Perhaps he could have been a poet, a minor provincial flaneur; but all he was was a modest shopkeeper possessed by a consuming passion. That was his way, and that was the way I knew him, puffing away at his hookah, and ready to reveal moments of his life he would never tell his sons.

Soon everyone in the city knew: Halim was crazy for Zana. The women of the Maronite Christian community in Manaus, old and young, could not tolerate the notion of Zana marrying a Muslim. They held a vigil on the pavement outside the Biblos, and ordered

novenas to be said so that she wouldn't marry Halim. Anyone who
cared to listen could hear all kinds of gossip: he was a mere tinker, a
peddler, a roughneck, a Muslim from the mountains of southern
Lebanon who dressed like a pauper and advertised his wares in the
streets and squares of Manaus with a rattle. Galib went on the offensive, and shooed the fanatics off: "Leave my daughter in peace, this
rubbish is bad for business." Zana retired to her room. The customers wanted to see her, and the only topic at lunch was the girl's
withdrawal, and the Muslim's mad love for her. They made up stories that Halim had offered the widower a dowry, and other slanderous concoctions; stories bounced back and forth all over the place. It
was a plague: put two words together and everyone believes them.

Halim laughed: "That's passion in the provinces," he'd say.
"It's like being onstage, listening to the audience booing two actors
playing two lovers. The more they booed, the more perfume I put
on the marriage sheets."

Zana listened neither to the booing nor the advice; she listened
to her own voice reciting Abbas's *gazals*. That was the way it stayed
for two weeks: neither yes nor no. She was the light of her father's
eyes; he took her her meals, told her the latest gossip, the stories the
customers recounted, or news of a murder that had shocked the city.
He didn't touch on Halim, and she, with her eyes, asked him to let
her decide on her own.

Years later, I understood why Zana let Halim talk as much as he
wanted. She waited with her head half bowed, her face serene, and
then spoke, in perfect control, once only, the words coming out in a
torrent, with all the confidence of a fortune-teller. She had been like
this since she was fifteen. She was possessed by a silent, brooding
stubbornness, a slow-burning determination; armed with a powerful sense of conviction, she let the blow fall suddenly, and decided
everything, leaving everyone else dumbfounded. That's what she
did now. Alone, within four walls, entranced by Abbas's *gazals*,

Zana went to talk to her father. She had already decided to marry Halim, but they would have to live at home, in this house, and sleep in her room. She demanded this of Halim in front of her father. What was more, they must be married at the altar of Our Lady of Lebanon, and in the presence of every Maronite and Catholic woman in Manaus.

Galib invited some friends from the Catraia harbor, from the steps of Remédios Square: fishermen and fishmongers who supplied the Biblos, and his cronies from the lakes on Careiro Island and the Cambixe branch of the river. There were all kinds of people, with varied languages, origins, clothes, and appearances. They came together in the church of Our Lady of Remédios, and listened to Father Zoraier's homily. It was already nightfall when Abbas and Cid Tannus turned up, accompanied by two female singers from a cabaret in the Praça Pedro II. They didn't go into the church, but were photographed beside the couple and joined the dinner at the Biblos, which ended in a big party, accompanied by the hoarse voice of one of the singers and crates of French wine presented by Tannus.

Halim showed me the wedding album, and took out a photograph he was fond of; himself, elegantly dressed, kissing the dark-haired girl, both of them surrounded by white orchids: the kiss he'd waited for, for all to see, and no concessions to fanatical women or to Father Zoraier: Halim's lips glued to Zana's, and she, taken aback, her eyes wide open, not expecting such a ravenous kiss at the altar. "It was a greedy kiss, to get my own back," Halim told me. "I silenced those rattling tongues, and every one of Abbas's *gazals* was in that kiss."

So that was the way it was: Zana's word was law in the house, ruling over the maid and the children. He was all patience, a passionate, ardent Job, and he swallowed everything, always doing anything she wanted, and pampering her even in old age, "playing my flute just for her," as he used to say.

But he was a devil in bed and in the hammock. He recounted their lovemaking as naturally as could be, in a slow, husky voice, with a libidinous look on his face, lined with sweat, damp with the memory of the nights, afternoons, and mornings when the two would roll around in the hammock, their favorite bed for love, and where all Zana's power collapsed into a continuous melody of laughter and delight.

"The secret language of desire," Halim said over and again, quoting Abbas. He fanned the smoke from the hookah. It veiled his face and head, and the temporary disappearance of his features was accompanied by a silence, while he recovered a voice or an image, some part of life that time had swallowed up. Little by little, his speech returned; threads of the past interrupted by sudden images.

They didn't go away on a honeymoon. They spent three nights in the Hotel America, away from the world, luxuriating in their burning passion. Then Halim decided to spend a night in the open air, at the Tarumã waterfalls, near Manaus. When he came back to the Biblos, Zana suggested to her father that he should go to Lebanon, to see his relatives, the country, everything. That was music to Galib's ears. So he left, on board the *Hildebrand*, a colossus of a ship that had brought any number of immigrants to Amazonia. Galib, the widower: all that was left of him was a very old photograph, his face with its cheery look against a bluish background that imitated a painting; his mustache ended in slender twirls, and the grizzly mane of his hair grazed the edge of the gilded frame. In his daughter's face, his big eyes had grown even bigger. Galib's photo was hung in the drawing room, for everyone to admire.

He cooked and served the last lunch: it was a party for a man going back to his homeland. He was already dreaming of the

Mediterranean, of a country with sea and mountains. He dreamt of Cedros, his village. He went back there, found separate parts of his clan, the ones that had stayed behind, never venturing out to find another home. Zana got two letters from her father: he was living in Biblos, in the same house where Zana herself had been born. He celebrated his homecoming by cooking Amazonian delicacies: dried *pirarucu* with *farofa*, Brazil-nut cakes, things he had brought with him from the Amazon. Two letters, then silence. In Biblos, asleep in his house near the sea, he died. The news took time to come, and when Zana found out, she shut herself in her father's room, as if he was still there. Then, softly, she said to her husband: "Now I'm an orphan; I've lost my father and mother. I want children, three at least."

"She wept as if she was a widow," Halim told me. "She rubbed herself against her father's clothes, smelled everything that had belonged to Galib. She would cling to things, and I tried to tell her that mere things have no flesh or soul. Things are empty . . . but she didn't hear what I said."

Halim breathed in, blew smoke out through his nostrils, and coughed noisily. Again, he went silent, and this time I didn't know if it was forgetfulness or a pause for meditating. That was the way he was: he was never in a hurry, not even to speak. He must have made love that way, morsel by morsel, with no urgency, as if taking his time to enjoy every bit.

How was he going to get rich? He never saved a penny, not stinting on food, on presents for Zana, on things the children asked for. He invited friends over for games of *taule*, and it was a real feast, nights that went on into the early morning, with endless food.

"Imagine going back to your homeland and dying," Halim sighed. "You're better off staying put, keeping quiet where you've made up your mind to live."

She was two weeks shut in her room, two weeks without sleeping with Halim. She shouted out her father's name, dazed, out of her mind, completely unapproachable. The neighbors heard her and tried to bring comfort, but it was no use.

"The ocean, the crossing . . . How far away everything was!" Halim lamented. "When someone dies on the other side of the world, it's as if he's been killed in a war or a shipwreck. Our eyes couldn't see the dead man; there was no funeral. Nothing. Just a telegram, a letter . . . My biggest mistake was to send Yaqub alone to my family's village," he said to me in a whisper. "But Zana wanted it that way . . . she decided."

3

A letter from Yaqub would arrive from São Paulo punctually
at the end of every month. Zana made a ritual of reading it,
intoning it as if it were a psalm or a sura: her diction, filled
with emotion, was interrupted by pauses, as if she wanted to hear
the voice of her faraway son. Domingas remembered these reading sessions. They were not entirely sad, for Halim invited the
neighbors, and the reading was an excuse for a festive dinner.
Domingas understood Halim's ruse. Without the party, Zana would
get depressed, thinking of how cold her son must be, or of the leftovers the poor thing must be eating, alone at night in his damp room
in the Pension Veneza, in the center of São Paulo. Always laconic,
Yaqub described the rhythm of his life in the city. The loneliness
and cold didn't bother him; he talked about his studies, the chaos of
the big city, the seriousness of the people, and their enthusiasm for
work. From time to time, as he crossed the Praça da República, he
would stop to look at the enormous rubber tree. It was good to see

this Amazonian tree in the middle of São Paulo, but he never mentioned it again.

The letters revealed a growing fascination with this life, the new rhythm experienced by people separated from their families, and who live alone. He was no longer living in a village, but in a huge metropolis.

"My *paulista* son," Zana joked, proud and worried at the same time. She feared Yaqub would never come back. Little by little, the outsider perfected his capacity for abstraction. After six months in São Paulo he began to teach mathematics. The letters got shorter, two or three short paragraphs, or only one: just a sign of life, and some item of news to justify the letter. So, without boasting, almost in a whisper, the young teacher Yaqub told them of his entry into the University of São Paulo. He wasn't to be a mathematician, but an engineer. He was going to be an expert calculator, planning complex structures. Zana didn't properly understand what her son's future profession was, but engineer was more than enough for her: he had a doctorate. They sent him money and a telegram; he thanked them for the generous words and sent the money back. They got the message that their son would never need another cent. Even if he needed it, he wouldn't ask.

The letters came less often, and the news from São Paulo seemed to come from another world. The little he told them didn't warrant the fuss they made at home. A short, uninformative note might set off a party. Zana joined in the festivities, which to begin with happened every month, then got less frequent; Yaqub's few lines passed over Manaus like a fading comet. Flickering signals from the big city: daily life in the Pension Veneza, the cinemas on the Avenida São João, tram rides, the noise of the crowds on the Viaduto do Chá and the solemn professors in their ties, whom Yaqub worshipped. In the first photo he sent, he had a jacket and tie and a stiff, formal look, reminiscent of the swordsman in the Independence parade.

"He certainly looks different from the hillbilly I met in Rio," Halim commented, looking at the image.

"Your son is the hillbilly," Zana said. "Mine's the other one, the future engineer in front of the Opera House in São Paulo."

He was a different Yaqub, wearing the camouflage of everything that was modern about the other side of Brazil. He was becoming more refined, getting ready to take the big jump: a worm that wants to be a snake, is one way of putting it. He made it. He slid by silently under the foliage.

Outside, he really had changed. Inside, there was a real mystery: a silent person who never gave voice to his thoughts.

I grew up with Yaqub's photos, listening to his mother reading his letters. In one of the photos, he posed in an army uniform; a sword again, but this time the two-edged weapon made the reserve officer look all the more formidable. For years, this image of the dashing young man in uniform was imprinted on me. An army officer, a future engineer from the Polytechnic School . . .

Omar, on the other hand, was all too present: his body was there, sleeping on the porch. It shuttled back and forth between the torpor of his hangover and the euphoria of his nightly binges. All morning, he was dead to the world, motionless and wrapped in the hammock. In the early afternoon, he roared out with hunger—a bon vivant on hard times. On the surface, he couldn't care less about his brother's success. He didn't join in the letter readings, and ignored the reserve officer and engineer-to-be. However, he did poke fun at the photographs on show in the living room. "A twerp dressed up to look important," he said, with a voice so like his brother's that Domingas got a shock, and looked around the room for Yaqub in flesh and blood. He had the same voice, with the same inflection. The image I had of Yaqub in my mind was shaped by Omar's body and voice. He had both twins inside him, because he had always been around, spreading his presence in the house to blot out Yaqub's existence. When Rânia kissed the photos of her absent brother, Omar would get up to some monkey business, showing off like a contortionist to attract his sister's attention. But Yaqub's memory still won out. The photographs gave out strong waves: they had an aura of presence. Did Yaqub know this? He was there always, with his haughty expression, hair neatly combed, impeccable jacket, thick, arched eyebrows, and a reluctant, puzzling smile. The duel between the twins was a spark waiting to ignite.

"A duel? Better call it rivalry, something that went wrong between the twins, or between them and us," Halim said to me one day, looking at the ancient rubber tree in the garden.

The twins weren't born right after Galib's death. Halim wanted to enjoy life with Zana; he wanted everything, to live completely with her, just the two of them, drunk with their all-consuming passion. He exaggerated her beauty and laughed, saying she was more beautiful that way, in mourning, her father's widow.

Lying in the hammock, they talked about Galib, about Zana's early years in Biblos, interrupted when she was six and she and her father left for Brazil. Her father used to take her to swim in the Mediterranean, and then they would walk together around the villages, with a doctor who had studied in Athens, the only graduate in Biblos; they visited friends and acquaintances, Christians who were intimidated and even persecuted by the Ottomans. In every house they visited, the doctor looked after his patient, and Galib cooked a wonderfully tasty dish. The man who made his customers' mouths water in his restaurant in Manaus had already been an expert cook in his native Biblos. He used whatever was available in the stone houses on Jabal al Qaraquif, Jabal Haous, and Jabal Laqlouq, mountains where the snow shone under the intense blue sky. The mysterious, biblical beauty of the age-old cedars between the white drifts, sometimes golden in the winter sun—she paused, and her

eyes, wet with tears, swept over Halim's face. Whenever he visited a
house by the sea, Galib would bring away his favorite fish, the sultan
ibrahim, which he seasoned with a mixture of herbs whose secret he
never divulged. In the Manaus restaurant he used strong seasonings
with cayenne pepper and *murupi*, mixing them with *tucupi* and *jambu*
and pouring this sauce over the fish. He might also use other herbs,
like mint and *ʒatar*.

"Over in that corner was where he grew the Mediterranean
herbs," said Halim, pointing at a square patch of grass next to the
rubber tree.

In mourning, Zana avoided her husband's caresses and went
back to the subject, talking about her father's figure, his face, the
gestures of the man who had brought her up after her mother died.
It was quite some time before Galib's name left her lips. She
recounted her dreams: father and daughter hugging each other at
the edge of the sea, and going into the water that had taken her
mother—the two of them there, in the dream together, always near
the sea, staring at the dark rock like a beached, rusting hulk. She
remembered the day when she read the *gaʒals* to her father, and said,
point-blank, without a shadow of hesitation: "I'm going to marry
that Halim."

"I spent months that way, my boy," he said, shaking his head.
"Four or five months, I can't even remember. I thought she didn't
love me any longer, I thought of taking her to Biblos, digging Galib
up, and saying to her: 'Stay here with your father's remains, either
that or let's take this pile of bones back to Brazil, then you can talk
to his ashes for the rest of your life.'"

But he said nothing like that. He waited doggedly, as patiently as
could be. Then she suggested they open a small shop in the Rua dos
Barés, between the port and the church. It was a busy, crowded area,
with people coming and going day and night. They'd shut the
restaurant, because all those customers with their obscene anec-

dotes, stories of shipwrecks and magical creatures reminded Zana of her father. Halim agreed. He complied with everything, so long as all his acts of submission ended in the hammock or in bed, or even on the living-room carpet.

At the time they were opening the shop, a nun, a Little Sister of Jesus, offered them an orphan, already christened, who could read and write. Domingas, a lovely young native girl, grew up at the back of the house where there were two rooms, separated by palms and other trees.

"She was a tiny, shriveled-up little girl, with her head full of lice and Christian prayers," Halim remembered. "She went barefoot, and asked us to give her our blessing. She seemed a well-mannered girl with a good temperament: not withdrawn or forward. For a while, she gave us a lot of work, but Zana liked her. The two of them prayed together, one with the prayers she'd learned in Biblos, the other with the ones learned in the nuns' orphanage, here in Manaus." Halim smiled when he told me about his wife's closeness to the Indian girl. "What religion can do," he said. "It can bring opposites together, the earth and heaven, the maid and the mistress."

It was a little miracle, very convenient for the family and future generations, I thought. Domingas was useful; and she only stopped being useful when she died, as I saw her die, almost as shriveled-up as when she came to the house—for all I know, into the world. She was frightened by the racket her master and mistress made when they made love, and shocked that Zana, such a devout person, gave herself to Halim with such frenzy.

"It seems like all the filth in their bodies comes out," Domingas said to me, one afternoon when she was rinsing their sheets in the washtub.

With time, she got used to the two shameless, entwined bodies, with no set time or place for their encounters. On Sunday mornings, Zana resisted Halim's advances and ran to the church of Nossa

Senhora dos Remédios. But when she got back home, with her soul purified and the taste of the Host on her palate, Halim lifted her over the threshold and carried her upstairs, with her arms around his neck. On his way up, he left his slippers and bathrobe on the staircase, along with her shoes, stockings, petticoat, and dress, so they were almost naked by the time they reached the bedroom perfumed with white orchids.

"Oh Lord, I could never take commerce seriously," said he, in a tone of false lamentation. "I haven't the time or the brain for it. I know I was remiss in my business life, but I put too much energy into my love life."

He didn't want three children; in fact, had it been up to him, he'd have had none. He said this over and over, irritated, chewing the mouthpiece of his hookah. They could have lived trouble-free, without a care in the world, because a couple in love, with no children, can survive poverty or any other kind of disaster. However, he had to give in to his wife's silence, and to the imperious tone of the sentence after the silence. She knew how to be insistent, without making a show:

"You mean to say we're going to spend all our lives alone in this big house? Just us two and the Indian girl in the yard? That's selfish, Halim."

"Children are killjoys," he said, seriously.

"Three, love. Three children, no more, no less," she insisted slyly as she was putting the hammock up in the bedroom, scattering the pillows on the floor, just as he liked.

"They'll change our lives, they'll take the hammock down . . ." Halim complained.

"If my father was alive, he wouldn't believe his ears."

Halim backed down whenever she mentioned her father, and Zana saw that. She didn't give up: she alternated between silence and perseverance, and gave herself to Halim with the promises of a woman head over heels in love. Did he not see the ambiguity in Zana's attitude? He let himself be carried away by nights of love, with no shortage of docile phrases—nights that always ended in the happy promise that they would fill the house with children.

Yaqub and Omar were born two years after Domingas appeared in the house. Halim got a shock when he saw the midwife, with her two fingers, announcing the arrival of twins. They were born at home, Omar a few minutes later. He was the younger, the *caçula*. He was often ill in the first few months of life. Also, he was a little darker, and had more hair. He grew up in the jealous care of his mother, morbidly concerned about him; she saw imminent death in her son's fragile complexion.

Zana hardly left his side, and the other child was left to the care of Domingas, the shriveled Indian girl, half slave, half nurse, "desperate to be free," as she said to me once, tired, defeated, caught up in the family's spell, and not much different from the other maids in the neighborhood, taught to read and write and educated by the nuns in the missions, but all of them living at the back of some house, right next to the fence or the wall, where they slept with their dreams of freedom.

"Desperate to be free": dead words. No one can free themselves with words alone. She stayed here in the house, dreaming of a freedom that receded into the future. One day, I said to her: "To hell with dreams; if you don't make a move, you'll get a dig in the ribs from death, and in death there are no dreams. Our dreams are all here," and she looked at me, brimful of words she'd stored up, with the urgent desire to say something.

But she didn't have the courage—or rather, she had and she hadn't. Hesitant, she preferred to give in, did nothing, and was overtaken by inertia: inertia, and her involvement with the twins, above all with Yaqub as a child, and, four years later, with Rânia. With Yaqub the ties were stronger: it was a substitute mother's love, incomplete, perhaps simply impossible. Zana luxuriated in Omar's company, and took him everywhere: tram rides to the Praça da Matriz, the boulevards, the Seringal Mirim neighborhood, the big holiday homes out in the Vila Municipal. She took him to see the jugglers at the Gran Circo Mexicano, or to romp around at the children's dances at the Rio Negro Club, where at the age of two he was photographed in fancy dress as a pet monkey; Zana kept the costume as a relic.

Domingas stayed with Yaqub and played with him, reduced to his level, going back to the childhood she had spent by a riverbank far from Manaus. She took him to other places: beaches left by the river in the dry season, where they explored the stranded boats, abandoned at the gully's edge. They went around the city too, going from square to square as far as the island of São Vicente, where Yaqub stared at the fort, climbed on the cannons, and imitated the rigid pose of the sentinels. When it rained, the two of them, so Domingas told me, hid in the bronze ships in the Praça de São Sebastião, and then went to see the animals and fish in the Praça das Acácias. Zana trusted her, but sometimes the neighbors' comments gave her a fright. These Indian girls cast a spell on the children: hadn't there been cases of strangulation, vampirism, poisoning, and even worse? But then Zana remembered that they prayed together, worshipped the same god, the same saints, and to that extent were like sisters. When they prayed, before the altar in the living room, they were together, kneeling, venerating the plaster saint Domingas dusted every morning.

When the boys were born, Halim spent two months without touching Zana's body. He told me how much he suffered: he thought this time of prohibition absurd, and his wife's mad devotion to Omar even more ridiculous. He spent the day in the shop, passing the time with the customers and layabouts that wandered around the port area, teaching them to play backgammon, drinking arrack from the bottle, just like when he was courting Zana and reciting Abbas's *gazals*. Sometimes he came back home merry, his breath reeking of aniseed, and one or two couplets of love poetry on his tongue: maybe that way she would emerge from her self-imposed quarantine. In the end, convinced that the twins' birth had interfered with his nights of love quite as much as Galib's death, he had recourse to the same wiles and gallantries he'd used when his father-in-law died. He reconquered Zana, but said goodbye to the times when they shuddered with pleasure in every corner of the house or the yard.

"Right there, under the rubber tree," he pointed with the index finger, his hand wrinkled, but still firm. "That was our leaf bed. It really made you itch, because the undergrowth was full of nettles. That was how it was before the twins were born."

Halim no longer had any peace when the boys began to walk. They meddled with the tobacco in the hookah, brought dead lizards into the house, and filled the hammocks with nettles and crickets. Omar was the more daring: he went into his parents' bedroom during the siesta and did somersaults on the bed until he got rid of Halim. He only quieted down when Zana left the room to come and play with him in the yard. The two of them sat in the shade of the rubber tree, while Halim, irritated, had the urge to lock Omar in the chicken coop, empty since Galib's departure. "What poor Halim went through with Omar," said Domingas, remembering the time when he tried to steady his son. When he was riled, he used to chase Omar around the house; the boy would climb into the jackfruit tree and threaten to throw one of the huge fruits onto his father's head. Zana laughed: "You look as childish as Omar."

One night Halim woke coughing and short of breath. He lit the kerosene lamp, and saw a yellow spider's web reflected in the bedroom mirror; he smelled smoke and thought the mosquito net was slowly burning by his side. He jumped out of bed and saw Omar curled up next to Zana. He yelled at him and shooed him out, waking everyone up, and accused Omar of being an arsonist, while Zana repeated: "It was a nightmare, our son would never do that." They had an argument in the middle of the night, until he left the house, banging the door behind him. Zana and Domingas went after him, and caught up with him near a newsstand in the Municipal Market. He was standing, smoking, looking at the lighted fishing boats that had just tied up in the Escadaria harbor. He told the two women he would come back later, and spent the rest of the night thinking over the nightmare, fixing his gaze on the boats and the river Negro, until the voices and laughter of the dawn brought him back to reality. He was barefoot, in his pajamas, and the first fishermen of the morning thought he was mad. One of them brought him back home, leading him by the arm as if he was sleepwalking. He slept for two nights in the storeroom of the shop, and refused to accept his son's presence in the room; he would not put up with interference in the marriage bed. Later, when he was calmer, he even suggested that they should make love in Omar's presence. Zana, without losing her cool, said: "Fine, in front of the children, Domingas, and the whole neighborhood. Then I'll say we're going to have another child."

By the time Rânia was born, Halim was resigned to the limited space in the bedroom. On Zana's rare visits to the shop, he dismissed the customers and backgammon players, shut the doors, and went up with her into the little attic storeroom, where a small window looks out over the river Negro. They spent hours there, far from the three children and the orphan that acted as their maidservant, far from practical jokes and interruptions. The two of them alone, as he liked. A breeze wafted in from the river, bringing the whiff of fish and the scent of fruits and pepper. He liked this smell, which mingled with others: the sweat of their bodies, the mustiness of the piles of cloth, leather sandals, cotton hammocks, and the rolls of tobacco. When he opened the shop again, he celebrated the event by having a sale of all the stuff littered around the little room. It was a real jamboree, but it happened less and less often.

The children had invaded Halim's life, and he never got used to the fact. Still, they were children, and he spent time with them, told them stories, and looked after them every so often. He took them fishing in the Puraquecoara Lake, and they went rowing in the Cambixe branch of the river, where Halim knew cattle farmers and owners of small plantations. He was what you could call a father, but one who was aware that his children had robbed him of a large part of his privacy and pleasure. Years later, they would rob him of his serenity and good humor. He warned his wife that she was spoiling Omar, the delicate boy who had nearly died of pneumonia.

"My little black monkey, my hairy little boy," Zana said to Omar, to Halim's despair. The little hairy boy grew up, and when he was ten he already had the strength and bravery of a grown man.

"Omar got up to all kinds . . . I don't want to talk about it," he said, clenching his fists. "Some episodes really make me angry. For an old man like me, it's best to remember other things, all the things that have given me pleasure. That's best: remembering what makes me live a little longer."

He kept quiet about the episode of the scar. He also kept quiet about Domingas's life. However, when I really pressed her, I extracted a few moments of confession.

4

I knew nothing about myself, how I came into the world, or where I had come from: my origin, or origins. My past, pulsating in some way in the life of my ancestors, I knew nothing at all about. My infancy carried no trace of its origins. It's like forgetting a child in a boat on an empty river, waiting for one of the banks to give him shelter. Years later, I began to suspect that one of the twins was my father. Domingas dissembled whenever I touched on the subject; she left me in a state of uncertainty, thinking one day I might discover the truth. Her silence hurt me; on our walks, when she took me to the aviary by the cathedral or along the riverfront, she would begin a sentence, but only to interrupt it and look at me, upset, and overcome by a weakness that inhibited sincerity. Often she would try, but faltered, hesitated, and ended up saying nothing. When I asked the question, her look bade me be quiet, and her eyes were sad.

Once, on a Saturday, worn out and fed up with routine, she wanted to get out of the house and the city. She asked Zana if she could have Sunday off. Her mistress was surprised, but let her go, so long as she didn't come back late. It was the only time I went out of Manaus with my mother. It was still dark when she shook my hammock; she had already prepared breakfast and was singing under her breath. She didn't want to wake the others, and was keen to get going. We walked to the harbor at Catraia and got into a motorboat taking some musicians to a wedding party on the banks of the Acajatuba, a tributary of the Negro. On the journey, Domingas was almost childishly happy; it was as if she were in charge of her own body and voice. Sitting at the prow, her face to the sun, she seemed free; she said: "Look at the *batuíras* and *jaçanãs*," pointing at the birds skimming over the dark water, or splashing over the matted vegetation. She pointed to the hoatzins nestling in the twisted branches of the *aturiás*, and *jacamins*, uttering strange cries as they cut across the magnificent sky, heavy with clouds. My mother had not forgotten these birds: she recognized their sounds and names, and looked eagerly at the vast horizon up the river, recalling the place where she had been born, near the village of São João, on the banks of the Jurubaxi, an arm of the Negro, far away from there. "My place," Domingas remembered. She didn't want to leave São João, or her father and brother; she helped the women of the village to grate manioc to make flour, and looked after her younger brother while her father worked on his plot in the jungle. Her mother . . . Domingas didn't remember, but her father said: your mother was born in Santa Isabel, she was pretty, with a happy laugh; at the housewarming parties and nights when there were dances she was the prettiest of all. One day, very early, Domingas's father went out to cut piassava and other Brazil nuts. It was June, the day before St. John's night, the canoe carrying the saint's image was being brought down to the river, and the *gambeiros* were beating drums, singing, and begging for alms for St. John. The village of Jurubaxi was already lively, with prayers and dances, and from the nearby towns and even from Santa Isabel on the river Negro Indians and half-castes were coming for the festival. Then, the sounds of the drums were drowned by grunts, and Domingas saw a wild boar kicking, trembling, suffocating, frothing at the snout with the poisonous juice of the wild manioc. "A man threw boiling water and hit the animal over the head a few times with a cudgel. Then he pulled out the hairs so the meat could be prepared," Domingas told me. "I ran inside our hut, where my brother was playing. I stayed there, shaking with fear, crying . . . I waited for my father . . . He was late . . . Nobody knew anything."

There was no festival for her. Her father had been found dead by the piassava palms where he had been working. She still remembered his face, the funeral in the little cemetery, on the opposite bank of the Jurubaxi. She never forgot the morning when she left for the orphanage in Manaus, accompanied by a nun from the missions of Santa Isabel do Rio Negro, or the nights she slept in the orphanage, the prayers she had to learn by heart, and woe to anyone who forgot a prayer, or the name of a saint. Two years or so she was there, learning to read and write, praying at dawn and dusk, cleaning the bathrooms and the refectory, sewing and embroidering for the missions' bazaars. The nights were the unhappiest time; the boarders couldn't go near the windows, and had to keep quiet, in bed in the dark; at eight Sister Damasceno opened the door, crossed the dormitory, and prowled around the beds, stopping near each girl. The nun loomed up in front of her; she held a ferule in her hand. Sister Damasceno was tall, grim, dressed all in black, and terrified everyone. Domingas shut her eyes and pretended to be asleep, remembering her father and brother. She cried when she remembered her father, the little wooden animals he made for her, the songs he sang for his children. She wept with frustration. She would never see her brother again; she could never go back to Jurubaxi. The nuns wouldn't let her; nobody could leave the orphanage. The sisters were on guard all the time. She watched the girls from the Normal School walking in the square, free, in groups . . . flirting. It made her want to escape. Two of the boarders, the oldest, managed to escape early one morning: they climbed over the wall at the back, jumped into Simón Bolívar Alley, and disappeared into the woods. They had courage. Domingas thought about escaping, but the nuns saw, and said God would punish her. The stink of the bathrooms, the smell of disinfectant, and the nuns' sweaty, greasy clothes: Domingas could bear it no longer. One day Sister Damasceno ordered her to have a real bath, wash her hair with coconut soap, and cut her fingernails and toenails. She had to be clean and sweet-smelling! Domingas put on a brown skirt and a white blouse that she herself ironed and starched. The sister put a coif on her head and the two left the orphanage, went as far as the Avenida Joaquim Nabuco and into a tree-lined street leading to Nossa Senhora dos Remédios Square. They stopped in front of an old two-story house, painted dark green. High up, right in the middle of the facade, there was a square of blue and white Portuguese tiles with the image of Our Lady of the Conception. A young, pretty woman, her hair in clusters of curls, came to welcome them. "I've brought an Indian girl for you," said the sister. "She knows how to do everything, she can read and write properly, but if she's any nuisance, back she'll go to the orphanage and never get out again." They went into the living room, where there were wooden tables and chairs piled up in a corner. "This all belonged to my father's restaurant," said the woman, "but now you can take them to the orphanage." Sister Damasceno thanked her. She seemed to be expecting something else. She looked at Domingas and said: "Dona Zana, your mistress, is very generous, so don't blot your copybook, my girl." Zana took an envelope off the little altar and gave it to the sister. The two of them went to the door and Domingas was left alone, happy to be free of that grim woman. If she'd stayed in the orphanage, she'd have spent her life cleaning the toilets, washing petticoats, and sewing. She detested the orphanage and never went to visit the Little Sisters of Jesus. They called her ungrateful and selfish, but she wanted to keep well away from the nuns; she wouldn't even walk along the street where the orphanage was. The sight of the building depressed her. How many times had Damasceno beaten her! You never knew when she'd get the ferule out. She was educating the Indian girls, she said. In Zana's house the work was the same, but she had more freedom . . . She prayed when she wanted, she could talk, disagree, and she had her own little corner. She saw the twins born, she looked after Yaqub, and they played together . . . When he left for Lebanon she missed him. He was only just a teenager, and didn't want to go away. Halim gave in to his wife, and let his son go away alone. "Omar stayed close to his mother's skirts," Domingas said. "He used to come to my room to complain, and called Halim selfish . . . The two of them never got on."

When we got off at the village on the banks of the Acajatuba, my mother's mood changed. I don't know what made her so gloomy. Perhaps it was the setting, or something about the place that was painful for her to see or feel. She didn't want to go to the wedding, much less wait for the festivities, the fireworks, the fish barbecue by the side of the river. My mother was frightened of getting back late to Manaus. Or, who knows, she was afraid of staying there forever, thirsting for the past, entangled in her own memories.

We came back in the same motorboat, with ten or so inhabitants of Acajatuba who were going to sell pigs, fish, chickens, and manioc in Manaus. I noticed that my mother talked less the closer we got to the city. She looked at the edges of the river, and said nothing. The vendors watched over their animals, the chickens flapped around in improvised cages, the pigs were tied to one another. The end of the journey was horrible. It began to pour when the boat was passing near Tarumã. It was a real storm, with bursts of torrential rain. Everything went dark, the boundary between the sky and the river was blotted out, the boat pitched back and forth, jumping as it cut through the waves. The rain flooded the deck and the bridge, and the captain asked us to lie down. Everyone began to shout, there were no floats, and the only thing to do was grip the gunwales. My mother was the first to be sick. Then it was my turn; we both brought everything up, all our breakfast and the tapioca balls we'd eaten on the journey. I saw everyone with their mouths open, weeping, vomiting on the pigs and chickens. No one knew what was happening, and the screams and shouts mixed in with grunts and cackles; I tried to protect my mother from the pigs shaking and kicking right next to us. They were squealing terribly, trying to run but slipping, and piled on top of each other in desperation, as if they were going to die. More than half an hour of thunder, squalls of wind, and rain; first, I thought we were going to go under, then I couldn't think of anything, I felt so sick. The only things I didn't bring up were my soul and my eyes: they seemed all I had left in me. My poor little mother was gasping for breath, with no strength left. She was sobbing, her head hung down, and she dribbled saliva as she gripped my hands. I began to give up as the boat shook, and the bursts of water from river and sky hit my body, but I didn't let go of my mother. The animals didn't let up, I felt like throwing them in the river, but their owners held tight onto the cages and the pigs; they were their only means of livelihood.

We arrived at nightfall, when it was still raining hard. The quay of the little harbor of Escadaria was awash with mud, and we had to get off at the edge of the beach and walk through canvas tents and overturned shacks. We were in a terrible state, soaked through, dirty, stinking of vomit. We went into the house by the wicket gate in the back fence. Domingas went straight to her room, lay down in her hammock, and asked me to stay with her. I dozed on the floor, my head swimming and with a sour taste in my mouth. In the middle of the night I awoke to hear Domingas asking if I liked Yaqub, if I remembered him, what his face looked like. I heard nothing more. At five she was ready to go to the Municipal Market.

We never went on a boat trip again: the trip to Acajatuba was the only one I ever went on with my mother. I thought she nearly got the strength or courage to say something about my father. She avoided the subject and forgot the questions she'd asked me during that Sunday night. She swore she'd never uttered Yaqub's name. At bottom, she knew I would never stop asking her about the twins. Perhaps because of an agreement or some kind of pact with Zana, or Halim, she was forced to keep quiet about which of the two was my father.

After our boat journey Halim suggested I occupy the other little room at the back. He told Domingas I was too old now to sleep in the same room as my mother, and she ought to break away from me a little. I myself helped to clean the room and paint it. From then on, it became my refuge, the bit of the back garden that belonged to me. Now I only heard the echo of the song my mother sang when she couldn't sleep. Sometimes, when I was studying, bent over a table, I saw Domingas's face at the window, her smooth, copper-colored hair over her dark shoulders, her eyes fixed on me, as if asking me to come and sleep with her, in the same hammock, in each other's arms. When I went out at night through the back fence, she was waiting for me, on watch, like a sentinel listening for some nocturnal threat. She was frightened that my destiny would follow Omar's, like two untamed, raging rivers: rushing onwards with no respite.

On Sundays, when Zana sent me to buy beef offal at the Catraia harbor, I took time off, wandering aimlessly around the city, crossing the metal bridges, roaming in the areas beside the creeks, in the neighborhoods that were expanding in those days, surrounding the center of Manaus. I saw another world in these areas, the city we don't see, or don't want to see: a hidden, secret world, full of people who had to improvise everything to survive, some just vegetating, like the packs of squalid dogs prowling under the stilts of the houses built over the mud. I saw women whose faces and gestures reminded me of my mother's, children who one day would be taken to the orphanage Domingas hated. Then I went around the squares in the center of town, walking around the streets and alleys of the Aparecida neighborhood, and watching the canoes crossing Catraia harbor. It was already busy at that hour of the morning. Everything was sold at the side of São Raimundo creek: fruit, fish, gherkins, okra, tin toys. The old building of the German Brewery glittered over in the neighborhood of Colina, on the other side of the creek. Immense and all white, it drew my gaze and seemed to flatten the huts surrounding it. But the sight of the dozens of small boats lined up in file was even more fascinating. Halfway across you could smell the beef offal and the guts: the whiff of innards. The boatmen rowed slowly, and the pairs of canoes looked like an immense reptile approaching the shore. When they came alongside, the tripe sellers unloaded boxes and trays full of entrails. I bought the offal for Zana; the strong smell, thousands of flies, all of this nauseated me, and I left the edge of the water and walked as far as the island of São Vicente. I looked at the river. Its dark, slightly rippled surface brought me a feeling of relief, and a sense of freedom in my cramped existence. Just looking at the river made me breathe more easily. It meant a great deal, almost everything in fact, on my afternoons off. Sometimes Halim gave me some change and I had a ball. I went to a cinema, listened to the audience shouting, felt giddy at the sight of so many moving pictures, so much light in the darkness.

Then I nodded and went to sleep for one or two programs and was woken by a man with a flashlight shaking my shoulder. It was the end: the end of all the programs, and of my Sunday.

I was allowed in the main part of the house, and could sit on the gray sofa and the wicker chairs in the living room. I didn't often sit at table with the family, but I could eat and drink anything they did; they didn't mind. When I wasn't at school, I worked at home, helped with the housework, cleaned the yard, cleared up the dead leaves, and mended the back fence. I went out to do shopping at any time, and tried to help my mother, who never stopped for a minute. It was one thing on top of another. Zana invented thousands of tasks every day; she couldn't bear to see any dirt, or an insect on the walls, the floor, or the furniture. The statue of the saint on the little altar had to be polished every day, and once a week I went up onto the low wall surrounding the roof to clean the tiles at the front. Also, there were the neighbors. They were a lazy bunch, and kept asking Zana to do little favors, and off I would go to buy flowers at a house out in the Vila Municipal, or a piece of organdy from the Casa Colombo, or take a message to the other side of the city. They never gave me money for the journey, and sometimes didn't even thank me. Estelita Reinoso, the only one who was really rich, was the stingiest. Her mansion was sumptuous, its rooms full of Persian carpets, French chairs, and mirrors; the glasses and goblets sparkled in the cabinet, and everything had to be cleaned a hundred times a day. The gilded pendulum shone, though the clock had long ago gone silent. To go into the Reinosos' kitchen I had to take off my sandals; that was the rule. In the house there were maids that Estelita always complained about to Zana. They were so clumsy, so careless, no use at all! There was no point in trying to educate these savages; they were all lost cases, an utter waste of time! Calisto, a stocky lad from the slum at the back of the house, looked after the Reinosos' animals, above all the monkeys, which squealed and jumped around in huge wire cubes in the garden. They were funny, docile, played tricks for the visitors, and didn't involve that much work. The trained monkeys were Estelita's living treasure.

For all the battalion of servants at her command, this blood-sucker was the worst of all the neighbors, the one who tortured me most. She seemed to do it on purpose. "Zana," she said in saccharine tones, "could your boy pick up a jug of milk for me?" I went out to get the milk and had the urge to piss and spit into the jug. Sometimes, after lunch, when I was sitting down to do school homework, I heard the click of Estelita's high heels echoing on the wooden floor. The clatter woke everyone up. Zana shut the bedroom door so her neighbor wouldn't hear Halim swearing. I knew what was in store for me. I saw her sleepy face, all made up and already blurred with sweat, her hair stuck up with lacquer like a painted gourd, and heard her croaking voice announce that the gray upholstery on the sofa was stained, the chandelier out of date, and the carpet worn through. Zana let herself be overawed by Estelita's past. Her grand-father, one of the tycoons of the Amazon, had appeared on the front of an American magazine, which his granddaughter showed off to all and sundry. She also showed the photographs of the firm's ves-sels, which had sailed up all the rivers in Amazonia, selling all kinds of things to the people living on the banks and the owners of stands of rubber trees. When talking to new acquaintances, she would begin the conversation by saying: "The King of the Belgians stayed at our house, and went for a trip on my grandfather's yacht." Now, the Reinosos lived off rented properties in Manaus and Rio de Janeiro. On one Saturday night a month, Estelita's house turned into a casino; it fairly exploded with light, for they were the only ones on the street with a generator. The neighbors were not invited to enter the illuminated palace, and stayed at the window, shrouded in darkness, admiring this fountain of light, and trying to guess who the guests were. On these occasions, Estelita had the effrontery to ask Zana for buckets full of ice. Once she asked for a roll of gauze. I went to take the ice and the gauze, and wondered who had cut themselves in the Reinosos' palace. Before I came back, I took a peep into the room where they were going to dine before the gambling started. The roll of gauze had been turned into little napkins the guests used to squeeze the lemon over the fish. I told Halim about this. "They're very refined, they belong to our aristocracy," he said. "That's why they love having those monkeys in cages in the garden." One day I got it into my head that I was no longer going to be the Reinosos' errand boy. My mother didn't have the courage to tell Zana that I wasn't someone else's employee. I myself told her, exaggerating a little, how Estelita messed up my life and I had no time to work at home. Halim agreed with me. And many years later, when Zana summarily expelled Estelita from the house, I was able to laugh right in the old vixen's face.

With Talib things were better; I got on with the widower. He asked for mint and spring onions to season the food his daughters prepared. Sometimes he wanted some tobacco and a little bottle of arrack. He always offered me a snack. "Come in, sit down a little, dear boy, come and try our raw *quibe*." Zahia was taller than her father and much more inquisitive than her sister. When Zahia swayed her body or sang, Nahda imitated her movements and her voice. The timid little girl, all shy and retiring, opened her mouth in gales of laughter, revealing teeth so white they shone. The two sisters were a pair of stunning beauties. I had the impression they never tired; they never stopped for a moment, did everything in the house, and still helped their father in the bar. At noon, they appeared at the top of the street, in uniform, swinging their hips when they passed in front of Estelita's house. I devoured my raw *quibe* without taking my eyes off Zahia's crossed legs, covered with golden hairs. I fervently hoped she would take her uniform off and come back into the room in shorts and a T-shirt, and when this did happen, I gorged myself looking at her. Talib gave me a playful slap: "Do you want to swallow my daughter alive, you rascal?" I was embarrassed, and Zahia laughed. I didn't miss a night when they danced at home, where they were rivals for Rânia, and swung their hips for all they were worth.

On the day before Zana's birthday, Talib called me early in the morning. "Take this lamb to your house." Halim killed the animal, and my mother couldn't bear seeing the blood spurt from the animal's neck, she covered her ears; the bleats were sad and despairing, and the little beast seemed to cry out for help or pity. Domingas got out of the way and hid, overcome with pity, poor little lamb of God, she would say. The sight of the bloodied lamb hanging from the branch of the rubber tree upset her. From when I was very young I got used to skinning and gutting lambs. Halim cut the meat, which Zana prepared with her late father's seasoning. The head was kept for Talib, who ate it in a stew, with plenty of garlic. I spent the whole year waiting for the leg: I relished my own slices and my mother's. She scraped the bones of the little lamb of God for me.

What gave me some respite and a certain pleasure was a job that wasn't exactly a real job. When one of the houses in the street exploded with shouts, Zana told me to snoop around the area, and I ferreted everywhere, gnawing at the neighbors' rotten bones. I was as subtle as a snake. I memorized the scenes, and told Zana everything; she loved it, and her eyes bulged in curiosity: "Come on, boy, tell me, but slowly . . . no hurry." I took care over the details, inventing things, with here and there a pause, abstracted, as though I was trying hard to remember, until it came to me. The widower Talib's girls, not his daughters: the others, the ones he picked up around the warehouses. Once, his daughters caught him flagrante delicto with an Indian girl behind the bar at the Flores do Minho. He wasn't expecting that, and couldn't have thought that one day all his daughters' teachers would be off work at the same time. They gave their father a beating; we could hear the widower's howls echoing all down the block, and when I came up to the house I saw him lying on the floor, writhing under the plump, strong arms of his daughters, begging over and over: "I was just having a little fun, girls . . ." He was beaten by the two of them like a condemned man; they were dreadfully jealous, and couldn't bear seeing him near a woman. They feared the nocturnal visits of Cid Tannus, the old bachelor, and dogged their father's footsteps, spying on him, only letting him go and play billiards in Balma's shop if Halim went with him. But when they danced, Talib shed tears of pride; his belly trembled with so much pleasure. He called them "my dark-skinned warriors, my lovely Amazons." They were his flowers from the banks of the Minho, for their mother had been born in Portugal.

In the Reinosos' house it was worse; Zana could hardly breathe, and asked me to recount every little detail. When the trouble started, the servants turned the generator on to drown the squealing from the monkeys and Abelardo Reinoso's shouts. The noise shook the whole street, and all the busybodies ran to see Estelita beating her husband in broad daylight. I saw him cornered, squatting, at the back of the monkeys' wire cube, listening to Estelita's threats and curses, all because of her sister, the intruder, Lívia's mother. Estelita ordered the maids not to feed the good-for-nothing: no water, not even a banana. "You'll rot in there," she shouted. "My monkeys are too good for you." The next morning, on the way to school, I climbed into the mango tree in Talib's garden to see poor Abelardo suffering among the animals. During the night the widower would throw biscuits into the wire cage, and I saw the monkeys' shadows moving like gigantic spiders around Abelardo. Estelita was unconcerned about the gossip. She was proud, thought herself superior to her immigrant neighbors, and sustained herself on the legends of the family's past; the visit of the King of the Belgians never left her brain. She showed off the ivory necklaces and bracelets that the king had given her grandmother.

When the neighbors had quieted down, Zana sent me to Talib's bar and a dozen other places to buy some trivial item or other. She bought on credit, and only paid at the end of the month; she didn't trust me or anyone else. She would scold me: "That's not what I wanted; run back there and bring what I asked for." I tried to argue, but it was no use, she was stubborn and felt better when she was giving orders. I counted the seconds till it was time for school; it was a relief. But I missed classes two or three times a week. With my uniform on and ready to go, Zana's orders put an end to my morning in school: "You've got to pick up the dresses from the seamstress and then go by Au Bon Marché to pay the bills." I could easily do those things in the afternoon, but she brooked no refusal. My homework was late; the teachers reprimanded me and called me thickhead, lazybones, and worse. I did everything in a hurry; even now I can see myself rushing from morning till night, desperate to get some peace, to sit in my room far from voices, threats, and orders. And then there was Omar. That was a real mess, hell from start to finish. I couldn't eat at the table with him. He wanted the table to himself, and had lunch and dinner when he felt like it. Alone. One day I was having lunch when he came in and gave orders: I was to leave, and eat in the kitchen. Halim was nearby, and said to me: "No, eat right there, that table is for all of us." Omar snorted, and took his revenge later. He could never bear seeing me study late into the night, concentrating in the stuffy little room. Nights were my distant hope. When Omar went on his drunken sprees, he caused havoc. Sometimes he came in so slewed he lost his balance and fell over, completely smashed. But if he came in half lucid, with the energy to create more mayhem, he woke the women up, and off I went to help Zana and my mother. "Bring a basin of cold water . . . His arm's bleeding . . . Hurry up, go and get the Mercurochrome! Careful not to wake Halim . . . Boil a little water, he needs to drink some tea . . ." They kept on asking for things, while Omar writhed around, belching, wishing everyone to hell, making a show of himself: a raging bull. He groped my mother, touched her, patted her on the backside, and I jumped on top of him, wanting to strangle him; he shoved me away, kicked me, everyone started shouting and getting involved, Zana sent me to my room, Domingas came to my assistance, crying and hugging me. Rânia put her arms around her brother, "Stop this, for Heaven's sake!" But he wouldn't quiet down, he wanted to ruin everyone's night, everyone had to be on the receiving end; he wanted to wake up everyone in the slum at the back, in the street, the whole neighborhood. What he most wanted was for his father to come. Halim rarely came down. He cleared his throat, put the light on, and we saw his elongated shadow, immense, on the wall upstairs. The shadow moved, then stopped, and disappeared. He slammed the door, making a terrific noise. The next day nobody spoke; everyone was riled at everyone else, nothing but scowls and bad temper. And hatred. I hated these sleepless nights, all of them lost through Omar. The tickings-off I got from Zana because I didn't understand her son, poor thing, so muddled he couldn't even study. She took advantage of Halim's absence and invented onerous tasks, doubled my workload so that I hardly had time to be with my mother. How many times I thought of running away! Once I went onto an Italian ship and hid—I'd made up my mind: I was going away, two weeks later I'd get off in Genoa, when all I knew was that it was a port in Italy. I had sudden urges to go, maybe to Santarém or Belém; that would be easier. I looked at all the boats and ships moored in Manaus Harbor and put the journey off. I pictured my mother; I didn't want to leave her there at the back of the house, couldn't face it . . . She never wanted to take the risk. "Are you mad? It gives me the shakes just to think about it, you have to be patient with Zana, with Omar. Halim likes you." Domingas bought the patience myth, though she cried when she saw me running around, hard at work, missing school, swallowing insults. So I stayed with her and put up with our fate. I started meddling in everything. I saw Halim and Zana with their legs in the air, immersed in frenzied licks and kisses, scenes I saw when I was ten or eleven, that amused me and frightened me, because Halim let out bellows and guffaws, and Zana, for all the holier-than-thou face she put on at breakfast, was a devil in bed, a volcano, erotic to the tips of her toes. Sometimes they forgot to shut the door, or there wasn't time, and there, through the crack, my left eye followed their bodies as they rolled, and her breasts as they disappeared into Halim's mouth.

Perhaps he forgot things, and omitted some strange scenes, but memory invents, even when it wants to be faithful to the past. Once I tried to coax a recollection out of him: didn't he recite Abbas's poetry before he went courting? He looked me right in the eyes, and then his head turned around towards the garden, his gaze fixed on the old, half dead rubber tree. All there was was silence. Lost in the past, his memory was hovering around the far-off afternoon when I saw him reciting Abbas's *gazals*. It was an overture, and Zana was excited by the deep, melodious voice, which must have touched her soul before delirium took hold of their bodies. Omissions, lacunae, forgetfulness; the desire to forget. But I remember; I've always had a thirst for memories, for an unknown past, abandoned on some beach by the river.

Yaqub had already been living in São Paulo for some six years, more and more proud of himself, more and more of a genius. But he didn't boast; he let it be known what road he had taken, and it was always the right one. At the end of every line, an arrow pointed to a glorious destiny, and marriage was part of that destiny. What did not enter the surveyor's sights was Omar going to São Paulo. In that year, 1956, Omar had already abandoned the Vandals' Cockpit, and there was no mention of studies, diplomas, anything like that. Antenor Laval brought him books and invited him to read poems in the pension where he lived. He admired Omar's intonation; after Omar recited one of his friend's poems, he would say: "That's the voice of your perfect reader." The two of them didn't stay indoors long, and Omar emptied his mother's purse and dragged Laval to the pavement in front of the Café Mocambo, where veterans and novices from the Rui Barbosa Lyceum passed by.

He was living it up as much as ever, and one night came home with a new girl, from the slum in the street at the back, Calisto's sister. The two of them had a ball: they danced around the altar, smoked the hookah, and drank as much as they wanted. In the early morning, Halim smelled cooked peach palm and jackfruit; he saw bottles of arrack and clothes scattered on the floor, fruit stones and peel on the Bible open on the carpet in front of the altar, and saw his son and the girl, naked, sleeping on the gray sofa. Slowly the father came down, the girl woke up, frightened and ashamed, and Halim, halfway downstairs, waited for her to get dressed and get out. Then he went over to his son, who was pretending to be asleep, dragged him to the edge of the table, and then I saw Omar, now a mature man, take one slap, just one; his father's huge hand swung and fell hard, like an oar, on his son's face. All of Halim's vain entreaties, all his rude replies were concentrated in that blow. It was like a hammer falling on hollow wood. What a hand! And what an aim!

The tough guy, the night owl, the whoremonger was sprawled out on the carpet. Omar didn't get up. His father chained him to the lock of the steel safe, sat for a few minutes on the gray sofa, took a deep breath, and went out. He disappeared for two days. Zana couldn't interfere; she had no time to come to her son's aid. She blustered, shouted, and felt ill when she saw her son chained, leaning against the rusty safe, his cheek swollen up in high relief. Deep inside, that slap echoed like part of my revenge too.

Rânia put arnica onto the bloated cheek, his mother fed her little chick through his pursed mouth, and Domingas got the chamber pot in position so he could piss: three slaves for one captive. Zana went after Halim and found the shop locked up. I was charged with combing the city center: I went into the stalls scattered around the harbor in Remédios Square, the little restaurants hidden at the top of the gullies, and the cheap bars in the labyrinth of the Floating City, where he used to go for a chat with one of his cronies. No one had sighted him, and even if I had found him, I wouldn't have said a thing. Right at the end of the Escadaria harbor, tethered to a canoe, a dog was barking—the poor beast was foaming at the mouth in its distress; this time I really laughed, for the sight of the tethered dog reminded me of the prisoner with the swollen face. Every tough guy has his weak points. Did Halim, calm as he was, know that? He gave his son's face a good thump and left. He only came back home two days later. For the two nights he was captive, we heard Omar bellowing, the sound of him pointlessly kicking the solid safe, and the harsh clanking of the metal chain. A blowtorch would have freed him, but no one thought of that, least of all me, ignorant as I was of the existence of blowtorches and only thinking vaguely of revenge. But who could I exact vengeance on?

It was only after the episode of the Silver Woman that Halim decided to send Omar to São Paulo. Yaqub was now married and, once again, hadn't accepted a penny from his parents; he would have turned down a gift from the hand of God. He didn't reveal his wife's name, and only gave notice of the wedding by telegram. Zana bit her lip. For her, a son married might as well be lost or kidnapped. She pretended not to be interested in her daughter-in-law's name, and danced attendance on Omar even more; she was attracted to him like iron filings to an immense magnet.

On Zana's birthday, the day dawned with the vases in the living room full of flowers and affectionate notes from Omar, flowers and words that awoke in Rânia a passion that she had never experienced. For a moment, on that single morning of the year, Rânia forgot the mocking, sarcastic good-time boy, and saw the ghost of a fantasy lover in her brother's noble gesture. She hugged and kissed him, but caressing a ghost is a fleeting affair, and Omar reappeared, flesh and blood, smiling cynically at his sister. He smiled, tickled her around the waist, on her bottom, and one of his hands felt its way up between her legs. Rânia sweated, bristled, and kept clear of her brother; she went to her room in a flash. Before dinner, when the neighbors were already chatting and drinking in the living room, she would reappear. She was the best-dressed woman of the evening, almost more beautiful than her mother, and the neighbors looked at her, wondering why that woman insisted on sleeping alone in a narrow bed. Rânia could have gone to the open-air parties in the city, to St. John's night, to Carnival balls, to the parties by the lake at the Rio Negro Athletic Club, but she avoided all that. On the few occasions she appeared at the Benemous' party, she stayed aloof, beautiful and much admired, showered with confetti and streamers by smooth-chinned lads and gray-haired men. Zana, still quite young, kept herself to one side and sulked. Domingas, who had known her since she was born, remembered the afternoon when mother and daughter fell out. The bouquets of flowers with messages for Rânia faded in the living room until they smelled of mourning. My mother didn't find out what had happened, and I only got to know something years later, during an unexpected, memorable encounter. She had been a happy, vivacious girl, Domingas said, but from that day on Rânia only touched two men: the twins. She no longer went to the dance halls in the city; she stopped promenading around the squares where she met old friends from the Ginásio Amazonense to go to matinees at the Odeon, the Guarany, or the Polytheama; she became a recluse, retiring to the nocturnal solitude of her little room. No one knew what she did within those four walls. Rânia became this cloistered being, and woe betide anyone who disturbed her after eight o'clock, when she withdrew from the world. She left her room on the night of her mother's birthday and for Christmas dinner. She abandoned the university in the first semester, and asked her father if she could work in the shop. Halim agreed. What he expected from Omar came from Rânia; the result of this unexpected turn of events was a hawk-eyed businesswoman. In a short time, Rânia began to sell, buy, and exchange merchandise. She knew all the most powerful river traders, and without leaving Manaus, without even leaving the Rua dos Barés, she knew who was selling clothes to the most distant villages. She struck a deal with these traders, who at the start despised her; then, they thought or pretended to think that Halim was behind this astute haggler. It wasn't uncommon to see her display her almost instantaneous smile of false familiarity to the customers. She knew how to attract them, giving them a slow, languid, captivating look, which contrasted with the rapid, efficient gestures of the practiced saleswoman.

A photograph of Yaqub with six words on the back sharpened the urges of this compulsive letter writer. However, she didn't answer the love letters sent by doctors and lawyers, which Zana read in tender tones, and with some degree of hope. Rânia tore them all up, and threw the pieces into the brazier.

"Is that a way to treat your suitors?" her mother said.

"Smoke! They all turn into smoke and ashes," she replied with a smile, biting her lip.

In secret, Zana would invite some suitor for dinner on her birthday; she did this every year, for I saw lots of men come into the house with two bouquets, one for the mother, one for the daughter. The next morning, the leaves in the garden were sprinkled with petals. Rânia shredded the letters and took the petals off the flowers quite naturally, and, when she did it in front of Zana, even with a certain pleasure. Her mother warned her—"You'll become an old maid. It's sad to see a girl aging that way"—but to no avail.

Old age was still a way off, and if there was any bitterness, Rânia knew how to hide it. She hid a lot of things: her thoughts, her ideas, her sense of humor, and even a good part of her body, which I always admired. However, she was a virtuoso when it came to more humble matters, and in that regard she was always a help to me. It's sad to think she only used those dark hands with their long, perfect fingers to change a lightbulb, mend a leaking tap, or unblock a grate. Or to do the accounts and count the money: maybe that was why the shop stayed open for so long, even when business was thin; then, she would go out with a box of trinkets, for the sustenance of the house and the family. She did all this during the day. After dinner she shut herself in her room, where the night awaited her.

Who knows what happened in that mysterious encounter? Probably not even the night pried into her gestures and thoughts. But Zana's birthday party was, for Rânia, a break in her nocturnal confinement. This was the night when she made one of her suitors hopeful, and he was the one who would not return to the house on next year's birthday. She led them all on, one by one, on every festive occasion, as her mother got older. I smelled Rânia's scent before I heard her footsteps along the corridor on the upper floor. She let herself be admired at the top of the stairs; then, with meticulous movements, she came down, and one by one there came into view her shapely legs, her plump, bare arms, the wavy hair covering her shoulders, and her low neckline, which emphasized her breathing. We saw her dark-skinned body, almost as tall as the twins, with makeup and lipstick on for this one night of the year, and her eyes, mystified or stunned, seemed to ask why on earth she was coming into this room full of people. Rânia brought shivers to my almost adolescent body. I had the urge to kiss and bite those arms. Anxiously, I awaited her close embrace, the only one of the year. Waiting was torture. I kept quiet, but inside I was ablaze. Then the minx came over to me, gave me a squeeze, and I felt her breasts pressing against my nose. I smelled the jasmine, and spent the rest of the night intoxicated by the scent. When she went away, she stroked my chin as if the beard was already there, and kissed my eyes with lips wet with saliva, and I had to run away to my room.

Talib had the hots for her. The widower pushed to the front, and was the first to greet her with unrestrained kisses on her hands, her arms, and face. Zahia and Nahda jealously ran to pull him away from Rânia, as he shouted to Halim: "By God, I'd exchange my two daughters for yours."

I envied the suitor of the evening when Rânia put out her hands to accept the bouquet. Afterwards, she moved away with an ethereal, enigmatic look, which made her gallant look bashful. But she accepted the invitation to dance, pretending to be shy and distant during the first steps; gradually her dusky arms twined round his back, her hands gripped his waist, and, with her eyes closed, she rested her chin on the dancer's right shoulder. At that moment, Zana turned the lights off in the room, and prayed that a love affair, or the promise of an engagement, might come out of the dance. All that came out of it was a resentful man, who saw Rânia suddenly interrupt the dance and throw herself into Omar's arms when he entered the room. The suitor, openmouthed at this intimacy between brother and sister, went off in a huff; some didn't even say goodbye to Zana. Omar called them boobies, stuck-up imbeciles, groveling idiots with nothing to them; for none of them had Omar's eyes, voluptuous and devouring. Perhaps Rânia wanted to grab one of these imbeciles and say: "Look at my brother Omar; now look carefully at the photograph of my beloved Yaqub. Put the two together, and that'll be my fiancé."

She never found this compound. She contented herself with idolizing the twins, in the knowledge that their blood ties could never cancel out their enmity. Even so, Rânia's admiration for both was, for a long time, visceral and almost symmetrical. She talked to Yaqub's image, kissed his face on the dull paper, and whispered one thing after another to him—words she would put in her letter.

Year after year I heard Zana say to her daughter, on the day after the birthday party: "You missed a fine figure of a man, dear. You're throwing your future out of the window." Rânia reacted angrily: "You know very well . . . He wasn't what I wanted. I've never felt attracted to any of the idiots that come around here."

What for her mother was a blow of fate, for her was nothing more than a pleasure that lasted for three dances or fifteen minutes. Unlike Zana, she managed to conceal the jealous feelings she felt for Omar, and both women did everything possible to be the queen of the ball when he appeared with a new girlfriend. But on the night of the episode of the Silver Woman, they didn't reign alone.

There were rumors that Omar was courting a woman older than himself. It was Zahia Talib who brought the news, on the night of Zana's birthday. The two sisters and their father came early. Talib had brought a drum, the *darbuk*, and said he was going to play for his daughters to dance at the party. Zana thanked him and stopped smiling when she heard Zahia's voice:

"It seems Omar's found a woman and a half. They say they spend the whole night dancing in the Acapulco . . ."

"A woman and a half? In the Acapulco? Heavens, Zahia, you can't think much of my Omar. Omar, what's more . . . he's always admired your looks."

Zahia's news left Zana impatient. She showed every guest the flowers, still fresh, and the love note written by her son. She knew that sooner or later, Omar would arrive, accompanied by a woman. He came at ten, before the Talib sisters' dance. He opened his arms, saying in Arabic, "Happy birthday, my queen." It was a phrase he'd learned by heart, but it was perfectly pronounced. He kissed her with passion, and at that moment Zana shed tears, partly out of emotion, partly because Omar, after the kiss, introduced his new girlfriend.

This time she decided not to pretend: she faced this woman with a sweet smile and a look of contempt, knowing she would never be her son's wife; she was the rival defeated in advance. At heart, Zana didn't pay much attention to the women Omar brought back home. He didn't discriminate; never got enthusiastic about the color of their eyes or hair. He wooed nameless women, women of whom nobody in the neighborhood could say: she's the daughter, granddaughter, or niece of so-and-so. They were unknown women, who never went to the fashionable beauty salons, much less to the Green Salon in the Ideal Club; he courted girls who had never left Manaus, never gone to Rio de Janeiro. All the same, Omar's anonymous women brought surprises, and he cultivated these surprises, taking pleasure in other people's reactions. Halim prayed for one of these women to take his son far from home, or for one of Talib's daughters, preferably Zahia, the more beautiful, sensual, and perceptive of the two, to ensnare him. But he sensed that Zana was stronger, more audacious, and more powerful.

The jealousy, fear, envy, and pity that Omar's women caused! Like the Peruvian girl from Iquitos, small and dainty, who sang in Spanish all night, pouting at Halim, until Zana said, loud so that everyone could hear: "Son, is your little girl looking for a job?"

They were all Zana's victims. All, except two. The one I knew and saw close-up rises up again in front of me, as if that distant evening were coming alive again in this present one.

The others, eager and compliant, were no match for Zana, and came nowhere near threatening her mother's love. Apart from that, they had no names, that is, Omar only called them love or princess, to the delight of the queen mother, secure on her throne. But that night the woman had a name: Dália. She was introduced to everyone, one by one. A first name wasn't enough. Omar revealed her surname, which I've forgotten. The rest, that is, all Dália's charms, were her own. What a duel there was between Zana and the aspiring daughter-in-law! It was silent, and witnessed by very few: such was the dissembling power of the false laughter and the bows and curtsies.

But Dália's strength began with her body and flowed into her flaming red dress, more rebellious, sensual, and full-blooded than the seed of the *guaraná*. She attracted more looks than Rânia. She attracted them, but kept herself to herself, mysterious, molding herself to our imagination. Little by little, the looks moved away from her dress to her face, with its effortless smile. Omar and Dália settled in one corner of the room, and at that moment Zana went over to talk to her. Omar went off and left them alone. It's not known what they said, but each was sounding out the other's territory, their gestures carefully disguised, both of them very nervous, like an actress on an opening night. Dália's words prevailed, both in tone and timbre, captivating sounds, slightly lilting, and not at all false. Zana felt herself threatened, and looked for another corner. It was her first defeat, though still a partial one, before midnight.

After the dessert Rânia retired, for even her suitor was overcome with Dália's presence. It was not Rânia's night. She left without saying good night, and as she slowly crossed the room to the staircase, she tried to glean some flattering remark, but this time her beauty was ignored.

It was then that the night began. The lights in the room went out. From the veranda, the glimmering moonlight outlined seated silhouettes. The sound of lutes and drums filled the room, the house, and, to my ears, seemed to fill the whole world. Then Talib's two girls came out of the shadows. Their arms, then their hips and bellies, undulated to the rhythm of the music, which seemed to multiply the movements of the dancers' bodies. Their gestures were similar, rehearsed, perhaps predictable, a calculated sensuality, such was the skill of the dancing sisters. They repeated the steps and the turns, under the spell of the music, and were just suddenly stiffening their bodies in an unexpected pause in the drumbeats when out of the dark there arose a clear, tall figure who moved towards the center of the room, with sensuous, symmetrical twirls, and then we saw a slim female body, barefoot, dancing like a goddess, throwing her face and shoulders back, curved like a bow, and now the music was accompanied by claps and the click of heels on the floor. The atmosphere was already close, hot, almost suffocating, when a shaft of light from a lantern lit up the dancer's face. Then we saw the smile, the full lips with no lipstick, the eyes turned to the corner of the room where Omar, in ecstasy, held the lantern. What magic there was in the light licking Dália: the light from Omar's trembling hand. She attracted everyone's looks, and danced that way for quite a time, her silvery body maddened by the rhythm of the drums, the clapping, and the lute, and we—stunned by the sensual turns of this body that drew us away from our usual night—we envied Omar, the disputed twin.

But Omar was making the mistake of betraying the woman who had never betrayed him. Zana stirred in her seat when she saw her son coming near Dália, the light from the lantern gradually illuminating the dancer's face, until the infatuated exhibitionist theatrically kissed his lover in the middle of the room, and then asked for applause for her. Everyone clapped in time to the drum, played by the widower Talib. Only Zana stayed aloof from all this homage. She refused to let them sing "Happy Birthday," ignored the cake that she and Domingas had prepared, and left the little candles that

Halim had arranged with his wife's name lit on top of it. Zana's name kept burning on the iced cake, and the image of the red flames is still vivid in my memory. Halim understood and went up to the bedroom. My mother signaled to me to go with her, but I pretended not to notice and stayed there. She disappeared into the back of the house. The neighbors said goodbye, and Talib was the last one to go out, with his drum. There was no more music: Omar and Dália dragged themselves around the room, glued to one another, while Zana, sitting on the rocking chair, her fan motionless in her hand, accompanied their silent dance.

Never, on these festive occasions, had he danced so long with his face and body stuck to a woman. It was an affront to his mother, Omar's great betrayal. Zana waited for the bodies to begin to stagger with exhaustion, and for the right moment for the dénouement, which couldn't be long in coming. She put her fan on one side, got up, turned all the lights on, and sweetly asked if the dancer would mind giving her a hand, and help her to clean the table. Omar approved of this intimacy. He lay down in the red hammock, not far from me. I don't think he saw me: he only had eyes for the Silver Woman. The two of them began to take plates and glasses from the table, and went from the living room to the kitchen; sometimes they talked as they went, and in one of these comings and goings, Zana gripped the other woman's arm hard and whispered. Dália went into the toilet. She reappeared in the red dress, holding a small bag where she had put the silvery one. I only got a glance at her face, but I could see it was no longer the same as when she came into the house, nor of the dancer that had magnetized so many eyes. It was the face of a humiliated woman. She stopped in the room, and before she left, said out loud: "We'll see, we'll see."

Omar, sleepy, sat up in the hammock and heard the front door slam. He ran into the street, and disappeared into the night, after the woman.

. . .

We found out that Dália was one of the Silver Women who were on show on Sundays at the Maloca dos Barés. They were Amazonian dancers, but said they were from Rio, thinking this lie would enlarge their audiences. Zana did everything to convince her engineer son to give lodging to the good-time boy. "He wants to get hooked to a hustler from the Maloca, a dancing girl who made a show of herself on the night of my birthday. If he doesn't spend some time in São Paulo, he'll let everything go: his studies, his home, his family," she wrote to him.

Yaqub refused to put his brother up. He wrote to his mother that he could rent a room in a pension for Omar and matriculate him in a private school. He agreed to send news of Omar's life in São Paulo, but he was not going to have him sleeping under his roof. "Let him find his own road, but away from me, way away from my patch."

When Omar found out about the plan, he spent several days out of the house. He slept and ate out, and sent an abusive letter, calling his brother a "wimp, a scoundrel, a hypocrite." He tried in vain to fix a meeting with Dália and his mother. Zana discovered what kind of roof the dancer had over her head: a tumbledown house in Vila Saturnina, to the north, where Manaus came to an end. It was the last little house in the town, in a bit of wasteland full of the remains of carts and rusty bicycle wheels. The red flowers of the *jambo* trees covered a dirt track that linked the street to the town. Dália lived with two aunts, a seamstress and a confectioner, and the three of them lived on the verge of poverty. The state of the house was pitiful: the beginnings of a slum, with twisted wooden partitions separating a mass of tiny rooms and compartments. I went to visit them on Zana's orders. Even in daylight, without her makeup and her silvery costume, Dália was beautiful. She was in shorts and a T-shirt, sitting on the ground, with a pile of colored bobbins between her brown thighs. When she saw me, her smile disappeared; she stuck her needle into her frayed sleeve and left the room. I still got a close view of her breasts, which showed through the worn cotton. My mission was contemptible, but Omar's going to São Paulo, and his absence, even temporary, would benefit me, and bring me a little peace. I offered Dália's aunts the money Zana had sent. They were reluctant, but orders for sweets and dresses were few and far between at that time. The other end of Brazil was growing at a dizzying rate, as Yaqub wanted. But in stagnant Manaus, any offer of money was manna from heaven. The aunts accepted the offer and maybe changed the broken tiles and rotten beams in the roofing. That way, I spared them some of the discomforts of the rainy season, soothed a mother's heart, and even got a little money myself as a tip.

Dália disappeared from the Maloca dos Barés, from the house in Vila Saturnina, from the city. We never found out if she departed this world altogether, and even Omar never found out, or, if he did, he said nothing when he reappeared one wet afternoon. He had no shoes or shirt, and his trousers were soaking. He was like a scarecrow coming in from the rain, and so drunk he bumped into the two porcelain vases before falling into the red hammock. Zana didn't budge. Domingas and Rânia were concerned, and wanted to help him, but a sharp look prevented them. He slept out of doors in the damp air, and woke with a cough, so worn out he could hardly move. He was already feverish when he heard his mother say:

"All this because of a common dancing girl. That snake would have taken you to hell with her, love. Your brother'll help you in São Paulo."

"My brother?" he shouted in exasperation.

Halim came over to his son:

"You're going to study in São Paulo, you're going to have to work at it just like your brother . . ."

"Calm down, Halim . . . our little boy's burning with fever," said Zana, embracing her son. "He needs some rest, then he can go, spend a few months in São Paulo, and come back."

Omar fixed his bloodshot eyes on his father's face, tried to get up, but Halim pushed him down hard and turned his back on his son. They didn't speak to each other until the day he left. Zana repented her decision, and wanted to put her son's journey off; she looked as if she was in mourning, and prayed for everything to turn out right for Omar; the separation had something of death about it.

He went under protest, rebellious and angry. There were six months of peace and quiet at home, and of relief for Halim. Omar's books, the novels and poems he read in the hammock, fell into my hands; his books, notepaper, his pens, everything, except for the room, which was his and his alone. In his chaotic bedroom, the old mattress and the sheets were changed. But before he left, Omar had asked Domingas to leave the objects on the shelves; she put a sheet over the collection of ashtrays, glasses, bottles of sand, panties, bras, red seeds, stubs of lipstick, and stained cigarette butts. Domingas, cleaning out the wardrobe, discovered an Indian oar, dark and polished. On the blade, there were women's names carved with a knife. Domingas smoothed the dark blade, pronouncing one name after another and sat on Omar's bed, half in a trance, maybe missing him. Now she could go into his room, live with the things he had left behind, open the window and see the horizon he saw every evening before he left for his nightly entertainment. She went through all the furniture in the room, and kept on finding objects, photographs, toys, the old worn-out uniform from the Vandals' Cockpit. It was different from Yaqub's room, empty, with no rubbish: a place to put your body, and nothing more. I don't know which of the two my mother preferred to clean. The fact is that every day, in good or bad mood, she went into each room and lingered there before she started cleaning.

And if the oar and the junk excited her, the severity of Yaqub's room cooled her head. Perhaps my mother liked the contrast.

Zana gave me her son's uniform; it was loose on me and made people laugh. I swallowed the laughter, and gave the clothes back before Zana ate me with her eyes—she couldn't bear seeing the uniform on another body. And thanks to Halim, I went to the Vandals' Cockpit.

At the school I found traces of Omar: ex-girlfriends, stories of shindigs, heroic scenes, challenges, duels. On the toilet walls was graffiti composed by him. Wherever he went, he left a daring gesture, some act of bravado, an epigram, words of humor and irony. I finished the course he had abandoned in the final year. In fact, Omar never finished anything, he would never go to a university, despised diplomas, and was ignorant of anything that didn't give him an intense, powerful pleasure, in his endless quest for adventure.

Halim and Zana thought that their graduate son could straighten him out, and that sooner or later the tough life of São Paulo would tame him. For months they believed Omar's letters: he was fine, it had taken him a while to get used to the cold, but now he was studying, getting up early to go to the college, having his dinner in the pension in the Rua Tamandaré, hardly leaving his room. It was a different Omar, diligent, never playing truant, though he did feel a bit out of place among the other pupils, being so grown up. On the last Saturday in August, Yaqub's maid visited Omar's pension to give him clothes and sweets Zana had sent. Two coats, a pullover, and a pair of velvet trousers, so that her little hairy boy wouldn't suffer from the cold and drizzle; and a tin full of Arabic sweets, to remember his mother by. Omar acknowledged the gift: "Thanks very much, brother. It's the first time I've enjoyed my food since I came to São Paulo. Only my mother could give me so much pleasure." Yaqub said nothing when the maid told him that Omar, sitting on the bed, devoured the sweets.

This other Omar existed for a few months. On Republic Day, November 15, before he went to Santos with his wife, Yaqub decided to go to the Liberdade area, where Omar lived. Years later, Yaqub told his father that he didn't want to speak to his brother, or even see him. He had passed in front of the pension to see the miserable house inhabited by students from other cities and regions. He thought of the lonely nights of the first months when he, Yaqub, had lived in São Paulo. On Saturdays he would go to Porto Geral and the Rua 25 de Março, and go into the little clothes shops and haberdashers'; he heard the conversations of the Armenian and Arab immigrants, and laughed to himself, or felt bitter as he remembered his childhood in the port area of Manaus, where he had heard those same sounds. Then, in the Damascus Emporium, he spent a good while sniffing the strong odor of the spices, devouring with his eyes the delicacies he couldn't buy; he thought of the restaurants and clubs he couldn't go to, of the shop windows he stared at on his way to and fro between the Pension Veneza and the Polytechnic School; he thought of the boredom of Sundays and holidays in a city, with no friends or family. Extreme solitude would tame a savage like Omar. Yaqub believed that suffering, hard work, changed habits, and the despair of solitude would be decisive in Omar's education. He wasn't going to help him. He believed that having to fend for oneself brings out the best in people. But he was curious to know something about his brother's life. How was he getting on? How was he behaving at school? How could he live far from Manaus, where he knew every street and was greeted and fussed over in the posh clubs and the brothels? Where home cooking and the comforts and affections of the women of the house spurred on his insolence even more? In Manaus, Omar would never be just anybody. For Yaqub, though, anonymity was a challenge.

A week after the holiday, he decided to go to the school where his brother was studying. He talked to the teachers and pupils. He was strange, they said; an impulsive boy, a daredevil, who liked overcoming obstacles. Omar faithfully came to classes, went to the labs, though he was a bit overenthusiastic in the physical education classes. He was getting on well: why had he stopped coming to school? Was he ill? Yaqub stood openmouthed: since when hadn't he come to school? Since the holiday he hadn't come to a single class.

He went to the pension on the Rua Tamandaré and learned that his brother had abandoned his room with no explanation, without even paying for it. He went into Omar's room and saw an empty suitcase on the floor, the clothes hanging on makeshift hangers, and a map of the United States on the writing desk. No note, not a word, not a sign. Yaqub thought there might have been an accident, a disaster. He looked for his brother in the hospitals, police stations, and morgues of São Paulo. His wife advised him: "Whatever you do, don't mention his disappearance to your parents. He'll come back. If he doesn't, it's not your fault."

They thought he might come back at any moment; they might as well wait one or two weeks. Boxes of sweets went on arriving from Manaus. In December they got the first postcard.

5

Incredible things happened in Omar's life, or he let them happen, as if welcoming any opportunity for adventure with open arms. Some people are like that. They don't even need to go looking for life's unpredictable side; they just let themselves be swept along by chance, or anything unusual that happens.

Yaqub only revealed the truth about his brother when he visited the family for the first time since he'd left for São Paulo.

When I found out he was coming, I had a strange sensation, and got quite agitated. The image they gave of him was of a perfect being, or someone in search of perfection. I thought about this: if he's my father, then I'm the son of an almost perfect man. I was never worried by his expertise, or felt threatened by it. I thought of him as a determined man, respected at home, even praised by his father, who had no idea what his son was aiming for. Once, Halim told me Yaqub could hide everything: he was a man who would never lay himself bare; there were no chinks in his armor. You can expect anything of a son like that, his father said. Omar, on the other hand, laid himself completely open, and this was Zana's greatest weapon. I tried to find out which of the two had attracted my mother. I could see Domingas got nervous when Omar called me in arrogant tones and sent me with a message to the other end of the city. He even took advantage of Zana's protection to raise his voice, but when Halim was around he didn't dare, which was a relief for my mother. Now, with Yaqub's visit, she never let me out of her sight. When Yaqub saw me in the garden, holding hands with Domingas, he looked embarrassed, and didn't know who to embrace first. I was as happy as I was surprised. He embraced my mother, and I felt her hand sweaty and trembling, gripping my fingers. I had a vague memory of his voice, because he used to come into my mother's room and say things, words I didn't understand. What I do remember, very well, is the question Domingas asked him when she learned he was going to São Paulo. "Are you going to take that girl with you?" my mother asked several times. He didn't answer, and left the room without saying anything. Years later, my mother revealed who the girl was and told me Omar had cut his brother's face because of her.

Now I recognized the voice I had heard when I was four or five. He said he'd brought books for me. He didn't seem like a stranger—rather someone who couldn't feel at ease in the house where he'd been born.

Zana asked him why his wife hadn't come to Manaus, and he merely looked scornfully at his mother, knowing he could irritate her with his silence.

"You mean I'm not going to meet my daughter-in-law?" Zana insisted. "Is she afraid of the heat, or does she think we're animals?"

"Your other son'll give you a daughter-in-law, and then some," Yaqub said, drily. "Someone ideal, just like himself."

Zana preferred not to answer.

The day before Yaqub's arrival she'd dreamed the twins were chatting calmly in her room, but then suddenly she saw the young Yaqub at the quayside, with his back to a white ship, smiling coldly at her. He smiled and fixed his eyes on her, then slowly disappeared.

At breakfast she told Halim her dream. She was tense and flustered; stroking her hands, he said in an ironic tone:

"Zana, I swear, if I'd have had a little part in your dream, I'd have shooed the two out of our room and put up the hammock . . ."

"Even then, it would be a dream," she said bitterly. "What can I do? Our sons don't get on . . ."

"What can you do? Pay a bit of attention to your other son. It's years since we've seen Yaqub. Look what he's managed to do, alone in São Paulo. He's got his own existence, his own wife."

She feared a meeting between the two, and an explosion of insults in the household. She was on watch during the night until Omar came in; then Domingas helped carry him to his room; he emerged when his brother had already gone out. They did this for three consecutive nights, preventing Yaqub from encountering his brother in the red hammock on the veranda.

Yaqub's visit, though it was only short, let me get to know him a little. Something in his behavior escaped me: he left a mixed impression on me, of someone hard, resolute, and proud, but marked, at the same time, by an eagerness that was like a kind of affection. This uncertainty left me confused. Or perhaps it was I who was going up and down like a seesaw. A lot of what they said about Yaqub didn't fit with what I saw and felt. At home, with the family, he changed, and became wary. With me, however, his armor was incomplete, to use Halim's phrase about his son. As we walked around the city, and came near the harbor area, he seemed to find everything strange. He was dripping sweat, and irritated by the filth piled up in the streets. Gradually, this took on less importance. Near the Amazonas Hotel he stopped by Dona Deúsa's *tacacá* stall, and drank two gourds of the thick liquid, calmly swallowing the steaming pepper sauce, slowly chewing the spiced *jambu*, as if he wanted to recover a childhood treat. Then we went around the Escadaria harbor, where a canoeist took us to the Educandos creek. The low level of the river Negro left muddy beaches, with their motorboats, some stranded, others disused, their hulls upturned. Yaqub began to row, and at times lifted an oar and gestured to the inhabitants of the shanties built out over the mud. He laughed to see the children running through the alleyways of the slum, on the improvised football pitches, or clambering on the awnings of abandoned boats. "I played a lot around here," he said, "I came with your mother, we spent Sundays by the water there . . . hiding in the floating islands." He seemed happy, and wasn't bothered by the smell of mud infesting the beaches along the creek. He pointed to a shack on the left bank, just before the metal bridge. We beached the canoe, Yaqub looked at the house with its legs in the mud, went up some steps, and called me. It was a shack that had been painted blue, but now its front was covered with gray blotches; inside were two small tables and stools: a woman who was setting the tables asked if we wanted to eat. Yaqub answered with a question: did she remember him? No, she had no idea: who was he? "This boy's mother and I used to come and eat fried *jaraqui* in your house. Then we used to swim in the creek . . . I played football and flew kites . . ." She stood back, looked him up and down, and asked when, was it a long time ago? "I am Halim's son."

From the Rua dos Barés? Our Lady in Heaven . . . that boy? Well . . . how you've grown! Wait a little." She brought out a black-and-white photograph: Yaqub and my mother together, in a canoe, in front of the shack, called the Bar da Margem. He looked at the image, quiet and thoughtful, and with his eyes searched for the place on the bank where one day he had been happy. Then he said he lived far away, in São Paulo; it was years since he'd visited the city. The woman wanted to strike up a conversation, but Yaqub hardly spoke;

his happiness gradually disappeared, and his face became serious. He briefly said goodbye; the woman offered him the photo, and he thanked her: he might come back to the Bar da Margem with Domingas. In the canoe, rowing to the little harbor, he told me he would never forget the day he left Manaus and was sent to Lebanon. It was horrible. "I was forced apart from everybody, everything . . . I didn't want to go."

His pain seemed stronger than his emotion at returning to his childhood world. He washed his face in river water, and asked the canoeist to go around the Floating City, where the flames of candles and kerosene lamps were already beginning to flicker. The jungle was going dark behind us, and the glow from the city grew as we rowed on through the humid night. In flashes, I saw Yaqub's unsmiling face, and imagined what must have happened to him during the time when he lived in the village in southern Lebanon. Nothing, perhaps, no wicked or aggressive act could have been as violent as Yaqub's brusque separation from his world. But, in those days he spent in Manaus, I noticed his mood often changed. His enthusiasm at rediscovering certain people, landscapes, smells, and tastes was soon stifled by the memory of a rift. Now, it's not so hard to think about these things. I can still see him jumping out of the canoe and going towards the Rua dos Barés; I can hear his voice, criticizing his father's out-of-date shop and his friends around the backgammon board.

"These people get in the way of the customers; they're like vultures with carrion, waiting for their afternoon snack to turn up. You'll not get very far that way."

Rânia agreed, but Halim, with his arms resting on the counter, asked:

"Why go that far? What about enjoying a game, or a chat?"

"Business doesn't flourish on chance pleasures like that," said Yaqub, addressing his sister.

Halim asked me to accompany him to Balma's shop.

"Tonight Issa and Talib are going to have a game of billiards, and I don't want to miss that particular game of chance."

I said goodbye to brother and sister, and only went to see Yaqub on the next day, the eve of his departure for São Paulo.

He came down early, had breakfast, and began reading an engineering textbook, about the building of "large structures"; when Rânia showed him the framed photographs, he shut the books and admired these images of himself. Rânia had gotten thinner, and prettier, with her large, almond-shaped eyes, long neck, and face like her mother's, almost completely smooth. She would grow old like that, hostile to men, revealing as each year passed the remains of a beauty that never ceased to have its effect on me. She spoiled the twins and let herself be caressed by them, as on that morning when Yaqub took her onto his lap. Her legs, dark-skinned and firm, brushed against her brother's; she caressed his face with the tips of her fingers, and Yaqub, enraptured, began to look less serious. How sensual she became in her brother's presence! They made a promising couple, whether she was with him or the other one.

During the four days of his visit she dolled herself up as never before, and all her sensuality, held back for so long, seemed to be suddenly bursting forth for the visitor. Rânia, and not her mother, got the best presents from him: a pearl necklace and a silver bracelet, which she never wore in our presence.

It was still raining hard when I saw her go up the stairs, holding hands with Yaqub; they went into her room, someone shut the door, and then my imagination ran riot. They only came down to eat.

They had lunch with their parents, and Talib and his two daughters. Yaqub was almost formal in his behavior; his attitude to the neighbors was humble, friendly without being effusive. He smoked with a cigarette holder, and was annoyed when Zana filled up his plate again with lentils and slices of leg of lamb. He blew out a cloud of smoke and left the table without touching the food.

They had coffee under the rubber tree in the garden, and he said nothing about engineering, or his own feats. There was no need: everything in his life went so smoothly that the upsets and the purgatory of daily existence only happened to other people. "Other people" meant us: us and the rest of humanity.

Then the unexpected happened: Talib, with a heavy, thundering voice, put his finger on the wound:

"Don't you miss Lebanon?"

Yaqub went pale and took some time to answer. He didn't answer, he asked:

"What Lebanon?"

Halim took another sip of coffee and frowned, looking gravely at his son. Zana bit her lip, Rânia searched for the song of a red oriole, on a branch of the rubber tree near me, until she found it.

"As far as I know, there's only one Lebanon," Talib replied. "Or rather, there are many, and one of them is here inside." He pointed to his heart.

Zahia got up, Talib gestured, and she quietly sat down again. Nahda didn't know where to look, and nobody knew what to say.

"I didn't live in Lebanon, Talib." The voice began calmly and in a monotone, but sounded as if it would soon be raised. It was, so much so that the words that followed shocked everyone: "They sent me to a village in the south, and I've forgotten the time I spent there. That's it, I've forgotten almost everything: the village, the people, the name of the village, and the relatives. The only thing I've not forgotten is the language . . ."

"Talib, let's not talk—"

"There's something else I couldn't forget," Yaqub excitedly interrupted his father. "I couldn't forget . . ." he repeated, hesitating, and then went silent.

Zana invited the neighbors to have a liqueur in the drawing room, but Talib thanked her, said he was going to take a siesta; he had a headache. He and his daughters said goodbye, and right away the family made themselves scarce. Only Yaqub stayed beneath the rubber tree, with his uncompleted sentence, his reticence, and the mystery of his life. Yaqub, cornered in this way, looked more human, or less perfect, less finished. I could see he was nervous, smoking hard, his eyes on the ground. I didn't go over to him; I didn't dare. He was transfigured; he looked as if he were grinding his teeth right down to the quick.

At nightfall, he wanted to talk to Halim; the two of them went out for dinner and came back late. I only saw him on the Sunday, before his return to São Paulo. He no longer looked haggard, and showed no signs of weakness or suffering. He hugged me tight, then stood back and looked straight at me, examining my height, observing my face.

Rânia insisted on taking him to the airport. They were already in the street when Domingas gave Yaqub a packet of manioc flour and a bunch of *pacovã* bananas. She embraced him, and sobbed when she saw him go. It was the most moving scene of Yaqub's visit.

He had revealed to his father some episodes connected with Omar's disappearance from São Paulo. Halim knew nothing. Zana and he misguidedly thought he had gone to one of the best schools in the city, and that for a whole semester he had burned the midnight oil, applying himself, bent over a book-covered desk. That's why he came back speaking a bit of English and Spanish, they thought.

"*Majnun!* Omar's a madman!" said Halim, taking a swig of arrack.

He'd taken me to a small bar at the very end of the Floating City. There, we could see the shanties of the Educandos, and the huge creek separating this amphibious neighborhood from the center of Manaus. It was the busy time of day. The labyrinth of houses built on wooden posts was humming; a swarm of canoes wound their way between the floating houses as the inhabitants returned from work, walking in single file along the narrow planks that allow people to circulate in this labyrinth. The more daring carried a large flagon, a child, or sacks of manioc flour; they had to be acrobats not to fall into the Negro. From time to time, one would disappear into the darkness of the river and turn into a news item.

I had explored the Floating City on my Sundays off. However, Halim knew the area better than I did; knew and was known. When he had sold more than usual, he shut up shop early and went into the tangle of alleyways in the crowded neighborhood. He went from house to house, greeting acquaintances here and there, and sat at the table of the most distant bar, where he had a drink or two and bought fresh fish from his cronies coming back from the lakes.

Before our conversation, he offered a coil of tobacco to a friend from Janauacá Lake, Pocu, who came to Manaus to sell star apples, piassava fiber, and manioc flour. When he couldn't sell his goods, he exchanged them for salt, coffee, sugar, and fishing tackle. He always brought some fried fish for an appetizer, and told stories; as a ship's captain, he had traveled along many of the rivers of the area. We heard a small part of a story even Halim hadn't heard: about a pair of brothers who lived in an abandoned boat, hidden, permanently stranded, near the mouth of the river Preto da Eva: two people with the same blood, brothers, living far from anywhere, without a sign of human life anywhere near. One afternoon, at the end of a great day's fishing, Pocu met them and talked with them.

"Animals . . ." murmured Pocu. "They lived just like animals."

"Animals?" Halim shook his head, looked at the swell on the river and the boats piled up in the little harbor by the steps of Remédios Square.

"That's right, animals. Except they looked happy."

"I know an animal, but one without much courage." Halim loosened his tongue, took another swig of arrack, and rolled a cigarette as his gaze wandered between the Floating City and the jungle.

Now we could hear the racket of people carrying their nets, the shouts of the boatmen, grunting pigs, voices nearby, children crying, all the noises of nightfall.

"An animal without much courage," he said again, with a cigarette in his mouth. He fixed a time to meet Pocu, for him to come by the shop next day, before the heat got too intense. The ex-sailor left the bar, and for a moment I began to imagine what the end of the story of the brother lovers might be. Had Pocu made it up? How much truth, or how many lies are there in the words of a sailor? He recounted these events with a keen conviction, as if it were an intimate truth, so much so that I went on thinking about the two brothers, mated, in a boat.

"That's it, *majnun*, a real madman." Halim snapped his fingers, then stroked the gray stubble on his chin, which made his face look even older. "Omar wants to live a life of excitement. He won't give up on that, he wants to feel excitement at every moment of his existence. Zana thought our son . . ." Halim looked at the riverbank, as if trying to remember something. "Do you know something? I too . . . I believed he'd studied for a whole semester in a top-flight school and later he'd get into a university. Not even São Paulo could mend Omar's ways! What's more, there's no saint or city could put him to rights."

Yaqub told the truth, then, or his version of it. He only told his father, who let him get things off his chest. The laconic engineer this time really let loose, and vilified his brother: "He's ungrateful, primitive, irrational, rotten to the core. He insulted me and my wife."

Halim had listened to his graduate son with a serious, sober look on his face. Now, at the bar table, his face puckered up and he let out a frightening laugh.

What had happened was this: Omar sent the first postcard from Miami; later he sent others, from Tampa, Mobile, and New Orleans, recounting the fun and games he'd had in each city. Yaqub had torn up all his postcards except for one, which he handed to his father: "Dear brother and sister-in-law, Louisiana is America in the raw, really rough, and the Mississippi is the local version of the Amazon. Why not take a little trip here? Savage it may be, but Louisiana is more civilized than the two of you put together. If you come, be sure you dye your hair blond: that way you'll be one of the elite. Brother: your wife, who's been pretty in her time, might look really young with toasted-blond hair. And you can make of lot of money here in America. Cheers from your brother, Omar."

"For a hundred days your son was disciplined in a way he'd never been in almost thirty years, but they were a hundred days of farce," Yaqub said to his father. "He stole my passport and went to the United States. My passport, a silk tie, and two Irish linen shirts!"

Yaqub found out about this for certain when he got the first postcard. He'd already dismissed the maid, because she'd taken Omar into the apartment when he and his wife were in Santos over the Republic Day holiday, November 15. The maid had confessed almost everything: Omar had taken her out to the Trianon and the Luz Garden; they'd had lunch in the Brás, and in restaurants in the city center. A couple of layabouts! All this with the money you were sending, said Yaqub, furious. Then Yaqub remembered the two dust-covered old volumes of integral and differential calculus, books he'd bought for a song in a secondhand bookshop in the Rua Aurora. He opened the books with foreboding, a sense of having been debased. He gritted his teeth, and his hands were shaking so much they could hardly leaf through the first volume, where several one-dollar bills had been hidden; the twenty-dollar bills had been put in the other volume. He checked the two books, page by page, shook them, and one-dollar bills fell out. The bastard! OK, the swine had taken his passport, the silk tie, the linen shirts, but money . . . "He left the rubbish behind, and rubbish is what he is. That's what your son is. A *harami*, a thief!"

"He shouted 'thief' so many times I thought he meant me," said Halim. "Well, he was talking about my son, and to an extent that rubbed off on me. But I let Yaqub talk; I wanted him to unburden himself. Then I said: 'Is there no chance of you forgetting this? Can't you forgive him?' My God, that was worse!"

From the accusation, Yaqub went on to demanding compensation. He wouldn't rest until his brother returned the eight hundred and twenty dollars he'd robbed. A fortune! It was his savings from a year's work; a year spent working out the structures of buildings in São Paulo, and other cities in the state; a year inspecting building sites. Zana should be told about this, then she'd understand the real character of her little favorite, her fragile little monkey: "Go on, spoil the wretch until he ruins you! Sell the shop and the house! Sell Domingas; sell everything to encourage his filthy tricks!"

"Over and over again, he cursed the son my wife had spoiled; he couldn't stop. It seems the devil makes the mother choose one of the two children . . ." Halim looked straight at me: his misty eyes seemed to want to say more. He sat up. "He wasn't just angry because of the dollars. The maid had already told Omar who Yaqub's wife was. He was furious because Omar had entered his apartment, rummaged everywhere, and found the wedding photos, holiday snaps, and must have seen other things too. I was the only one who knew that Lívia, Yaqub's first girlfriend, had gone to São Paulo at his request. He wanted to keep the secret, but Omar finally found out. I don't know which of the two was the more jealous, but anyway, Yaqub never forgave the obscene drawings Omar did on the wedding photos . . ."

Halim put his hands on his head and said: "That's right: Omar covered Lívia's face with obscenities, wrote swearwords and drawings on the wedding album ... Yaqub went mad ... He'd never forgiven his brother's attack when they were young, the scar ... It had never left his mind. He swore one day he'd get his revenge."

He seemed melancholy now, and was drinking arrack with ice; he hardly ever drank anything else. Two little blue bottles on the table, with the Zahle label, bought from a smuggler. He took three or four swigs and rolled another cigarette. The river and the sky were blurred, and, far off, a procession of lighted canoes formed a sinuous line in the darkness. The wind brought the smell of the nearby jungle. The sound of voices was dying down, and the Floating City was going quiet.

Was Halim going to stop talking? He faced me one more time, and angrily bit his lower lip. He banged his fist on the table as if asking for silence.

"Do you know what I did after these accusations?" He seemed upset, half drunk, maybe a bit of both. "Do you know what's the best thing to do when a son, a relative, or anyone else makes a fuss over money? Do you know?"

"No," I said, hardly understanding.

"Well then ... I let Yaqub finish. He was angry; I'd never seen my son that way. After he'd given vent to his feelings, he went quiet, his energy gone, like a plant out of water. Then I said: 'All right, I'm going to fix this.' He thought I was going to go after his brother, or tell Zana everything. I got up, went back home, filled all the vases in the bedroom with orchids, put the hammock up, and shouted my wife's name ... Sons, what sons! For heaven's sake, all I wanted to do was to forget all this garbage, the eight hundred and twenty dollars, the passport, the tie, the shirts, and bloody Louisiana ... Zana came into the room and saw me naked in the hammock. She saw me and understood. I recited some of Abbas's words ... It was the signal ..."

It was the first time I saw Halim tottering; he was canned, and very nearly fell off the chair. He decided to stay there for a few more minutes, without making a single noise. A small motorboat approached the stakes, the captain threw the ropes, and I helped him tie them down. He moored near the bar, and the boat's searchlight slowly swung to and fro, lighting up the wooden posts, our table, or Halim's face. I saw his lower lip was very red, where he'd bitten it, and his face was burning. I asked the captain to point the light at our table, and helped Halim get up. I went back home with him; the two of us together, arms around one another, along the narrow alleys, and across the bowed planks of the Floating City. From time to time someone called out to him, but he didn't reply, and walked on with me in the darkness. Halim was silent. I already suspected what his greatest fear was. The engineer was getting more important, making money. And the other twin had no need of money to be what he was and do what he did.

And how! Those five or six years: the time between Omar's flight and Yaqub's visit to Manaus. Only afterwards we found out that Yaqub had prospered: maybe he aspired to a place at the top. He had moved, and the area of São Paulo where he lived spoke volumes: the area, and the apartment, because the photographs sent nowadays showed imposing interiors that made the human beings look so small they almost disappeared. Rânia complained: "They want to show the décor; they've forgotten to show their faces," she said.

It was true; the couple kept their distance from the camera lens. His wife, who only existed in my imagination, now appeared in these images as a tall, slim body, as thin as a razor blade. Omar had said that his wife dragged Yaqub to the smart clubs, where he met clients and sealed transactions. "She can't have children," Omar said, crudely. "But they'll have other offspring, you wait and see."

Even so, Rânia framed the photographs and her mother showed them to her friends. Zana was proud of her graduate son, but when she was chatting to the neighbors she worshipped Omar. She put the twins on a seesaw, and sang Omar's praises in blind adoration. But Zana wasn't blind. She saw a lot, from every angle, from near and far off, directly and obliquely, and there was wisdom in what she saw. Only, she was the victim of excessive jealousy. She pretended not to be devastated by her son's marriage: she managed to control herself, but she didn't rest till she found out who her daughter-in-law was. Little by little, her curiosity grew with her jealousy. The daughter-in-law sent boxes of presents for Halim from São Paulo. Bottles of arrack, boxes of tobacco for his hookah, bags of pistachios, dried figs, almonds, and dates. Halim, who loved food, was in his element. "What a woman! What a wonderful daughter-in-law!" Zana turned away; she felt like throwing everything in the rubbish, but ended up eating the delicacies on the sly. It's common knowledge: the way to a man's heart is through his stomach. Omar impertinently wanted the best of everything. They picked out the fish bones so he didn't have to bother; the tapioca pudding with grated coconut had to be baked just right; any food that wasn't cooked enough, he would chew and then go and spit it out in the henhouse. I relished the pudding Omar only picked at. My mother would also hide a handful of dates and almonds behind the wooden animals. I ate them before I went to bed; she didn't touch any of it and left everything for me: she wanted me to be fit, as sturdy as a horse.

Halim never wanted more than was necessary to eat, and eat well. He was never bothered by leaks, or by the bats that sheltered in the roof space under the broken tiles and flew low over us in the many nights when there was no electricity. There were blackouts in the north of Brazil, while the country's new capital was being inaugurated. The euphoria from this far-off country was nothing more than a tepid breeze when it reached Manaus. And the future, or the notion that it held out great promise, melted in the sultry Amazon air. We were far away from the industrial age, and even further from our glorious past. Zana, who in her youth had enjoyed some of the dregs of that past, now got irritated at the fridge run on kerosene, the brazier, and the oldest jeep in Manaus, an ancient banger with a filthy exhaust.

At this time, Rânia decided to modernize the shop, decorate it, and enlarge its range. Halim made a tired gesture; maybe he was indifferent. They had no money to renovate either the house or the shop, much less the two rooms at the back where my mother and I slept. Just when we least expected it, the magician waved his wand. Yaqub took action, and he was generous. Years later, at the most tragic moment of his life, and perhaps without intending it, I would reciprocate this generosity, which in some way changed my life. He didn't ignore the rest of the world; on the contrary, he kept an eye on everything, as I gradually came to realize. In his short visit to Manaus, he must have seen and made a mental note of all the things lacking in the household, for the family and the servants. The man who had had a fit over eight hundred and twenty dollars and a few other possessions transformed the house.

Halim was given no time to refuse this providential help. A fine selection of the products of the industry and progress of São Paulo parked in front of the house. The neighbors came around to see the truck full of sealed wooden boxes; the word FRAGILE, in red paint on one of the sides, hit you in the eye. We saw the spanking new machines, like gifts from the gods, enameled, all lined up in the room. If the inauguration of Brasília had produced national euphoria, the arrival of these objects was the great event in our household. The biggest problem was the almost daily electricity outages, so Zana decided to keep the kerosene fridge running. Domingas, at the end of the afternoon, before the blackout, took everything out of the new fridge and transferred it to the old one. Everything new, even if it had limited uses, made an impression. Yaqub surprised us even more: he sent money to restore the house and paint the shop.

Now, a modern look put a new shine on our humble dwellings: ours, because my room and my mother's were renovated too. I changed the laths in the ceiling, filled the holes in the wall with plaster and painted them white, and built slightly sloping eaves to protect the windows from the rain: from then on, I could sleep and study without hearing dripping water, and I was free of the mold and mildew that made it difficult for me to breathe when the nights were most humid. I opened the two windows, one giving onto the garden, the other onto the veranda, and let the sun warm the walls and the floor. When it rained, short of a downpour, Domingas would come into my room and I helped her take the bark off a piece of brazilwood, which she would then carve with skill and patience. She was scared to change a lamp, but she could transform a shapeless piece of wood into a *saurá*. Thanks to Yaqub, our rooms became habitable all year round: the rainy months were no longer a menace, and our conversations were more relaxed.

Rânia oversaw the renovation of the shop. I helped her to rough-plaster the front and smooth it down, and she herself picked up the brushes and painted all the walls green. My contribution wasn't useless, but anyone who worked with Rânia got the feeling they were getting in the way. She wanted to do everything on her own; nothing was too much for her energy and enthusiasm. She was as strong as an ox, and as patient as her father, who looked on mystified, surrounded by his partners at backgammon and his drinking pals. After the renovation, Rânia took more pleasure in the shop. She ran the place from top to bottom, looked after the profits, the stock, and the bad debts. She finally finished with selling on credit: "Charity doesn't mix with business." She put ads in the papers and on the radio stations, and had leaflets printed. She had a sale, and got rid of the unsold merchandise, the old stuff belonging to another time.

She believed in style, and revered the latest fashions.

I was suspicious of Rânia's burst of enthusiasm, and realized it took its cue from Yaqub's opinions and actions. In less than six months the shop changed course, and anticipated the economic euphoria that would not be long coming.

Omar was contemptuous of the renovation of the house and the shop. He didn't allow them to paint his room, and deprived himself of any signs of material comfort coming from his brother. He ate out. His mother went crazy when he wasn't in his room in the morning. He was still faithful to his old habits, his adventures, and the nightclubs where he was known and made a fuss over. When he wasn't there, the neon fan on the Acapulco lost some of its shine. At Carnival time, his room reeked of alcohol and perfume for squirting at other revelers. He had extravagant costumes, and stuck color photographs onto the bedroom walls in which he figured, entwined with half-naked odalisques or Columbines. His mother got amusement from the pictures: looking at him in a photo surrounded by almost naked women was preferable to seeing him in flesh and blood, with one fully dressed woman. The high brought on by the perfume led Omar to purloin part of the money for the market and the local fairs. He did this several times. Later, I saw Domingas take one or two yellowing bills, thinking her mistress would put the theft down to her son. She didn't blame anyone: Zana let herself be hoodwinked. Sometimes, when her son was combing his hair in front of the living-room mirror, she came up to him, sniffed his neck, and as he shivered, vain and possessed by maternal love, she adjusted his shirt collar; then Zana's hand went lower, gripped his belt, at the same time managing to slip a roll of notes into his trouser pocket.

Omar preferred not to know that a part of that money came from São Paulo. Money, and consumer goods: Yaqub knew some of the manufacturers of the city and the interior of São Paulo state, people who went to the same clubs as he did, and for whom he had built houses and apartment blocks. Rânia accepted the samples, chose the fabrics, T-shirts, wallets, and handbags. When Halim woke up to the fact, he was no longer selling most of the things he had always sold: hammocks, nets, boxes of matches, machetes, rolls of tobacco, bait for troll fishing, lanterns, and night lamps. With these changes, he was no longer so close to the people from the hinterland, up the rivers, who used to come to the door, or into the shop to buy or exchange goods, or simply chat: to Halim it hardly mattered.

Now the storefront sported wide windows, and there was almost nothing left to remind one of the old dry goods store less than two hundred yards from the beach of the Negro. The smell did remain: it survived the plastering, the paint, and modernity in general. The attic, a tiny space where Halim sometimes prayed or retired with his wife, had not been renovated. There he piled up his bric-a-brac, and there he took refuge, alone now, without Zana. From time to time I saw him in the window, chopping tobacco and rolling a cigarette, gazing at the Rua dos Barés with its kiosks, vendors, beggars, and drunkards amidst the black vultures, watching the movement of the street, which was an extension of the market and the moorings of the little harbor.

I don't think he saw me; he looked in my direction and didn't notice me, or mistook me for any passerby, one of the many who had haunted the harbor area forever, wandering aimlessly around the streets or the edge of the river, stopping in a bar to have a drink or eat some fried fish. That was what Halim loved: the sight of the Municipal Market and its surroundings; the fruit and fish, the rotten logs and planks, bits of dead matter that insisted on being reborn through their smell.

"That smell," said Halim in his hideaway in the attic, "and all those people, the fishermen, the carters, the porters I knew when I was very young, before I started going to Galib's restaurant."

They passed in front of the Municipal Market, already old, bent over, still carrying bags of flour and piles of bunches of *pacovã* bananas; they waved to Halim, but no longer stopped by the shop to drink water or *guaraná*. They went on up to the top of the square, where they unloaded their burden. Then they returned to the steps of the small harbor, went into the boats, and began again. How long had they been doing this?

"For more than half a century," he went on. "I was a kid, and they were there, kids too, already carrying everything; they went from the boats to the top of the square, from morning till night. I sold everything, from door to door. I went into hundreds of houses in Manaus, and when I didn't sell anything, they offered me *guaraná*, fried banana, coffee, and a bowl of tapioca. In the early twenties, more or less, I went to Galib's restaurant and saw Zana . . . Later, Galib died, the twins were born . . ."

He didn't mention Domingas. I put off the question about my birth: my father. I kept on putting it off, maybe out of fear. I got wound up in conjectures, brooding, suspecting Omar; I said to myself, Yaqub is my father, but it could be Omar, he challenges me, gives himself away by the way he looks at me, mockingly like that. Halim always refused to talk about it; he never even hinted at anything. He must have feared something. All the better, then, that he didn't see the worst of it. The vilest thing, the bottom of the abyss Halim feared so much, only happened some years after the story of Pau-Mulato.

Pau-Mulato: a lovely tree with a dark, smooth trunk, a member of the Rubiaceae. But what a nickname for a woman!

The nickname was the least of it. After Dália, Zana thought Omar would have been done with loving anyone. He wasn't; he wasn't as weak as that. Anyway, the women in the house didn't slake

Omar's thirst. The adventurer, just when he least expects it, falls into the trap and gets ensnared.

This time Halim seemed floored. He didn't drink and didn't want to talk. He told one story after another, about the twins, his own life, and Zana, and I put the separate pieces together, trying to put the fabric of the past back together.

"There are some things that shouldn't be told," he said, looking into my eyes.

He really was reluctant, and persisted in his silence. But he had to get it off his chest to someone. I was his confidant; one way or another I was a member of the family, Halim's grandson.

Omar hid with Pau-Mulato. He didn't bring her home, and for a good while stopped going to the nightclubs. He would return calm, without the dissipated look and the drunken stumbling. He began to sleep in his own room. The life and soul of the party was now a model of discretion. It felt as if he was overdoing it. Omar woke up in his room, in peace, without a hangover, without the wide-eyed, staring look from his mad sleepless nights. This man turned angel frightened his mother; instead of bringing her comfort, the change unsettled her. Zana found it strange seeing her son at the meal table; the man who had never worked getting up early, shaving, putting on his best clothes, and going to a foreign bank. It was a plum job, and his travels around Florida and Louisiana must have had something to do with it. He didn't look like an American, much less an Englishman, but he wore a tie, and anyone seeing him from a distance, tall, erect, his hair slicked and parted in the middle, might have confused him with Yaqub. That is, in appearance he was like his brother, though he was himself. His body had lost its spontaneity and its slovenliness; and the impetuosity of the risk taker, the adventurer who hopes that the greatest challenge, the dangerous, exciting gamble will come his way, no longer quivered inside him. Had he been tamed, mastered? The blaze that had lit up the nights of Manaus turned into a candle flame, a little gleam of light unruffled in the darkness. Now Omar was a man obedient to the norms and rules of routine work, with a gold watch on his wrist, firm in his exits and entrances.

It was all Rânia could do not to devour this new brother. She spent more time in his company; they chatted over breakfast, when she and her mother laid siege to him and made suggestions about his clothes, his perfume, the color of his tie and shoes. The morning Zahia saw him spruced up and turned into a gentleman, his mother and sister wouldn't let him alone, or take their eyes off the low-cut dress on Talib's elder daughter.

"This time Omar'll have loads of girls after him . . ." said Zahia, kissing his cheek.

"He doesn't need it," said Rânia.

"And what use is a girlfriend, dear? He's so happy as he is," Zana added. "It's my daughter needs a boyfriend. You too, Zahia . . . What'll you be, next birthday? Good heavens, when I remember the two of you as children . . ."

"True enough, I do need a boyfriend," Zahia agreed. "Who knows if he doesn't live here, in this house?"

"Halim's much too old for you, dear," Zana laughed, squeezing Omar on the cheeks. "And Domingas's son is very young, and only interested in books."

Zahia's dark eyes lighted on me, at the kitchen door.

"He's only interested in books, but he's as sharp as can be," she said, laughing, fixing me with a burning look, the one she used when she danced at birthday parties in Zana's house, and balls at Sultana Benemou's. Zahia knew there was no husband in our house for her or her sister, but she didn't know what was happening to Omar, dressed in white linen, with a contented air, talking less and smiling much more, so much so that he surprised the Reinosos and anyone who came to the house. "A fine boy, that son of yours, eh, Zana?" sighed Estelita. "What a change from that layabout! I'll slit my throat if a woman's not at the bottom of this." Zana gave a nervous laugh. "You'd better slit it now then, Estelita. Omar's no one's fool, not like Yaqub."

We no longer saw him with his legs in the air in the red hammock, with long dirty nails waiting for Domingas's scissors, or heard his voice huskily demanding certain fish stuffed a certain way. For a while, my mother was free of his crude groping and absurd demands. He stopped his hungry growling when he awoke at midday, and I was released from the messages he sent to women in various distant parts of the city. He came back sober from his nights out, and when he didn't go straight to his room, he sat in the garden, breathing in the humid air, meditating. He would laugh to himself. On moonlit nights, while I was burning the midnight oil to finish a lesson, I saw Omar's head erect, his face lit by a smile. We didn't speak to each other. He was lost in ecstasy, and I was concentrating on my reading and my equations. The odd time, I saw Zana watching him from the living room, aggrieved. He ignored her.

"Zana was very suspicious," said Halim. He hesitated, and I didn't know if he was going to keep quiet or tell all. He had given up on making peace between his sons, but not on having some influence on Omar's destiny; he was a grown man, but with plenty of rough corners. "He was unpredictable . . . He brought this overdressed Englishman to the house, with a name like Wyckham or Weakhand, who said he was the manager of a foreign bank. He ate like a girl, sat at table with a pose like a debutante, and was afraid of trying the sauce, the fish and even the *tabule*. Afraid of trying good food, I ask you!"

Wyckham nibbled at Domingas's delicacies, refused the dessert, and must have gotten up from the table hungry. When he left, Omar went with him, and then we saw at the front of the house an

Oldsmobile convertible, silver, with its seats upholstered in blue denim. It was some car! And, to our surprise, it was Omar's.

The two of them got into the convertible, and the neighbors observed the scene from their windows, astonished, taken aback by so much luxury and formality. It was truly impressive! Impeccable clothes, chrome-capped shoes, an imported car. It all seemed like the reverse of Omar; nothing seemed like him. Up to the last moment, no one knew what was going on, not even Halim. Zana, yes; she was the first to see, and she fought the final battle with determination. My God! What an explosion. But how had she found out?

"How?" Halim bit his lip. "She didn't need to go after Omar; she went after the car . . . a load of gleaming scrap iron. Omar could have been living with that woman till this very day. As far as I'm concerned, he could have lived with any woman, pretty, ugly, even if she was a whore . . . with anyone, or lots at the same time, so long as he left me in peace with mine . . ."

Halim's son: he was strong and virile with all kinds of women, but with his mother he was either aquiver, or trembling like young bamboo. There's no understanding the power of a mother: of Zana, in particular. She was the only one who didn't swallow the story of the English bank. Omar duped everyone; who wouldn't believe in such a convincing facade, in the British punctuality, and the Englishman himself? What about his voice, his thoroughly rehearsed gestures, his short sentences, his hesitation as he ended them: all these signs of the gentleman? Wyckham, a big man with enormously long arms, and a round face full of red spots, was, as Zana eventually found out, an impostor, a big-time smuggler. His gestures, his voice, his manner of eating, everything was real, except his profession. Omar worked with Wyckham; he was his right-hand man. The two of them had a female partner in crime, and that's where the convertible and the woman came into it. Zana went rummaging, imagining, divining, like an architect in reverse: she uncovered the secret hiding places they'd built themselves. The building was unfinished, but it had monumental ambitions.

First, the easy part: she found out that the job in the British bank was pure farce. Then, stalking around the Port Authority and in the warehouses of Manaus Harbor, she greased the palms of employees and stevedores. Patiently, she spread her net, and caught her fish, small fry and big boys. She also found her way around the system, the smuggling network Omar had gotten mixed up in. Halim only found out about the story when it was near its end. That was why he looked so solemn in the final weeks, before our conversation in the shop storeroom.

"When a son's fate's at stake, no detective in the world can find more clues than a mother," he said. "She did everything on the quiet, silently, like a shadow."

Zana went to the harbor every morning. Several times she saw her son, without being seen. Not at the harbor itself, but in the warehouse where the goods were piled up, to be sidetracked to their final uncertain destination. She found out where it had come from and where it was going. The stuff was carried in the Booth Line's ships; Omar checked everything in warehouse number nine and went out alone in the convertible, while the small fry took the merchandise to a house in the suburbs: Swiss chocolate, English clothes and toffees, Japanese cameras, pens, American sneakers. Everything that at that time couldn't be found in any Brazilian city: foreign shape, color, labels, and packaging—foreign smell. Wyckham understood this. He sensed the thirst for novelty, for consumption, the spellbinding power each thing carries with it. What was his part in the business? Was he making money? Halim didn't know. But what Zana found out was that her little hairy monkey had been attracted by a woman. He was never seen with her in daylight. They hid it, the two of them, deep inside a nocturnal shell, in love; the two of them, and no one else.

"Just as I always wanted." Halim smiled at last, and said hello to a fishmonger. "This time he did take after his father, but Zana spoiled everything."

She discovered a guy with a strange name, Zanuri, who came around to the house one night. He really was a strange one, wily, somewhat forward, almost smiling, a guy full of somewhats and almosts, with a twisted nose in a rather gaunt face—a man with no look in his eyes, as if he had no soul. A Panama hat tied with a yellow ribbon, slouched over his head, gave him an almost comic air.

"Almost, because he was an incomplete being from top to toe. That Zanuri didn't even have a man's fiber," Halim muttered. "He was a coward; couldn't even stroke an animal."

Halim disliked him from the start, from the moment he saw him whispering with Zana, just once, in the iron kiosk in the Adolpho Lisboa market. His aversion grew, and became unbearable when Zanuri entered the house without knocking, when it was dark, something you might expect of a neighbor of many years' standing, but not from someone like him. Halim was in the hammock with Zana, both of them dead to the world, quietly drifting among the slow caresses of incipient old age. They were taking advantage of the silence and the cool, damp night air. Rânia had already shut herself in her room. Domingas, overcome with fatigue, was stretched out in the hammock in her room. From my hiding place, I could see the almost-smile on the indistinct figure in the dark. I heard murmuring. Zana's voice prevailed. She was speaking in a low voice and gesticulating as if reprimanding someone. The shadow of her hands made strange shapes on the veranda wall; a subdued pitter-patter was heard on the stairs, and she went quiet. The shadow disappeared and the figure of Omar appeared in the middle of the room. He combed his hair in front of the mirror, arched his eyebrows, and smiled at his image. He was elegant; the white Irish linen suit smelled of essence of Pará, and a stronger smell came from his body. These assorted scents, essences from here, there, and everywhere, filled the house. Only the slightest whiff reached my hiding place: a smell that faded in the caladiums where I was ensconced.

Halim saw his son leaving, and straight after him, the deplorable Zanuri.

"Nothing could upset me when I was with Zana in the hammock," Halim said to me, "but something bothered me, I was wary of what that Zanuri had come for, and decided to find out who the intruder was. He was an informer . . ."

Zanuri was a clerk in the law courts, but he made money from other services: he was a Peeping Tom. The pimp had made a tidy sum informing on couples who are a little too free with their enjoyments and excitements. Clandestine couples, shut in their rooms, were spied on by an invisible reptile. That was Zanuri: camouflaged, a chameleon hidden among the dark foliage.

Zanuri followed the convertible from afar. The Oldsmobile left the center of the city, crossed the metal bridges over the creeks, and went into the labyrinth of the Cachoeirinha. It went to the Rua da Matinha, feebly lit by streetlights: to the third house on the left, with no number. It was a wooden house, whitewashed, with vases on the sills of the two open windows. There was a lighted room, and an oval picture, Christ's face in a frame, on the wall next to the street. The door into the room was protected with wire netting. Omar parked the car some fifteen yards down the road. He walked towards the house; he seemed wary, looking behind him, and to every side. He stopped to comb his hair and straighten his collar. He took a flask out of his pocket and put on scent. Before entering the house, he looked at what was going on in the street: children playing around a bonfire, a couple under a mango tree, two old women sitting on the sidewalk, laughing and telling tall stories. He whistled a well-known song, a *chorinho*, and the room door opened. Nobody appeared: no doubt she was hiding behind the door. The room went dark, and

someone shut the windows. He spent some time in the shack. At ten
past three in the morning, he emerged. Or rather, they did. A giant-
ess. A bulky, rotund, tall, dark-skinned woman. A Pau-Mulato
trunk. Nearly pure African. A handsome, sculptural face, smooth
skin, and a tiny nose. A little, mouthwatering dimple on her chin. A
normal mouth. An easy, musical laugh, with more high notes than
low, and a debauched tone. Long, smoothed hair, but still frizzled. A
braid fell onto her right shoulder, sprinkled with tiny silvery points:
cheap jewelry, no doubt. But the rings were something else: they
were of precious metal. The necklace was made of little bits of
ivory, from the country of her ancestors. They kissed on the
mouth—for a good few minutes. Holding each other tight, they
walked to the convertible. They got in. Another kiss, a short one this
time, with no urgency. She took her blouse off, and Omar rubbed
her breasts, in no hurry. She let him, gave herself, half lying down
on the seat. Then her head disappeared, and one of her arms, the
right, too. I couldn't see, I can't swear to what she did. I know I
heard him mewing like a leopard in heat, but in stifled cries, biting,
sucking the fingers of her left hand. A drunk appeared on the other
side of the street. He was drinking from the bottle, quietly staggering and hiccuping to himself. He wound his way towards them, and
stopped right next to the convertible. He took a sidelong look at the
fun and games. A feast of flesh, alfresco. Stars twinkled above; here
below, a drunkard winked. This went on till five in the morning.
The first vendors, the last night owls, voices, people stirring. He
started the car, she got out. See you, love, she said. Ciao, precious,
he said. Then he said something in Arabic I didn't understand. And
went on his way. That was that.

   "That was that: the words of a drunkard," grumbled Halim,
pushing a sheet of paper away. "A pimp disguised as a drunkard.
And the wretch still had the brass neck to charge a fat sum for his
work. I should have shoved the Panama hat into his ugly mug."

Zanuri, the professional informer, noted everything down and then typed up the details of the clandestine encounter. The letters danced on the paper. Seven pages just for one meeting; some of the details were exaggerated: "Mountains of rubbish in the streets in Cachoeirinha. I smoked eight cigarettes waiting for the lovebirds to come out of their cage. Pau-Mulato walked tall, like the smooth, lofty trunk of a noble tree. A kite with a drawing of a skull on a white background, forgotten in the rubbish-littered street. With no tail . . ."

Zana read everything and analyzed it: the details, the digressions, and the scene of the encounter itself. She sent Zanuri on his way and went on the offensive, treading carefully. She began the battle by bringing home boxes of English toffee and Swiss chocolate. She gave Omar a present of a silk tie and an Irish linen jacket, "So you can go out more smartly dressed, more elegant for your nights in Cachoeirinha."

Omar understood the insult, and realized his mother had found everything out. He put on a show; they both did, and made a truce to put their thoughts in order. He put other things in order: his bedroom, for example. He also packed his clothes in a suitcase. Finally, he found a reason for leaving the house.

He decided to leave and be his own master, to all appearances. He would be secure in his decision, free of what he had been until that night, the man in the tie pretending to be a bank employee, high-minded, and with his studied gestures: the lord that never was.

Zana felt threatened, and shadowed her son.

"Where are you going? What trip is this?" she shouted, pulling at his jacket sleeve and looking him in the eye. "I know everything, Omar; this trip is a pretense, a lie. I know exactly who the woman is . . . she'll drain you dry, she'll bewitch you, you'll come back home in tatters . . . They're all the same, she'll send you mad . . . You're a sucker, a big silly boy, that's what you are . . . I can hardly believe you're my son."

She threatened him as far as she could, without taking her eyes off his face; she felt things were more serious now than the other time when he'd fallen in love. With a rapid gesture Omar took his jacket off and left it in his mother's hands, loose and crumpled. It gave off mingled scents: the same sweetish whiff. But it must have made her shudder.

From the top of the staircase Halim watched the scene, praying his son would go away. Omar listened to the scolding, and didn't shrink from his mother's gaze. Then, he snatched his jacket from Zana's hands, pointing his finger at her.

"You've got another son, who gives you nothing but joy, and has a good job. Now it's my turn to live . . . Me and my woman, far from you . . ." He lifted up his head and shouted to his father: "Far from you, too, far from this house . . . from the lot of you. Don't come after me, you'll get nowhere . . ."

He went out shouting like a madman, without saying goodbye to Rânia or Domingas. He would have hit out, broken everything if anyone had tried to stop him leaving. No one slept that night. Zana never ceased lamenting; she blamed herself, and then accused Halim: "You were never a father to him, never. He's gone because of your selfishness . . . That's right, selfishness." She went up and down the stairs, bewildered, demanding first my presence, then Domingas's. She didn't know what to ask for, or what to say to us. Sleepily, we awaited orders. But she couldn't make up her mind, and asked: "What do you think of this? My son besotted over a piece of trash! What do you think? Why doesn't Rânia come down? Instead of helping, gathering dust in that room." Finally, she commanded me to go and get her daughter out of bed. Rânia opened the door, with a scowl on her face. She wasn't asleep; the light was on in her room. The two of them prayed, made vows, lit candles. They lit everything: the lamps, their eyes, their souls. Time passed, and he didn't come back. Had he finally broken free? He had wings, and he was impulsive, but he hadn't the strength to fly high and lose himself in the immense sky of desire.

"Zana's son! He comes and goes, drunk with indecision, a lazybones when it comes to the crunch," Halim complained. "He lasted a good time, but at bottom I knew he wasn't going to make it. He had everything in his hands and heart: love, a colossal woman . . . He had pure gold; all he needed was courage. He did try, though. And how! He even tricked Zanuri the informer. All that money thrown away!"

Zana went into action. She wandered around the city in search of the convertible. Three taxi drivers went around the neighborhoods, looking in hidden garages, sheds at the bottom of gardens, old Manaus housing developments; in all kinds of no-man's-land, in the city and around its edges. It was impossible to inspect everywhere; the thousands of dwellings in the shantytowns built out over the muddy creeks, the Floating City, the rafts in the bay, the towns nearby, the boats, the lakes, the rivers and the channels linking them.

She was miserable, muttering, "They've stolen my Omar"; she slept badly, had nightmares, and lost her energy. She hardly ate, just nibbled and sipped. But she didn't give up on the search, she wouldn't resign herself, sobbing in quiet desperation. She was a mother in mourning. Only, for her, this mourning had an end. Her son's return was a question of life, but never of death.

"It was such hard work," Halim sighed. "What I saw, what I understood, was that this woman, my wife, grew in stature when she felt she was going to lose her son. She picked herself up, and thought everything through again. What I mean is, she reshuffled all the cards until she found her king of spades."

One night, Zanuri reappeared, prying and sly as ever. She drove him out of the house with the fan for the fire. She insulted him in the two languages she spoke. Brainless burglar, thief, *harami*! Her eyes were burning, even if there were ashes in her heart. She said nothing to the neighbors, listened to none of the advice they wanted to give her; she shut her ears to everything. But inside, right at the bottom, the waves were swelling up. Halim, his mouth dry with so much desire, but also afraid, recoiled. Everybody knew about it now, the whole city, the settlements nearby: whispers in the air, fluttering down like confetti. No hunt like that can be anonymous. When a mother's on the prowl, it's a real storm; it turns the world upside down, a hurricane. Who knew what Zana was planning? Alone with herself, she was moving the sticks and blowing into the glowing embers. On her own, her voice quite calm as she chose her moment to pounce. She filled her basket with mysteries. She spent most of her time praying, with the other two faithful women, the three of them huddled together; she was the queen bee in the hive. Domingas joined this ritual every night. Did my mother want Omar back? I noticed a kind of desire in her, an anxiety she knew not how to hide, a shadow in her feelings. She left me in doubt; I lost my bearings when she bemoaned Omar's absence.

Oh, how she missed the lady-killer's body collapsed in the hammock! The runny sweat from the drinks and cocktails, and the heavy burst of sweating that came later, with its intoxicating aroma of strong, bitter alcohol, the whiff of a jaguar's skin. Her hands drying his face, his neck, his hairy chest; Omar, almost naked, sprawled out in the red hammock, as a yellow battalion of fire ants surrounded the whisky and rum bottles on the cement floor. The smell of arnica, cocoa butter, and *copaiba* on the blotches and bruises on his body. These smells mixed with others: that of the large leaves of the breadfruit tree, like green fans; of the heavy, ripe *cupuaçu*, like a yellow velvet casket protecting its silvery pulp, giving off a strange perfume. The wet leaves with which she covered the bruised parts of his body; the *cupuaçu* juice with seeds in it to suck that she made for him in the middle of the afternoon when, reinvigorated, he opened his arms to my mother and kissed her familiarly on both cheeks, before drinking in the thick liquid.

Was that what she missed? The body and the smells that surrounded him in the nights of a thousand binges? It seemed my mother thirsted after Omar's body, and no longer hid her longing for him to return. Domingas asked her mistress: "Can I prepare a dolphin's eye? You hang it around your neck, and Omar will come and kiss you . . . full of love for you." Of course Zana knew what to answer. She came close to my mother and turned her head towards the small oratory. The two of them, together, still preserved some of the beauty of their younger days. The Indian and the Levantine woman, side by side: their solemn faces, the fervor that had crossed oceans and rivers to throb there, in that room—all that devotion to bring him back, safe and sound, and above all alone, to the room that would always be his, and only his.

"That was when our lovemaking finally cooled off," murmured Halim, twisting some *tucum* fibers with his fingers. "We started to go without our little games; like going without life itself. All because of this business with Pau-Mulato."

Halim never spoke of death to me, except once, obliquely, skirting around the edges of the topic. He spoke when he already felt close to his end, some years after his son's affair with Pau-Mulato. He didn't see the worst, the final calamity. He didn't see it, but he did take omens seriously—all the prophecies he had heard from his *caboclo* friends, the offspring of solitude and the jungle. He had a naïve belief in these stories, and let himself be carried along by their plots and word magic. Halim was a faux naïf, an idolater of love and its ecstasies, in pursuit of the good life in the trivial world of the provinces. He took life as it came: any sugar, coarse or fine, was good enough for his coffee. But when it came to love, with Zana, he always wanted and always asked for more. In the days and months of Omar's absence, he began to hide away, begging for crumbs, starved and dizzy with pain. He acted, too. There were no tricks he didn't try, to see the back of the prayers, novenas, and suchlike mumbo jumbo. He didn't promise the earth: just one thing, the really tough act. He said: "I'm going to bring Omar back home. Either he comes back or takes that woman with him and finally gets the hell out."

6

alim was getting old: he was well over seventy, nearly
eighty—even he didn't know what day and year he'd been
born. He said: "I was born at the end of the last century,
some day in January . . . The best thing about it is that I'm aging
without knowing how old I am: that's what happens when you're an
immigrant." Still, the flab had to fight to take all the strength out of
his muscles. He was as strong as an ox, as he opened or shut up
the shop. He pulled and lifted the metal doors with real vigor, and
the cylinders crashed noisily as he did it. Rânia could have done the
work, but he got there first, displaying his muscles and showing off
to his daughter. Right up to a little before his death, he was discreet
when he was with friends, incapable of false laughter, generous
without thinking twice, but with an unpredictable, masculine bravado. He could give a good left hook to a hostile chin, and hurt.

That's what happened with one A. L. Azaz and his gang of
brutes, a year after the end of the Second World War. I have no

difficulty remembering the date because Domingas told me: "You were born when Halim had a fight in the public square, and was the talk of the town."

Everybody in the city heard about this fight, and remembered it, the anecdotes still circulated years later, distorted by time and its many voices.

What happened was that Azaz, a tough guy and a layabout, spread the tale that Halim spent his life chasing Indian girls, both his own maid and others in the neighborhood. He also said, this Azaz, that there were lots of children who asked for his blessing in secret. The carefree Halim was the last one to find out about this. He heard the slanderous tales when he was relaxing with friends in the Encalhe, a bar installed in the skeleton of a wreck below the Educandos neighborhood, then settled by former rubber tappers, almost all of them very poor. There were always two or three with a machete or a sharpened knife in their pocket. But Halim liked the Encalhe, the fried manioc and fish they served at makeshift tables, and already in those days he was inseparable from his bottle of arrack and the backgammon board. Halim heard the rumors, stopped laughing, and pushed the grimy dice away.

A. L. Azaz had no fixed address: he was an idler who found shelter in big abandoned houses, where he broke in and lived for a stretch, pretending to be the owner. He picked up leftovers from rich people's banquets, and afterwards boasted about his tawdry sexual exploits in the Encalhe. But he looked like a ruffian, and he was a famous slanderer, always to be found gossiping in the early evening, when poison creeps into the voice, and evil silences good judgment. He was stocky, with crinkly blondish hair and tight trousers, the pockets always full of sharpened bits of metal.

Halim closed the board, put the dice away, and paid the bill. He looked at one of his friends: "You mean this Azaz hasn't a home?

Then he should come alone, unarmed, on Sunday at three, to the Praça General Osório." Everyone found out. Who can resist a duel? There was even an audience, people from the Educandos, the customers from the Encalhe, the peddlers from the market, all of them there, sitting in the shade of the *oitizeiros* around the edge of the square: an immense, green oval arena, a setting for many festivals in the June season.

A. L. Azaz arrived before three. He waited for his foe in the middle of the open, sunlit square. His white T-shirt got wet, and they say he rubbed his hands and looked around him like a restless hawk, daring anyone to come and get him. But the audience, silent and attentive, didn't move. Azaz's gaze swept around the square to see if his opponent would appear. Halim took his time, pretending he'd given up, or was a coward. Then, at half-past three, Azaz, bathed in sweat, laughed out loud, drunk with his triumph. He showed off: turning around, he walked towards the audience. He shouted out challenges and war cries, and punched the air, cracking his knuckles and pummeling and kicking imaginary foes. He was grunting, making a complete idiot of himself, looking like a crazed howler monkey. He tried to terrify the Encalhe's customers: panting for breath, he screamed insults at his adversary. Then, calmly, from among the group of his friends, Halim appeared. He got up, quite slowly, and made his way through the crowd. Azaz, when he saw him, stopped short, nailed to the spot: he tried to pull himself together, and then, as they said, the howler turned into a squirrel monkey. Azaz had no time to think, let alone defend himself. He was exhausted by his celebration of the delayed duel, by the supposed cowardice of his enemy. Halim came forward a few paces, and wasn't put off by the knife in his adversary's hand. He too had his weapon: the steel chain he pulled from his waist with a single movement. Azaz, when he saw he was at a disadvantage, pulled back and

stammered: "Let's put down our arms, and fight hand to hand."
Halim ignored these words, and advanced, cautious but determined,
shaking the chain, his eyes fixed on the enemy's face.

There was a pool of blood on the arena in the square: that's what
they said, and still say. Both of them, bleeding, put their weapons on
one side and went at each other until the thirst for vengeance was
slaked. The customers of the Encalhe were astonished by their
placid rival at backgammon. They prevented Halim from cutting
A. L. Azaz's tongue out. They couldn't prevent the knife thrusts and
the blows with the steel chain. As evening came on, just before the
fight ended, there were people gathered all along the sides of the
arena. No one interfered. In duels like that, God is the only referee.

Azaz, lamed, died three years later, knifed in the middle of a
smaller, less public arena: a poolroom frequented by sailors and
whores, near the harbor, where Manaus's small-time ruffians ended
up. It's said that Halim, when he heard, was neither pleased nor
sorry; he simply said: "If you want the glory, you have to pay for it."

But he didn't talk about the duel. He let the stories do the
rounds, ignoring new versions in which he or his enemy were
reborn as heroes or cowards. Azaz, when he was dead, was resur-
rected more than once, described as courageous and unbeatable. It
didn't worry Halim. The worst thing, Domingas told me, was after
the fight, when he got home and saw his wife clinging to Omar's
waist, saying, "For the love of God, Omar, leave your brother in
peace," and saw Yaqub cornered, on his knees under the stairs,
listening to his brother's threats: he was an intruder, he sucked up
to the priests, he couldn't even speak Portuguese properly, and
deserved a good sock on the jaw. Halim saw the scene, swung his
steel chain, and shouted: "Now it's your turn . . . That's right, two
big boys against their father, let's see if you're men."

Omar went quiet when he saw his father's back and shoulders
bleeding, covered with slits and gashes from Azaz's knife. Frightened,

Zana let go of Omar, and begged Halim to calm down; then, trembling, she asked again and again who had wounded him, and he replied, "A slanderer . . . who went around saying I had children with lots of Indian girls. Now I think about it, it wouldn't worry me if I did have half a dozen kids running around out there." He went over to Omar and told him: "Go up to your room and don't dare put your foot outside the door unless I tell you." Yaqub waited for his brother to go upstairs, crawled out of his hiding place, and then ran to Domingas's room. Halim lay facedown on the drawing-room floor and felt for the knife marks.

"Domingas," shouted Zana, "leave your baby with Yaqub and come and help me."

My mother, at the kitchen door, shuddered when she saw so much blood. Halim spent the night groaning, and for some weeks was the most spoiled person in the family, Domingas told me. Zana looked after him, bandaging his back and shoulders, pouring an infusion of *crajiru* onto the wounds before she put the dressings on. She was afraid of him getting an infection, and he said: "No, the knife was perfectly clean, the filth was only in Azaz's mouth, and the garbage he spread around . . ."

Even after he was better he complained of the pain, the itching on his back, and the twinges in his shoulders. Zana saw through the ruse:

"Children with Indian girls? What's all this then?"

"Look at the marks on my back and shoulders," he said. "If it wasn't a lie, do you think I'd have confronted a giant like that, with a knife in his hand?"

These children, his supposed offspring, never appeared. He wouldn't put up with slander, nor did he explode with every stray spark; the great battle of his life was with his sons.

Now what he needed to do was hook Omar, or get him to remove himself far away, with his siren. If they weren't in the city, it would be almost impossible to find them. Months of searching . . . And anyway, where was he to begin? There were so many villages and towns on the banks of each river and its tributaries . . . But nothing happens there, and it would be death for a nocturnal animal like Omar. Then Halim thought of Wyckham, the smuggler.

He found him on board a ship of the Booth Line. He asked about his son: he hadn't seen him for a good while, and wanted news. Where was he? Wyckham was genial, and crafty. He spoke well of Omar, and said that both of them had left the foreign bank and were planning to open a supermarket for imported goods. That was why Omar had gone to the United States, but he'd had no news of him so far. It might come at any moment, when you least expected it, the way things happened with Omar.

"Good God, I wanted to give the liar a punch on the nose," Halim grumbled. "He calculated every word, and spoke with all the conviction of a preacher."

Then he remembered Cid Tannus, who played backgammon with Halim himself, and was his companion in years gone by. Tannus, with two bright eyes in his little grasshopper face, didn't often come by Halim's shop. Rânia didn't like him, said he got in the way of the customers, because his short visits got longer and longer, and the two men, in loud voices, remembered the good old times of the casinos and Polish girls. Zana, too, picked quarrels with him:

"All that old bachelor thinks about is orgies."

For Tannus was, and always had been, one for seeking out tenth-rate clubs, shacks with no lock on the door, nothing but a few wooden poles with a roof on top. As he wandered around from one party to another, he would see Omar, and sometimes they would have a drink together, just for the pleasure of it, with no women at the table. They had a chat, and Tannus always asked him to give Halim a hug from him, but Omar never did anything of the sort.

"He never told me about those meetings," Halim said. "And anyway, he never talked to me. He only opened his mouth for his mother."

"He must have for other women," Cid Tannus said, laughing.

"This Pau-Mulato . . . It seems Omar is really crazy about her. The two of them have disappeared."

Halim wanted to find them before Zana did, and maybe Tannus knew where his son was hiding with Pau-Mulato. His friend laughed again, shook his head, but agreed. The two of them searched around every den in the city; they spent three nights going to the smart clubs in the center and the lively nocturnal haunts of the Manaus suburbs. On the fourth night they ended up in a bar on the Colina, near the German Brewery. Not a sign of Omar. They sat at a table, Tannus opened a bottle of whisky, filled the glass without putting any ice in, and said: "Real nectar, Halim. Know who gave me it? Lord Wyckham."

Halim found out more about the Englishman, and a few little facts about Omar. He found out he wasn't English, and certainly wasn't called Wyckham. His real name was Francisco Keller, or Chico Quelé, as he was known in the quay area by pilots, sailors, and stevedores. He was the grandson of poor Germans, people who had gotten rich and then lost everything. Hadn't he been a bank manager? Yes, he had worked in banks, in various departments, but Quelé doesn't last the pace, he hates regular hours, detests clocking in and saying good morning and good afternoon to the same people every day, all your life. He's a deserter from routine. Quelé had met Omar in the Verônica, a huge sauna-cum-brothel, full of lamps with lilac tissue-paper shades. Omar and Quelé drank together in the Verônica, at the same table, larking about with the same girls. Quelé. Francisco Alves Keller, tall, blond from his father's side, and delicate. He had the sweet talk to attract the Indian girls and half-breeds, lovely dark-skinned beauties, almost like children, smiling with their milk teeth. Quelé had other things too: the best whisky, English toffees in his pockets. Silk blouses. Bottles of French perfume. More than that, topping it all: an Oldsmobile. An ancient car, just a shell. Quelé scavenged the engine, the wheels, the windows, and the bumpers from another car. From the shell he made a kind of stunted convertible: a monster intended to impress. He only went to the Verônica in the convertible; the Oldsmobile arrived quietly, sliding down the soft, sandy slope, with its engine off, the headlights illuminating the lilac-colored building, surrounded by assai palms. The car looked like an old steamer, one of those ones with wheels, like from the Mississippi, from earlier times: "our time, Halim," said Tannus. The girls left their clients in the middle of the room, ran to the car, and right there, on the sand, Quelé handed out bottles of perfume, sweets, blouses, and kisses. He got fresh with the girls on the edge of the jungle, among the wet caladiums; they caressed him and begged him to take them for a spin in the Oldsmobile. Quelé never went any farther. He never went to the huts at the back of the Verônica. He didn't like the smell of other bodies having fun on the kapok-stuffed mattress. He didn't go out with the girls; what he really liked was a bit of fun, with languishing looks and bites—the quirks of a strange man.

"But your son's game for anything, Halim. He'll pluck the rarest orchid, but he won't turn down the commonest plant from the mudflats."

One night, when Omar was enjoying himself at the Verônica, he heard the noise of the girls, and followed the fluttering wings and the clamor as they rushed out to the convertible. He got up, curious: where were they all going, the prettiest of all among them? He saw the scene, then came closer to where the fun was, and admired the convertible. He stuck around, drinking rum from the bottle. He waited for the owner of the Oldsmobile to calm down, and the girls to leave him alone. Then, with a glance, he saw the woman sitting on the back seat. She didn't get out of the car. Yes, it was the woman Quelé had brought. And she wasn't from the Verônica: she didn't look as if she was from the Amazon at all. Tall, and dignified. Her breasts, shoulders, and head hinted at her beauty. She seemed indifferent to the precocious twittering of the other girls, poor and too knowing for their age. Omar, with the bottle of rum in his hand, gazed happily at the woman. With a look like that, he must have seen the red hammock ready and waiting. But she stayed still, with her statuesque head, bronze, with delicate features. Omar was spellbound. Chico Quelé, who was drinking, came up to the car. The two of them talked. Quelé took Omar's bottle, threw it into the trees, and brought out a bottle of whisky, real nectar. Then the three of them left the Verônica for some nightspot.

Tannus saw the trio on other occasions, always at night, in the convertible. Then, it was just the two of them: the woman and Omar. Not at the Verônica, or any whorehouse or nightclub; he saw them, twice, on the road to the Bolivia bridge. In the ravines around the Cachoeirinha, on three consecutive nights. And, once only, in this bar, sitting at this very table. Omar, perfumed and elegant, talkative and with the look of the besotted lover who's surrendered everything, heart and soul, and his whole body. She sat quietly, serenely aware of how to receive his attentions. They drank and looked at each other, drank and touched each other, completely absorbed. They looked at the road bordered with shacks that ended at the ravine. Beyond it, the strip of light coming from the floating platforms in the bay of the river Negro. A motorboat passed by, a noise on the river, a light moving in the night. Children from the neighborhood were touching the convertible, marveling at such a wonderful car; like a machine from another world. Stunted, rickety, but still seductive. The Oldsmobile left its tracks; that was the trail the two of them left. The convertible disappeared. Omar and the woman disappeared. It was almost impossible to find them in that world of islands, lakes, and endless rivers.

"Sometimes, it's wiser to give up . . . let the two of them live their lives. Let's hope your son finally takes off, Halim! Let's hope he really does get intoxicated with the happiness of a free woman."

"That's what I wanted," said Halim. "But Omar wants much more, he wants everything. He's a prisoner of his own desires."

He was prepared to take a boat upriver for weeks to find his son. At heart, he was thinking of all the nights he'd lost because of Omar. Halim rented a motorboat and enlisted Captain Pocu: he wanted to search all around the edges of the lakes and the branches of the river. He asked for my help, and insisted on Tannus going with us. We spent weeks going around in circles. We would go out early in the morning, go around Marapatá Island, and cross the branch of the Xiborena to Marchanteria Island. Now we were on the river Solimões, and we went up the Careiro branch, making an arc until we reached the Amazon. We would ask the river dwellers and fishermen if they had seen the couple. Halim showed photos of his son, and Tannus described the woman. The river dwellers looked at the photographs with furrowed brows, struggling, but: no sir, we've had no strangers around here. Halim said over and over: "I'm going to bring Omar back by hook or by crook, you'll see." He only needed to see a house on stilts, an isolated shack, or a raft, and he would ask Pocu to take the boat across. This went on for days. Tannus said that Halim was losing his head: he wasn't searching for his son, he was persecuting him. We no longer knew what day of the week or month it was; we disembarked in Manaus at night-fall and at five on the dot Halim woke me, and off we went, on foot, to the small harbor. We went all along the coast of Terra Nova, of Marimba, of Murumurutuba . . . We went around the lakes of Careiro Island: Joanico, Parun, Alencorne, Imanha, Marinho, Acará, Pagão . . . Not a sign of Omar. Pocu used the trips to hunt hoatzins and wild duck; he set up a net in a lake, and on the way back picked up the fish, which he later sold in the street markets in Manaus. On the Parauá branch, an old man very solemnly said: "The dolphin's got them, you'll see; they must be enchanted, at the bottom of the river." We went from black to muddy waters, moored dozens of times on the shore of the Cambixe branch. Halim and I visited the little farms, he asked the questions, got the answers, but all to no avail. One day, Pocu, tired of all this, reminded Halim that they had already gone around the same places seven times. "We're burning fuel for nothing," said the captain. Then Halim took it into his head to look on the Madeira, they might be in Humaitá, who knows? Or they might be on the Colombian border, or in Peru, in Iquitos . . . Then suddenly, worn out, he would change his mind: no, maybe in Itacoatiara, or some island near Parintins. But there were hundreds of them. He thought of Santarém, where Abbas the poet was known, and Abbas would help him, he knew the middle and lower reaches of the Amazon—he was forever sailing up and down the river in those parts.

His friends who lived on the lakes helped in the search too. The first month extended into others. In the bars in the Floating City, his pals avoided the topic; it was a hopeless case. They swore they were not on the lakes, or in any of the towns around Manaus.

Tannus felt sorry for his tormented friend. He insisted he should give up: the two of them were nowhere to be found. "They're in the clouds, having a good time under a tree, eating fried fish."

Did he give up?

He was waiting, a little naïvely, like someone waiting for a little miracle: suddenly to see a chance flicker of light, when there's nothing left to hope for.

No such flicker came. Only the fireflies glimmered in the darkness of the garden; and, in the living room, the candles on the altar.

Halim, averse to any kind of fanaticism, looked gloomily at his wife. None of this fervor attracted him; he never surrendered to religious ecstasy. His prayers, always calm and serene, seemed to contain doubts about things beyond the grave. When there was no carpet to kneel on, he would put off any urge for transcendence. Life's finale had no need for such rituals. If it hadn't been for the fights between the twins, and Zana's crazy possessiveness where Omar was concerned, he'd have had nothing to worry about. He could have spent the rest of his life, his final days and years, between the bars around the harbor, the labyrinth of the Floating City, and the marriage bed.

Rânia, who looked after the shop, had tightened the links with São Paulo, and the novelties displayed in the window all came from there. As well as being astute in business, she knew how to control the household expenses, noting down every penny that was spent; but she gave in, against her will, to excessive purchases of fish.

We never ate so well. The most varied kinds of fish, with unusual flavors, covered the table: grilled ribs of *tambaqui*, fried *tucunaré*, yellow fish stuffed with *farofa*. *Pacu*, *matrinxã*, *curimatã*, tender, thick steaks of *surubim*. Even piranha stew, with pepper sauce, came steaming to the table. Then there was mashed manioc, and soup made of fish leftovers, flour made with the bones and heads, or *pirarucu* balls with parsley and onion.

"Wasn't it strange, getting so much fish?" Halim said. "Zana filled the two fridges with fish. She gave fish away to the neighbors. I asked: '*Laysh?* Why? What's all this fish for?' She replied, 'It's good for the bones, our skeletons are rickety.'"

There was something strange about this profusion of fish, because it wasn't the season for it: the river was far from reaching its lowest level, and we were a long way from Good Friday. We got sick of so much fish. There was a strong smell, the cats and the flies took up residence in the garden, beggars came after the leftovers, and all this superabundance of food, which made us generous with humans and animals, lasted through the months of the rainy season.

In March, when Zana was smiling and praying less, Halim switched his attention from the fish to Adamor, the fishmonger. We knew him. Old Toad-Leg, as he was called, had started to frequent our street again. He was one of the oldest fishmongers in the neighborhood. Before dawn, we heard his voice, in its amateur baritone, an echoing shout, drawing out the vowels of the words that gave him a living: "Fre-e-e-e-sh fi-ish!" It was the sound that ushered in the morning, a boom resounding through the mass of birds chattering in the tops of the enormous trees. It was Toad-Leg's signature tune. After the voice came the figure of the man, moving in short steps, little, calculated, symmetrical jumps, coming up to the door of a customer's house. There, alighting like a bird, Toad-Leg paused. His body, now visible in a world suddenly illuminated by the morning light, waited expectantly. On his spread-out hands was the tray. Stock still, he neither sang nor shouted: now it was dumb show. His left leg was crippled, half dead, and a swelling made it difficult to open his eyes. Little by little, Toad-Leg began to open his eyelids, and two very thin slits appeared in his sweaty face. The early sun, not yet hot, lit up angles, facades, trees, bodies in movement. Up above, the blocks of clouds dissolved with the morning breeze. Here below, on the dirty pavement, the figure of Domingas leaned over the tray, and her hands felt the eyes of a fish. She grumbled: "This *matrinxã* might have been fresh last week, now it's cat food." Adamor was irritated by Domingas's sallies. He wanted to empty his tray in our street, but my mother was niggling and fussy. She wouldn't buy smooth, scaleless fish: "They're no good, bad for the blood, they give you skin disease." The two of them quarreled, called the mistress of the house, and she backed Domingas. Choosing fish was my mother's big moment; she always won, and was proud of the fact.

All her cunning came out in the presence of Toad-Leg; all her boldness, suppressed in the house, came into its own on the pavement, for all to see. "Not today, Adamor, those fish decorated with parsley, spring onions, and tomatoes are all right for Dona Estelita . . . I don't like that kind of thing, they're just there to fool people." He dragged himself off with little jumps, calling my mother all the names he could think of: she was a stuck-up little Indian, keeping in with her mistress . . . But Domingas was not so hard on the pastry seller, a musical boy who played high-pitched notes on a steel triangle and sang tunes. Nor was she tightfisted with the *pitomba* and *sapoti* seller, an old man with a bronzed face whose time on earth was spent selling fruit purloined from waste plots and the gardens of ruined houses.

She even helped these unfortunates, as poor as poor can be. She would call the pastry seller over, give him some of yesterday's tapioca, and while the boy was eating, look at his dirty nails, filthy feet, and frayed trousers. How could he work like that? Wasn't he ashamed to be so dirty? When she had scolded him, she would choose some pastries for me, then give him a coin or two, and some advice: have a shower before you come out in the morning. But Toad-Leg, the seasonal fishmonger, was her favorite target. From time to time, he would suddenly disappear—both the man and the voice. Then one morning he returned, shaking, bloated with *cachaça*, measuring every step, on the brink of falling over again. It might seem difficult to imagine any vestiges of pride in someone like that. However, what was missing in his body and appearance, he more than made up for in courage.

A little medallion of pride and bravery decorated his past. His story had been passed from mouth to mouth on our street, in the neighborhood, throughout the city. It was one of those stories that came downriver, from distant settlements, and were reborn in Manaus, with all the power of something really true. He was from the river Purus, from a place called Lábrea, where there are lots of cripples. He suffered from leprosy, the most dreaded of all illnesses, and the most shameful. He was a rubber tapper from wartime, when American ships and planes sailed the Amazon, and hummed in its skies; the time of huge, powerful cargo ships and seaplanes. They brought all kinds of things, and took rubber to America. Then, one day in 1943, a Catalina strayed from its course up the Purus. It disappeared. There was a thorough search, and small planes crisscrossed the area. They flew low, in increasing and decreasing circles. They scoured every mile from above, and followed vultures as they wheeled in, in their search for carrion: searching, maybe, for the remains of the two crewmen of the Catalina. That's the forest: fly over it, wonder at it, take fright, and give up. After two weeks searching, they gave up. In September, before Independence Day, the seventh, Adamor, rubber tapper and tracker, appeared in Lábrea carrying a body: or rather, dragging a heavy bundle behind him. The inhabitants crossed themselves, frightened, hardly believing their eyes. The survivor, wrapped in a hammock, had the strength to grip Adamor's hands and cry. Flight lieutenant A. P. Binford was a wreck, naked, grazed all over, his ribs broken, both his feet twisted; he looked like a *curupira*, or a ghost from the forest. Adamor nearly lost his left leg. It was infected, and permanently paralyzed. In Manaus he was a hero for a night: he got a medal for services rendered to the Allies. He had his photograph taken, gave an interview; Adamor and the flight lieutenant embraced, together again, for the last time, on the front page of the papers. The tracker thanked everyone, and refused a trip to the United States. He would no longer be able to clear moorings and paths in the forest. Never again would he be a wanderer, free to look for shortcuts through the jungle. He didn't return to Lábrea or the Purus: instead, he plunged into Manaus's labyrinth of alleyways, built a house on the mudflats, and rotted in the stink of the swamps. The man who saved the

American airman? What an achievement, saving a real hero! From a distance, the shine on the medal could be seen, pinned onto his ragged shirt. He trained his voice to produce bass notes and prolonged shouts; just as he had done in the forest, where the noise warded off the fear of solitude, animals, and ghosts. Another survivor. Adamor: Toad-Leg. No one's past is anonymous. He had his name and nickname; he was a real rubber tapper, and he was Zana's favorite fishmonger. "Yes ma'am. Of course, ma'am. I'll look for your son, ma'am."

"And he did," Halim recalled. "Adamor was a real ferret. Zana offered him a pile of photos of our son, but he wouldn't take them. He leafed through the album and said that Omar's face was already in his head."

In a short time, he did what Halim and Tannus hadn't managed in months of searching. Zana saw how insinuating Adamor was. She told him about her son's disappearance, hinted at the possibility of looking for him, sounded things out. Toad-Leg frowned attentively, moved by the story. He even shed tears, half sincere, half pretend. He wiped his eyes with his scaly hands, lifted up his head, and asked, in a serious voice, if madam would remove that mistrustful Indian woman. Domingas, obedient as ever, stopped feeling the fishes' eyes. Then Adamor began to offer madam the most expensive fish, and the ones he couldn't sell, from piranhas to small fry.

"All that was missing was for her to buy the tray and the rusty old medal," grumbled Halim. "She'd have bought everything: the river, the sun, the sky, and all the stars. Everything, absolutely everything."

In the early morning, Zana would station herself in the living room waiting for the fishmonger's deep-throated cry. Halim was in a nervous state, and spent sleepless nights in bed alone. Sometimes he got up and spied on her from the top of the staircase, but she was obsessed, and had no eyes for Halim; she was living in a world of her own, inhabited only by Omar's image. They even spent a whole night without speaking, facing one another, with her eyes fixed on his face—only her eyes, for the look in them was bottomless, without beginning or end. Another night, he remembered Abbas's *gazals*, recited the ones he knew by heart, and then begged, implored her to leave their son in peace with that woman . . . That's what Omar wanted, he himself had said it before he went away: he wanted to live far from everyone—who knows, maybe he'd even set up business with the woman, the two of them, like adults . . . Omar was a grown man; there was no sense in him living at home with his parents, ruining himself with drink and whores . . . That's the word, ruining himself . . . In no time he'll get sick, he'll rot, and no one can face watching their son go downhill. She listened, with her eyes on Halim's face. Nothing, not a blink, came from her impassive face. He gave a sigh and got up, seeing his words and his voice, with its lover's urgency, vanish into the night silence.

One Saturday morning he saw her go out with the fishmonger. Fine drizzle was falling after the night's downpour. Zana put on her best clothes. She had a little makeup, her hair was loose, and she wore her delicate jade earrings. Her eyes, protected by long lashes, and the perfect arch of her eyebrows, took Halim's breath away.

"Sixty years and more: nothing can hide that woman's beauty," he would say.

He said it over and over, until the end, as if she'd stopped aging. It was as if time were an abstraction, with no power over Zana's body. Right to the last, he was madly in love. Poor Halim! Well, not so poor as all that. He was a gourmet of carnal love: he turned small-time provincial life into a festival of pleasures.

That morning he waited for his son. He knew that Omar would be caught; it was inevitable. He was living in an old motorboat, rented, really cheap. They slept together, in a hammock. They also slept in the open air on deserted beaches, wherever they moored their boat. Could they go through life like this? Maybe. She, Pau-Mulato, set herself up as a palm reader, reading the callused hands of the river dwellers, getting manioc flour and a few coins in return for pipe dreams. They fished in the deserted branches of the Anavil-hanas, laying their net near the boat, gathering in the fish before dawn. They lived an amphibious existence, clandestine, both of them in a dignified poverty, with no set time for anything. Unfet-tered and free, their life had no fixed points.

But Toad-Leg sniffed them out. How did he find the lovers? It was hard enough to find Binford, because the plane had slipped down through some trees and plunged into the Purus. Adamor was astute: he observed every angle, every corner of the forest, and looked upwards, in search of broken branches, treetops broken off, bits of fuselage. Then all he had to do was follow the winding trail of debris till he found a quiet man by the side of the river: bags under his eyes, his face drawn and haggard, his teeth green with chewing so many leaves, and a pistol in his lap. A motionless body, with turtle eggs spread around on the beach. Adamor laughed when he saw the scene. Almost twenty years later, he laughed again when he saw Omar's boat hidden among heavy barges: a miserable little motorboat, of the kind that crisscross the bay of the river Negro every day; a dangerous boat to be in in a storm, and fragile in the fierce waves of a tidal bore. There it was, right behind the Adolpho Lisboa Market, ensconced and quite innocent, with the love ham-mock on display, set up under the little bridge, next to the catwalk; at the stern was a little Brazilian flag, limp and faded. There, three hundred yards from Halim's den—he'd imagined his son on some frontier, or in Iquitos, Santarém, or Belém. He'd thought he was in the south of Brazil, or North America, in the cold climate of the other hemisphere. He might have been anywhere, far away: any-where but where he was, in the crowded little harbor.

"Even Tannus didn't believe it," Halim said. "Who was going to look for the two of them here, in the Escadaria harbor? They were right under my nose . . ."

Toad-Leg didn't go after the boat: he preferred following the fish trail. He chatted to the fishmongers: who brought them fresh fish in small amounts? There were dozens of fishing boats, and Toad-Leg knew almost all of them. But it was the small fishermen, owners of canoes and small boats, who might lead to Omar. Toad-Leg, with money in his pocket, went to talk to the middlemen. He mentioned a novice fisherman. He sketched his manner: tall, dark, and with eyebrows like a tarantula. A wide forehead, broad shoulders, the easy laugh of a sociable fellow, and when he laughed out loud you could see down his throat. Oh, that bald guy with a thick beard? Stocky, smitten by that serious-looking woman? Maybe. Him? With a bottle in his hand, singing and dancing, showing off, mad as a hatter? That one? No one knew his name; he likes his fun, but he's not got many friends. Standoffish, not that he wants to be. Face half-covered, always wears dark glasses, even at night. Another Omar: his head shaven, a thick, graying beard, a prophet, a messianic madman. Doesn't appear for days. He beaches his boat in the early morning, cheerful, has his bit of fun, sells his fish for any old price, and pushes off. Very rarely, once a month or so, he appears in the boat, and it's the woman who gives him a bath, with a gourd shell, soaps him all over, a great big naked baby. Then she pulls the ropes in, gives the orders, and off they go. They're off before the fishermen, just as dawn's breaking, and it's a while before they're back.

"I think Adamor sold us the fish Omar and his ladylove had caught. That was all we needed!" Halim said.

Bald and bearded. Tanned, almost black from so much sun. He was thinner, slim in fact, with a necklace of *guaraná* seeds on his chest. Barefoot, he had dirty Bermudas on, full of holes. He didn't look like Zana's perfumed little monkey.

When I came in the house, I saw he was looking for his father upstairs, in the bathroom, everywhere. He had scratches on his arms and neck, and his staring eyes frightened Rânia and Domingas. He went into the garden, then into the rooms at the back, and came back into the living room with a metal chain. When the front door shut, he crouched near the stairs and lifted the chain. Rânia heard steps in the corridor and gave a shout. Zana went into the room in time to see her son fling the chain at the mirror. There was a crash; nothing was left. Part of the floor was covered with fragments of glass. Omar carried on in his fury, destroying everything: he dragged chairs out, broke the frames of his brother's portraits, and began to tear the photos; he tore, trampled, and kicked the pieces of frame, snorting, and shouting: "He's to blame . . . Him and my father . . . Where's the old man got to? Hidden in that filthy store? Why doesn't he come to sing the praises of the engineer . . . the genius, the brains of the family, the perfect son . . . You're to blame too, mother . . . you all let him do what he wanted . . . marry that woman . . . a pair of idiots . . ."

He went on and on cursing and swearing, swore at my mother and Rânia, calling them cows, nearly spitting in their faces, and he called me a son of a bitch, on the make, Halim's ass-licker, but I didn't back off, I got myself ready and clenched my fists as tight as I could; if the idiot had attacked me there'd have been nothing left of either of us. He was drooling and bellowing, the veins on his neck stood out, and spit dribbled down his chin. His visage with the thick gray beard and bald crown terrified everyone; the women ran this way and that, hiding from him, and he went after them, slipped, kicked everything, trying to wreak destruction on the whole room, the walls, the altar, the saint. But I didn't budge; I wanted to see how far Omar really would go in this little set piece, his pantomime . . . I couldn't wait for him to lay a hand on me, he'd have gotten a fistful right in front of his mother, he'd have been on his knees in front of me. But no; he was flagging now, calming down until he dropped. He held his head, panting. Rânia managed to save two photographs: the portraits in which Yaqub's face was largest and clearest. She tried to approach her brother, but he pushed her, threw her out of the room, and, when he went to lift his hand, Zana intervened, and bore down on him with a mother's authority. Now it was her turn. She cornered Omar right away; she wasn't going to let her son get mixed up with any piece of trash. "Trash, that's right! A *charmuta*, a whore! She can spend the rest of her life rotting on that filthy boat, but not with my son. A smuggler! A forger . . . an extortionist . . . I spent a fortune getting the details. Smuggling, the girls she procured for Quelé, the cardboard Englishman . . . Your hidey-hole in Cachoeirinha . . . The orgies . . . the goings-on . . . all that filth! I'd never have allowed it . . . never! Did you hear me? Never!" She lowered her voice and whispered sweetly, in a melancholy tone: "You've got everything here at home, my love." She began to sob and cry. She grasped his hands, combed his grizzled beard with her hands, and stroked his bald head, full of scratches. Then the two of them, hugging one another, went to the veranda; she frowned when she saw her own image distorted into a thousand pieces in the smashed mirror. She'd lost her precious mirror, but still, she sighed with happiness because her son was there, burned up inside, but now hers, and hers alone. She signaled to Domingas and me to clear the room up. Many objects were destroyed. The little altar, the hookah, and the glass cabinet had survived. There were pieces of mirror and frame on the gray sofa. The console and several chairs were smashed. Domingas and I had to sweep the floor and mend the chairs before Halim got back. The Venetian mirror was one of Zana's heirlooms, one of Galib's wedding presents. It was a relief for me, because I polished it with a flannel cloth every day, listening to the same litany: "Careful with my mirror, go around the frame with a feather duster."

There was almost nothing left of this relic. Later Halim bought another mirror, a huge one; I polished it less zealously.

At dawn on that Saturday morning when Zana and Toad-Leg went out together, Halim came into my bedroom and asked me to follow them. I was asleep; I'd spent part of the night studying for an exam at the Rui Barbosa Lyceum. Halim hadn't slept a wink; he sensed something was going to happen that day, and was sure of it when he saw Zana creeping out of the room. She was elegant, scented, and, in Halim's eyes, immensely attractive. He imagined her smiling and excited, and felt more jealous of his son than ever before.

Toad-Leg appeared without sounding his usual cry, hidden in the last vestiges of night. Neither did he knock at the door. He waited a few seconds and then left with the lady.

He was no longer the fishmonger, but the old ferret, a hunter in the urban jungle. He himself would tell his customers how he had set up the ambush and thought it through. On the Friday night, Adamor had gone to the Escadaria harbor with two bottles of whisky. He called a boy over: "offer them to the bald man with the beard for a street thief's price." Omar bought the two bottles and invited the boy to a party on board. They drank and danced to the accompaniment of Radio Voz da Amazônia. In the dawn light, Omar and the woman were groaning in the rocking hammock as if they were on a deserted beach on one of the thousands of islands in the Anavilhanas. They were foolhardy, inordinately happy, as if they owned the world. Finally they went to sleep, immersed in the magic. The beach in the little harbor smelled of oil and garbage. The dawn breeze brought the smell of the forest, still dark on the other bank of the river. And Zana's scent, the smell of jasmine. She was well known in the streets of the harbor area. She was Halim's wife, and the mother of Rânia, the one who ran the shop. Nobody understood why she was there, so early, in a place so full of poor people: boatmen looking for their first passengers, half-naked porters, vendors of sugarcane juice, and fruit sellers setting up their little canvas stalls. Elegant from her shoes to her hat, she was wearing a subdued gray dress, more suited to an evening reception than a morning encounter on a filthy quayside. However, it was an encounter with her son, as well as a struggle with this rival from God knows where. She walked decisively right down the middle of the walkway, her gaze moving over the boats and barges emerging from the night, like an archipelago in the middle of the river.

Her appearance imposed a silence, meaning either respect or surprise. Behind her, Toad-Leg, smiling, triumphant, waved at the boatmen squatting on the prows of their boats. From time to time sleepy faces poked out from the hammocks slung from the bridges of the vessels. Adamor stopped at the end of the walkway, where four thickset men were waiting for him. They exchanged words, gesticulated, and got up onto a barge that gave them access to Omar's boat. I followed some ways behind, watching their figures, small in the distance and hazy in the morning mist. Nearer the barge, I could make out the confusion on the motorboat's catwalk, bodies grappling, a hammock swinging, and the boat's prow swaying from side to side, setting off ripples in the black waters. I heard a woman's cries, then weeping, and Zana's voice: "Let that woman alone . . . leave her in the boat . . . My son's going home on his own."

I ran to the edge of the Escadaria harbor and watched through a gap in the red stone wall.

The outline of the quay, the silhouettes of the people, the slight nodding of the red prows, the multicolored hammocks, the lifting swell leaving oil-covered debris on the beach, the beggars dazed in the sun, the huge clouds wandering across the sky, the dark forest opening itself to the gaze: everything seemed to take on density, movement, life.

Then he appeared at the end of the walkway.

His grizzled beard and shorn head were less surprising than the look in his eyes. For a moment, the moment when he moved along the walkway, he could have been mistaken for the others; he might have been one more porter or fishmonger, or street seller with his trinkets—or just any poor devil. He could have been his own master, and given in to the temptation to free himself and live his adventure through to the end.

As he came nearer the beach, I saw him as a stranger, and I wanted Omar to be, really, a stranger. If he had been, I would perhaps have been less worried about the idea I had of him. I wouldn't have been there, behind the red wall, secretly watching this figure coming closer, his arms hanging loose, his shoulders and neck purple, a seedy figure that minutes later the neighbors looked on with pity. Omar didn't acknowledge them; he looked like a blind man who knew his way home by heart. This man, who always waved and smiled at the neighbors, now said nothing to anybody. He was covered in scratches, like a wild man, with fright in his eyes; a sharp movement of his head accentuated an imbalance, and echoed the rest of his body. At first, no one recognized him. Then, when Domingas welcomed him at the front door, and only then, the neighbors realized that Omar had come back.

He had lunch in the middle of the afternoon, alone, withdrawn. He spent several days without emerging from his room, brooding over his defeat. The recluse waited for his hair to grow, and then for a visit from the barber, who gave him back his original face: now again he was the gallant, the denizen of the night, and no longer the captive lover.

This loyalty to his mother deserved a reward. To Halim's despair, Omar was spoiled as never before. Certain things he didn't even have to ask for: his mother divined his wishes, and gave him everything, so long as he didn't go away. Nothing was free between them; it all had to be paid for. Rânia, to her irritation, had to open the shop safe; she gave way to her brother's whims, but reckoned every penny; she gave way, but preached sermons, listing all her expenses on the house and shop like an accountant or a skinflint. He heard the litany through, and began to stroke his sister: a kiss on the hands, a caress on her neck, a lick on each earlobe. He wound his arm around her, put her on his lap, looking at her like a suitor, full of desire. The words she would have loved to hear from a man, she heard from Omar, "the brother who was never far from you, who never abandoned you, sister," he whispered. Rânia melted, sensual and seductive, and her voice, slower, gradually gave way, until she faltered and said: "All right, I'll give you a little pocket money, so you can have your fun."

That was how he recovered the seductive power he'd lost during the time of his surrender to Pau-Mulato, in the boat his mother had cursed.

At bottom, Omar was the willing accomplice of his own weakness, of a choice that was stronger than him; there wasn't much he could do against his mother's will; a good part of his life and feeling came from her. He preferred whores and the comforts of home life to a humble, poverty-stricken life with the woman he loved. He tried to get used to the frustration, which he thought no longer bothered him, and never again dared give in to any woman.

He went back to the brothels, the nightclubs in the center and the suburbs; the early hours when he came in drunk, like a robot, sometimes stuttering the name of the two women he really had loved, or crying like a child that's lost something precious. He became half infantile, prematurely aged, with long silent intervals, like some children who reject maternal warmth or put off uttering the first intelligible word. He sat there on the veranda like a cornered animal, avoiding human contact, destroyed perhaps by the long hangovers, when his drinking continued at home until dawn. I wasn't sorry for him. It was he who had taught me that pity and sympathy were useless. I remembered one afternoon when Zana had sent me to the Praça da Saudade to get a dress at a seamstress's. I hadn't had lunch, and the strong sun made me dizzy. I sat down on a bench in the shade of a pergola. I was looking towards the Rua Simón Bolívar, at the back of the orphanage where my mother had lived. I thought of her, of the time she'd spent in that prison, and then remembered what Laval had said: there was an Indian cemetery beneath the square. The racket made by a group of men woke me up. As they came up to the pergola, one of them pointed at me and shouted: "That's my maid's son." They all laughed and went on their way. I've never forgotten. I had the urge to drag Omar to the most stinking creek I could find and chuck him into the mud, into the rotting debris of this city.

That was what I said to Halim; I had the courage to say it when he'd finished telling the story of Pau-Mulato.

He looked at me and turned his face to the storehouse window. Streaks of silver light flashed in the bright sun, dancing on the black water, amid the bustle of the little quay at the back of the Adolpho Lisboa Market on a lively Saturday morning.

I thought what I had said about Omar would mean the end of our conversation. His grayish eyes turned towards me, and he asked me about the Rui Barbosa Lyceum, and if it was worth going to this school, with its awful reputation. "It's always worthwhile finishing something," I said. "I learned a bit in the Vandals' Cockpit, and a lot reading the books Laval lent me, and talking to him after class."

"My son didn't want to study even in the Cockpit," Halim complained. "A weakling . . . he let my wife suck all his strength, all his fiber . . . his courage . . . she sucked out his heart, his soul . . . his will . . . I didn't want children, that's true . . . but Yaqub and Rânia, one way or another, let me live . . . I wanted to send the twins to Lebanon, they'd get to know another country, speak another language . . . That was what I really wanted . . . I told Zana, and she went to pieces, told me that Omar would be lost without her. It didn't work . . . either for the one that went away or the one that stayed here. When Yaqub came back, I still had hope . . . I brought Zana here, we fooled around as much as we wanted, we were free . . . What I didn't do to seduce that woman! Months and months . . . the *gazals*, the wine to overcome my shyness . . . Nobody wanted to accept it . . . Nobody thought a peddler could win over Galib's daughter. She had courage; she decided. And I believed . . . I thought only about her, only wanted her . . . Then life started giving twists and turns, closing in, cornering me . . . Life goes in a straight line, then suddenly it turns head over heels, and the thread has a knot in it you can't untie. That was the way it was . . . The death of her father, Galib . . . Death far away, the pain it causes, I can understand . . . A father . . . I never knew what it means . . . I never knew my father or mother . . . I came to Brazil with an uncle, Fadel. I was about twelve . . . He went away, disappeared, left me on my own in a room in the Pension Oriente . . . I clung to Zana, I wanted everything . . . things I couldn't have. It was a devouring passion, a bottomless abyss . . . After Galib died, Omar began to grow in her affections . . . She kept on saying he was going to die . . . It was an excuse; I knew nothing would happen to him . . . She went crazy, did everything for him, she's capable of dying at his side . . . When her son wasn't around, she was my wife, the woman I loved. I smelled her; I remembered our most passionate nights, the two of us rolling on top of those old pieces of cloth. In the early morning, we went to have coffee in the market kiosk; we'd walk barefoot on the beach . . . I had the urge to run away with her, get into a boat, go to

Belém, and leave the three children with your mother . . . I thought of that, I thought of everything . . . even of running away on my own . . . But I could never have done it; she'd have haunted my dreams . . . We had lots of nights of pleasure, right here, in the midst of all this mess . . . The problem was Omar, his love life, those two women . . . The second one was a real upset; Zana realized she might lose her son . . . The weakling! Coward . . . He'll never know . . . I can't even look at him . . . I don't want to hear his voice . . . I don't think I ever did, he makes me sick . . . If I had the strength, I'd give him another clout, I'd have given him a hundred or so when he broke the mirror Zana adored . . . A thousand, thousands . . ."

Rânia came up to see what was happening, but he wouldn't stop shouting: "I'd have given him a thousand, the coward!" She bent over, stroked his head, cleaned the sweat from his face and the saliva covering his mouth; he was drooling with hatred, he gagged, shook his head, began to cough, hawking up, gasping for breath, his eyes bulging, his hands searching for his cane. "Baba, are you better? Quiet down, the shop's full of customers." He looked at his daughter: "To hell with them all," he said. She went down. Halim got up, leaning on his cane. He stopped, looking at the rolls of frayed madras and chintz, full of clothes moths. He gave a few hesitant steps, and went very slowly down the iron staircase. I offered to help him, but he refused. He didn't say where he was going. He crossed the shop holding his cane to move the customers out of his way. I saw him stagger between the boats moored by the ramp. Soon after, only his white head was moving on the dark horizon of the river.

By that time of his life, it was difficult for him to walk from the house to the shop, go up the spiral staircase, and sit on the wicker chair near the window with its view over the bay. I accompanied him many times on this slow walk, and when someone greeted him or shouted his name, he lifted his stick and asked me who that madman was, and I replied, it was Ibrahim of the Kebabs, or, again, it's the son of Issa Azmar, or one of his friends who played backgammon in that bar, the Siren of the River. He'd stopped playing; his shaking hands stopped him toying with the dice before each throw. This ritual was a kind of secret magic, an infallible trick. Playing with the dice, feeling their corners, the lines on each side, the texture of the material, then watching them jump and roll over the felt rectangle; that ritual was over and done with. Sometimes Rânia invited two acquaintances to play in the little upstairs room, just so that her father would amuse himself and not stick his nose into her business, though he took practically no interest in the fate of the shop. Nor did Halim pay any attention to the players and their throws of the dice, because the other game, the big one, the real mainspring of his life, had ended when his son had met the woman in the lilac brothel. He let himself be lulled by the hot, humid air and the light, warm breezes coming in the storehouse window. And when he looked at the board, he soon turned his face away to the bay of the Negro, looking for calm in its waters and the huge white clouds mirrored in them.

In the last years of his life, Halim lived alone with this landscape in the little storeroom with its objects from the past, absorbed in the meanders of his memory; for he smiled and gesticulated, went serious and then smiled again, affirming or denying something indecipherable, or trying to keep hold of a memory that burst into his mind, some kind of scene that developed into others, like a film beginning in the middle of the story, and whose confused, jumbled images leap around in time and space.

That's how I saw Halim as an old man: a shipwrecked man clinging to a log, far from the banks of the river, pulled along by the current towards the calm waters of the end. Was he pretending to be cut off from everything? Sometimes he pretended to go blank, like someone floating in the air, above the things of this world. He listened to no one; it was as if he were deaf, but he had some energy left. He never stopped downing a few good mouthfuls of arrack. He drank, sweated, licked his lips, and watched Zana's gestures; he only had eyes for her, and stammered out a few words of love. And he was still around to witness some of the important events in our lives.

7

In the first week of January 1964, Antenor Laval came to our house to talk to Omar. The French teacher was flustered, asked me if I'd read the books he'd lent me, and reminded me, lowering his voice: classes at the lyceum begin straight after Carnival. He was talking like a robot; there were none of the calm and the pauses he had in class, and none of the humor that kept our attention when he was translating or commenting on a poem. My mother got a shock when she saw how low he was, like a corpse, and with the anguished expression of a cornered man. He refused coffee and *guaraná*, and smoked several cigarettes as he tried to convince Omar to take part in a poetry reading, but Omar first made a face, then joked: if it had been in the Shangri-la, I'd have been game. For Laval, this was no time for jokes: he frowned, went silent, cleared his throat, but soon asked Omar, begged him to go to the basement where he lived. Even then, Laval had to wait for his friend to have a bath to get rid of his hangover. The two of them left in a hurry, and Omar only came back at dawn the following day, when Zana was surprised her son was sober; there was something on his mind that he was hiding. She bombarded him with questions, but he gave no straight answers. Before lunch he asked his sister for some money. It was much more than he usually asked for, a large sum, which Rânia refused to give him: "Certainly not, Omar, no binge can cost that amount." He didn't give up, without his usual cynicism, or the seductive gestures that undid her resistance. Rather he insisted, with a tense face, a serious voice, and a sincere look in his eye. Zana, suspicious, interrupted her daughter, and told her to give him part of the money, or a little anyhow: maybe Omar was wanting to pay off a debt. "You two never stop asking for money. Why not spend a week behind the counter? Or a whole day, just once, in that furnace, putting up with drunken insults, boring customers, and Papa's rigmarole, just to top it all."

Rânia didn't give in. She was worried about a downturn in trade that January; things were almost at a standstill, and the dockworkers' strike was keeping the clientele away from the area around Escadaria harbor. She filled a box with samples of the latest things from São Paulo and asked me to chase up the best customers. "Get after those deserters; if anyone wants to buy, I'll take the goods to them myself." It was an immense list, and on every street I went into eight or ten houses to offer Rânia's wonders. I dealt with every kind of customer: indecisive, pedantic, demanding, spendthrift, aggressive, fearful, and impossible. Some asked me in for a snack, told endless stories, and then said goodbye as if I'd just paid them a polite visit. I remembered Halim's words: "More than anything else, trade is an exchange of words." Many were saving up for Carnival, but there was always someone who would buy, and I dragged a smile out of Rânia, and a bit of change as commission. She was euphoric, glowing, rolling her big eyes with the excitement. Business gave her a thrill, and she changed when she got orders, bit her lip and gave me a hug; I trembled just as I had done on the parties for Zana's birthday, which no longer took place. I spent the months of January and February going up and down streets, alleyways, and avenues. At nightfall, Rânia shut up shop and took over my work, while I went after Halim. Zana didn't want him to be out of the house at night. "He can't wander around alone out there, it's dangerous," she said. I would find him with a group of cronies in the Canto do Quintela, or at the house of an old, sick friend. He was reluctant to go back, let out a few Arabic swearwords, but then he'd mutter: "All right, dear boy, let's go, let's go . . . that's the way it is, I suppose."

The night we saw Rânia carrying a box and selling from door to door, he said angrily: "My poor daughter, killing herself to support that parasite." He could no longer bear to look at Omar. Even his son's voice irritated him, he said it gave him a stomachache, his heart burned, everything burned up inside him. I found out that he blocked his ears so as not to hear Omar's voice. When I was looking for Halim, I went by Laval's pension, but I couldn't see him in the basement. It was completely dark, and the deserted street was a little frightening. I remembered the few times I had taken part in the readings in the room. Piles of paper surrounded the hammock where he slept. From the ceiling there hung sculptures, mobiles and objects made of paper. Maybe he'd never thrown a single sheet out. He must have kept everything: letters, poems, and endless notes for his classes scrawled on sheets of paper, rolled up, folded, or loose, scattered over the dirty floor. In the dark corners there were piles of empty wine bottles, and on the cement floor shriveled bits of food mixed with cockroach wings. "This chaos is more loathsome than your worst nightmare, but I feed on it," Laval would say to his pupils. We left the basement carrying books and old class notes he gave us. He stayed there at night, smoking, drinking, and translating French poems.

I was surprised Laval hadn't asked me to take part in the poetry reading. Later, in March, he missed the first classes and only appeared in the third week of the month. He came into the room looking more depressed than when I'd seen him at home, his white jacket all stained, his teeth and the fingers of his left hand yellowed with smoking. "Forgive me, I'm very indisposed," he said in French. "What's more, a lot of people are pretty indisposed," he murmured, in Portuguese this time. He could hardly stand upright. His right hand, shaking, held a piece of chalk, the other a cigarette. We were expecting the usual "lecture," some fifty minutes he dedicated to the world surrounding the poet. He had always been that way: first the historical context, he said, then a conversation, and finally the work. It was the moment when he spoke in French, and needled and stimulated us, asking questions, wanting all of us to say something. Nobody, not even the shiest, was allowed to stay silent; passivity was taboo. He wanted argument, different, clashing opinions; he would follow all the voices, and speak at the end, arguing enthusiastically, remembering everything, every absurdity, insight, or doubt that had been expressed. But that morning he did nothing of the kind, he couldn't speak, he was choking, what a pain, he looked as if he was suffocating. We were openmouthed, not even the cheekiest and most rebellious among us managed to provoke him by making faces at the smell of his breath. "Let's see . . . let's . . . read something . . . translate . . ." His trembling hand began to write a poem on the blackboard; the chalk made scratches like arabesques, and all that could be read was the last line, which I copied: *"Je dis: Que cherchent-ils au Ciel, tous ces aveugles?"* The rest was illegible, he'd forgotten the title, and for a moment glanced at us strangely. Then he put the chalk down and left without saying a word. The French teacher never returned to the lyceum; one April morning we witnessed his arrest.

He had just come out of the Café Mocambo, and was slowly crossing the Praça das Acácias in the direction of the Vandals'

Cockpit. He was carrying the battered briefcase where he kept his books and papers. The same briefcase, the same books—the papers might have been different, because they had his scrawls on them. Laval would write a poem and hand it out to the pupils. He himself never kept what he wrote. He said: "A line by a great symbolist or Romantic is better than a cartload of rhetoric—my useless, miserable rhetoric," he insisted.

He was humiliated in the middle of the Praça das Acácias, punched as if he were a stray dog at the mercy of some ferocious gang. His white jacket was splashed with red, and he spun around inside the bandstand, his hands blindly searching for support, his swollen face turned up towards the sun, his body twisting aimlessly, staggering, stumbling down the steps until he fell at the edge of the pond in the square. The booing and the protests of the students and teachers from the lyceum had no effect on the police. Laval was dragged to an army vehicle, and the doors of the Café Mocambo were immediately closed. Many doors were shut when two days later we heard that Antenor Laval was dead. All this was in April, the first few days of April.

The morning the teacher was hunted down, I picked up his battered briefcase, dropped at the edge of the pond. Inside the case were his books and sheets with poems, full of blotches.

These were my memories of Laval: the lessons he gave, his accomplished calligraphy, the letters almost traced out; his words, carefully weighed and then weighed again. He had no desire to be called a poet; that wasn't his style. He detested pomposity, and laughed at the provincial politicians, the butt of his jokes in break time, but he refused to talk about such things in class. He said: "Politics is for the break; in class, we've higher things to discuss. Let's go back to what we were saying the other night . . ."

It rained a lot, a fearful downpour, on the day of his death. Even so, Laval's pupils and ex-pupils gathered in the bandstand, lit torches, and we all had at least one of the master's handwritten poems. The bandstand was full, lit by a circle of fire. Someone suggested a minute's silence in homage to the martyred schoolmaster. Then, an ex-pupil of the lyceum began to read one of Laval's poems. Omar was the last one to recite. He was moved and unhappy. The rain underlined the sadness, but it also incited rebellion. There were bloodstains on the bandstand floor. Omar wrote one of Laval's lines in red ink, and for a long time the words stayed there, firm and legible, a homage to the memory of one man, and perhaps of many more.

For once, this once only, I felt no anger towards Omar; I couldn't hate him on that rainswept afternoon, with our faces lit by torches, our ears attentive to the words of a dead man, our gaze fixed on the facade of the lyceum, on the black cloth hanging from the eaves down to the threshold. The school was in mourning for a master who had been murdered: that's how that April began for me, and for many of us.

I couldn't hate Omar. I thought: if our whole life could be summed up in that afternoon, we would be quits. But that wasn't the way things were. It was only that afternoon. He went back home so agitated that he didn't notice his brother's presence.

The city was half deserted; it was a time of fear, the day of a deluge. The house, too, was almost deserted. Rânia was in the shop, Halim wandering around the city, Zana somewhere in the neighborhood, maybe in Talib's house discussing cookery. Domingas, the custodian of the house, was starching the clothes in the little room at the back. I had gotten back earlier from the Praça das Acácias. I thought of Laval, of our conversations at night in his cave, as he called the basement where he lived alone. We knew very little about him: at midday and six in the afternoon the landlady left him his lunch or supper at the cave entrance. She did this every day, even on Sundays, when I passed by in front of the pension and glimpsed the plate of food at the threshold, swarming with fire ants and the stray cats from Manaus Creek. I could see Laval's silhouette through the basement's round window. The light of the sun hardly entered the cave, and a lamp hanging from the ceiling lit the master's head. He would move his hands nervously to smoke, write, or turn the pages of a book. He rarely ate at night: he began to drink after lunch, and came into the schoolroom still sober, but animated. The pupils who came to the evening classes smelled the sour reek of cheap wine on his breath. His pores exuded this unbearable vinegar. He sweated. However, he never lost his composure or his sense of humor. When there was an electricity outage, he lit a lamp and a lot of candles. He never failed to read a poem and comment on it enthusiastically. Sometimes he went silent, deliberately, quite suddenly in the middle of a lesson. The silence might be an interval; a pause for reflection, something the memory asks for and the voice accedes to. Or was it just the effect of the wine, a plunge into the abyss? Maybe that's what it was: something inexplicable. No one had reliable information about his life: he was like a little snail among pebbles. There was only one rumor that went around the corridors of the lyceum; a couple of bits of gossip about Laval. First, that he'd been a militant Red, one of the most daring, one of the real leaders, who'd spent time in Moscow. He neither confirmed nor denied it. He was silent when curiosity turned into a noisy clamor. The other rumor was much sadder. It was said that a long time ago Laval, a young lawyer, lived with a girl from the interior. A born leader and orator, he was called to a secret meeting in Rio. He took his lover and came back to Manaus alone. There was talk of betrayal and desertion. There were conflicting versions, some words that clashed, others that made sense . . . conjectures. What was known is that, from that moment on, Laval shut himself in the basement of a house next to Manaus Creek. Several times he was found in a corner of the cave, his face like a skeleton, and with the thick beard he kept until the day of his martyrdom. It wasn't a hunger strike, or lack of appetite; maybe it was despair. His poems, full of strange words, suggested nights of anguish, buried worlds, lives cut off from any escape. On Fridays he distributed them to his pupils, thinking no one would read them, always looking on the dark side. In his most intimate self, he was a pessimist, disenchanted, and he tried to make up for this disenchantment by his appearance, with his dandified manners. He rejected the label of poet, but it didn't bother him when someone called him eccentric or affected. I don't know which was the better description. Neither, perhaps. But he was a master. And a tormented man who wrote, knowing he wouldn't publish anything. His poems are lying around here and there, in forgotten drawers or in the memories of ex-pupils.

The worn-out leather briefcase was already dry, and I warmed Laval's papers in the steam from the iron Domingas used. The papers were wrinkled and stained. Only some words could be read. The poems, already short, became even shorter: almost isolated words, like looking at a tree and only seeing the fruit. I saw the fruit, which soon fell and vanished. And, looking into the living room, I made out a tall, thin figure; all I could think of was the poet, the ghost of the poet Antenor Laval.

It was Yaqub.

He gave me a fright as he came quietly into the house. He had just come from the airport, and he looked like a nabob. The youthful swordsman hadn't lost his poise: he was standing with his sleeves rolled up and smoking, enjoying the rain, hypnotized by the clatter of the heavy drops on the roof. Domingas put the iron down and went to greet the newcomer. She embraced him, and it was the longest embrace she gave to anyone in the house. Then she gave him rose-apple juice, put the hammock up on the veranda, and set a table with boiled peach palms and a pot of coffee. He lay down in the hammock and gestured to my mother to stay beside him.

I came over to the veranda to hear Yaqub's voice: a deep voice that uttered my name several times. My mother pointed to the bottom of the garden. I realized something in him had changed, for on his earlier visit he hadn't stayed so close to Domingas. Now the two of them seemed closer, chatting easily to one another. When the hammock brought him close to my mother, Yaqub ran his hand through her hair, and down to the nape of her neck. He only stopped laughing when Domingas unintentionally touched his scar with her fingers. Yaqub's face flushed, and he frowned, put his feet to the ground, stopped the hammock, and lit another cigarette. He can never have gotten used to this strange mark on his left cheek, and he tried to hide it with the palm of his hand. His face contracted; confusion and pain entered his gaze. He got up from the hammock when Omar entered the living room, soaking, barefoot, his clothes stuck to his body. He looked feverish, and the grief over Laval could still be seen on his face. I remembered Omar's voice reciting one of the dead man's poems, from the time when both of them, teacher and pupil, would go out together after class and into the woods near the Rua Frei José dos Inocentes, where the whores awaited them.

Yaqub's tense face turned around to look at his brother. Maybe this was the right moment for them to grapple, flay each other alive, the two of them torn and bleeding in front of my eyes and my mother's. Yaqub stammered out some words, but Omar didn't look him in the face; he ignored him and went upstairs, gripping the banisters. His cough and plodding steps echoed through the house, and before he went into his room he shouted Domingas's name. His voice sounded like an order, but my mother didn't leave Yaqub's side. She let the sick man yell like a madman, and I noticed a slow smile cross her face.

I took a good look at Yaqub; his face was much less irritated now. His body was upright, and he pulled himself together. I remembered the last time I had seen him at home, our walks around the city, and I was afraid of the long time that had gone by since I'd seen him: time that could have made him humble, cynical, or skeptical. I thought he might have become more arrogant, a know-it-all, certain of most things if not everything. I remembered my mother's words: "As soon he came back from Lebanon, he used to come to talk to me. He was the only one who came to talk to me, the only one who wanted to hear my story . . . He only kept quiet with the others."

He hadn't lost his disdainful air: the pride of someone who had decided to prove to himself and others that a rustic like him, a shepherd, a *ra'i* as his mother called him, could be a famous engineer, revered by the circle he moved in in São Paulo. Now he didn't want to be called "Doctor Yaqub"; he felt more at ease at home, without a jacket and tie. Nor did he behave like a guest. He was a son returning to the family home, where he had spent his childhood. He was chewing things over in the hammock when his father and mother came in almost at the same time. Zana was the first to see her son, to bend over and kiss him, but she soon left when she heard groans coming from Omar's room.

"I'm going to see what's happening to your brother," she said, flustered. "Halim, look who's come; what a surprise."

Halim was complaining that the city was flooded; there was a stir in the center of town, and confusion, and the Floating City was surrounded by soldiers.

"They're everywhere," he said, embracing his son. "Even in the trees in the bits of wasteland you can see bunches of soldiers."

"Those plots are asking to be occupied," Yaqub said, smiling. "Manaus is ripe for growth."

Halim wiped his face, looked in his son's eyes, and said with no enthusiasm:

"What I want is something else, Yaqub . . . I've done all the growing I'm going to do."

Yaqub turned his face away to look at the rain and got up; Rânia's voice got him out of his predicament. She was frightened by the deployment of troops in the port area, but the sight of Yaqub made her forget the political storm in Brazil. Halim left them alone. Zana was looking after her sick son: she spent hours in the room, and when she opened the door, we could hear her voice complaining: "Omar got caught in the rain, he got ill because of Laval, the mad poet." She put a hammock up in her son's room, and interrupted Rânia's conversation with Yaqub: "I'm going to call a doctor, poor Omar can hardly swallow his own saliva." Yaqub only followed Zana's movements out of the corner of his eye. He showed no warmth towards her; he behaved with a kind of distance that was neither neutral nor remote. He proved himself a master at keeping his cool in a tense situation. He didn't react in his youth, when a piece of glass cut his left cheek. Neither did he get used to the scar, however, passively accepting the work of fate. My mother thought Yaqub more and more decisive and energetic, "like a tree viper getting ready to strike." She sensed that he was planning something, and I thought the two of them might be meeting secretly, away from the house. They exchanged brief, almost instantaneous looks, but I could see her smile.

In those days, what impressed me most was Yaqub's obstinate dedication to his work, and his courage. He spent a good part of the night working, with the table in the living room covered with graph paper, full of numbers and drawings. He got up at five, when only Domingas and I were up. At six, he asked me to sit at the breakfast

table. He drank warm milk and tapioca, ate fried banana, French
toast, and mango compote; he ate almost greedily, getting food all
over his hands and mouth. At that hour, the scent of the damp
leaves, the fruit hanging off the palm tree, and the ripe jackfruit, was
more intense. Yaqub liked waiting for the sun to come up, and following the vegetation as it changed color, emerging slowly from
darkness into sunlight. It was the one moment of the day when he
was not in a hurry. That morning, he murmured: "I miss this dawn.
The smell . . . the garden." Then he told me about his work; he went
twice a month to the coast, where he was putting up buildings. "One
day you'll come and visit me, I'll take you to see the sea."

It was a promise, but I couldn't see much in that future; the sea
was a long way away, and my thoughts were stuck right here, in the
days and nights of the present, in the closed doors of the lyceum, in
Laval's death. Did Yaqub know that? He saw I was worried and sad.
What I told him was that I was afraid; I wasn't far off finishing my
courses at school. A teacher had been murdered, Antenor Laval . . .
He looked thoughtful, shaking his head. He looked at me: "I've got
a friend too . . . he was my teacher in São Paulo . . ." He stopped,
and looked at me as if I wouldn't understand what he was going to
say. Yaqub might have known Laval when he studied at the Salesian
college.

He knew that Manaus had become an occupied city. The schools
and cinemas had been closed, navy launches patroled the bay of the
Negro, and the radio stations were transmitting communiqués from
the Amazonia Military High Command. Rânia had to shut the shop
because the dockworkers' strike had been ended by a confrontation
with the military police. Halim advised me not to mention Laval's
name outside the house. Other names became taboo. The black
cloth covering part of the lyceum's facade had been torn down, and
the doors stayed shut for several weeks.

Even so, Yaqub was not frightened by the green vehicles surrounding the squares and Manaus Harbor, or the men in green occupying the avenues and the airport. The devil himself in green wouldn't have put him off. I didn't want to go out of the house, and didn't understand the reasons for the coup in the country, but I did know there had been conspiracies, troop movements, and protests all over the place—violence; it all made me afraid. But he insisted I accompany him: "I've been a soldier, I'm an officer in the reserve," he said to me proudly.

On the afternoon when we went out to photograph buildings and monuments in the central area of the city, we stopped in the Praça da Matriz, and I remembered the mass in memory of Laval, which had been forbidden. While Yaqub was taking pictures and making notes I went all around the square, and sat down on a stone bench entangled by the thick roots of a strangler tree. The afternoon heat made me dizzy, my mouth felt dry, and my lips were stuck together. There was no water gushing from the mouths of the bronze angels on the fountain. Near the church, I stopped to rest and admire the birds in the aviary. I saw they were alarmed, flying desperately all over the place, but soon a humming like insects began to bother me, a deep, monotonous noise that got louder and louder, and when I turned to look at the street, I froze: I saw a jeep bristling with bayonets. I thought of Laval, and his body, punched and trampled in the bandstand, and dragged to the edge of the pond. I waited for the military vehicle to disappear, but then came another, and another; lots of them, making a thunderous din. The soldiers were yelling, shouting hurrahs, and a racket of voices and horns spread alarm through the square. It was a convoy of trucks coming from the Praça General Osório, going in the direction of the quay. Out of the corner of my eye I followed the rumbling of this green monster along the cobbled street, and felt acute discomfort, a sharp pain in my forehead, and then an urge to vomit when I saw the seemingly endless line of green vehicles. The ground seemed to shake more and more, and now it was sirens and howls that buzzed around my head, and bayonets pointing at the church door, where my fellow students from the lyceum were raising their arms, throwing themselves on the ground and falling, and then pointing at Laval, writhing in the aviary full of dead birds, his right hand holding his battered briefcase, his left trying to catch the sheets of paper burning in the air. I tried to go into the aviary, but it was locked, and I could still see Laval right close to me, his face ripped apart with pain, his collar covered in blood, a sad look in his eye and his mouth open, incapable of uttering a word. He disappeared as night suddenly fell, and I began to shout for Yaqub; I shouted like a madman, and then saw my mother in front of me, her hands on my hot face, her eyes wide open, burning, anxious. Halim and Yaqub were behind her and looking at me, with fright in their eyes. I was shaking with fever and sweating: I was drenched. I wanted to know about the mass for the schoolmaster, but they avoided the subject. My mother didn't leave me; it was the only time I saw her night and day at my side. She left everything, all her daily tasks, and didn't even go up and see Omar.

During his last days in Manaus, Yaqub came to see me several times. He sat on a stool, put his hand on my arm and head, and said I was a little feverish. I still remember the worried look on his face, his voice wanting to call a doctor; he would pay for everything. Domingas wouldn't have it, she trusted in the copal balsam and other curative herbs. I spent some days in bed, and was pleased to know that Halim had been more concerned about his bastard grandson than his legitimate son. He hardly crossed the threshold of Omar's room. He came into my room several times, and on one of these occasions gave me a fountain pen, in silver, an eighteenth-birthday present. Not even Yaqub had remembered the date, but what he hadn't spent on the doctor, he offered to Domingas, and this time she accepted. It was a birthday I never forgot, with my mother, Halim, and Yaqub by my bed, all talking about me, my fever and my future. Upstairs, the other patient jealously tried to steal this celebration of my coming of age. We heard groans, shouts, knocks, metallic crashes: a frightful racket. Omar, furious, had kicked the chamber pot and the spittoon, messing up his own room as if he disowned the place he lived in. No, he wasn't going to let it pass; he wasn't going to let me hold sway in the house, even for one day. He coughed, complained of the heat, banged on the door, couldn't stand upright, turned his bed over, opened the windows, couldn't breathe. Rânia went up and down stairs with compresses and plates of food. Zana couldn't tear herself away from him; she resented Domingas and Halim, who hadn't gone to see Omar. My mother didn't go to see him. Halim couldn't bear listening to the whispers between Zana and her son. In my room, he said over and over, his head bent: "Do you understand that? Do you understand?" He seemed to be talking to himself, or, who knows, to an unknown person, someone not in the room. He lifted his head when Yaqub, ready to leave, came into my room. I didn't know if I would see him again. He didn't like prolonging goodbyes; he held my hands and said he would write and send me books. Then he grasped his father's hand, said he was in a hurry, but Halim hugged him tight and began to cry, his body bent over, his head leaning on Yaqub's shoulder, brokenly stammering: "This is your house, son . . ."

I'd hardly ever seen Halim so sad, his eyes tightly shut, his face tense, his wrinkled hands gripping Yaqub's back. The two of them went out of my room, and I got up to see them from the window. Zana and Rânia were waiting for them on the veranda. Halim asked his son to stay a few more days, and come back again with his wife.

Yaqub promised that on his next visit he'd bring his wife. I listened to his deep voice echoing: "You needn't worry, Mother, we'll stay in a hotel."

"What do you mean, stay in a hotel? Did you hear that, Halim? Our son wants to hide with his wife . . . He wants to be a stranger in his own country . . ."

Halim moved away: with a gesture of his hands, he asked to be left in peace.

"My wife doesn't have to put up with a sick man's tantrums," Yaqub said, in a loud voice.

Zana swallowed the words. She'd have swallowed anything to avoid a confrontation between the twins. She went with Yaqub to the door, and then I saw her going up the staircase, slow and hesitant, as if her thoughts hindered her steps. I nodded off for the rest of the morning and woke up with a continuous buzz in my ears that kept going for some seconds, then tailed off until it finally disappeared. It was Yaqub's plane that had just taken off. The midday flight to the south, as we said in those days.

I had a foreboding I would never see Yaqub again. I asked my mother what they had talked about when he went into her room. What was there between the two of them? I plucked up the courage to ask her if Yaqub was my father. I couldn't stand Omar; everything I saw and felt, everything Halim had told me was enough to make me detest him. I didn't understand why my mother didn't snub him once and for all, or at least keep her distance from him. Why did she have to put up with so much humiliation? She asked me to calm down: I ought to use these days to rest and read in bed. "You're thin and pale . . ." she said, her hands on my face. Domingas hid things as much as she could, and tried to console me with the last words she said before she left the room. Omar's health was more delicate than mine. He was a sick man; I was a convalescent. Laval's death was a blow for Omar and me. The groans and the violent reaction might seem exaggerated, but he had been affected by the master's death.

Antenor Laval, more than Chico Quelé, had been Omar's friend. It was a half-secret friendship, just as with Omar's two love affairs, or anything that gave him pleasure, desire, and self-confidence. He was a prisoner of these forbidden pleasures. He didn't forget Laval, and stayed shut up in his room even after his brother's departure. There was sincerity in the recluse. He wrote a "Manifesto against the Coup" and read it out loud. It was a courageous act, and it was a pity so much courage went to waste in an almost empty room; only I heard the daring phrases and harsh words.

When he emerged from his room, he looked like the ragged individual I'd seen coming down the walkway, coming towards me. He had the same fixed, staring look of a man in solitary confinement: nightmare eyes, lost in the darkest night.

Then he took up searching for rotten fruit in the garden, fruit and leaves he then swept, piled up, and put in bags. Domingas tried to help him, but impatiently, angrily, he shooed her away. He scratched the soil, planted palm cuttings, and pruned rebellious shoots twisting outside the pantry. He picked out the worm-eaten fruit, but wasted time with a burst jackfruit, observing the flies and larvae sheltering in its yellow flesh. It was strange to see him this way, so close to our living space, barefoot and dirty. He hardly knew how to use a rake, and got frustrated, his hands and feet swollen and red, his body scarred, covered with the bites of voracious ants.

Omar's strange mania let me study on Saturdays, but I was afraid of being called for some job in the house or the shop. Sometimes I would interrupt some reading to buy meat from Quim the butcher or take a dessert to someone's house; I waited for hours at the neighbors' front doors, because they wouldn't send the platter or the gourd pot back until they'd filled it in their turn. These friendly exchanges spoiled my Saturday afternoons, and maybe that's why I hated these mutual courtesies. On the way back, I used to cut a piece of pie or a slice of cake and take it to Domingas. I did it to save her effort too, because on Saturday mornings she was exhausted, her back aching, her voice hoarse. She began the week wanting to do everything, cleaning every corner of the house; the only reason she didn't clean out the hen coop built by Galib was because Zana didn't allow it; coyly ashamed of her own superstition, she said: "No, no one can go in my father's hen coop . . . it might bring bad luck." But Domingas devotedly looked after the rest of the house, and seemed distressed by Omar's mania, as he spent hours in the sun. From my room I secretly watched him as he clumsily cut branches, weeded, and piled up dry leaves. There was too much madness in this sudden enthusiasm for gardening. From time to time he dropped the rake and the machete to appreciate the beauties of our garden: the river Negro curassow that Domingas liked so much, roosting on a high branch of the old rubber tree; a chameleon crawling up the trunk of the breadfruit tree, stopping near a nest of black-tailed trogons, where the hen bird was sitting. On the ground, near the fence, Omar grubbed for the rose apples and red flowers that fell from the neighboring garden. He filled his hands with the little pink fruits, and hungrily bit into the ripe ones, purple and fleshy. The children from the slum came to plague him: a grown man like him, on all fours, smelling the flowers, twisting the *ingás* and sucking their white berries. He would stop, too, to dig in the earth, just for the sake of it, perhaps to get the smell of the humidity, strong after the rain. He enjoyed this freedom, and even made you feel like doing the same.

One Saturday afternoon, when I was amusing myself watching Omar's movements, Rânia sent a message for me to go to the shop to help her pile boxes of goods in the storeroom.

There weren't many people in the Rua dos Barés; over the loud-speaker of the Voz da Amazônia radio station came the sound of a famous bolero, and the two of us, inside the shop, listened to its echoes. She locked the doors so that no one could bother us. We sweated, she more than me, and hardly said anything. I carried so many boxes that the upper floor was jammed. There was no room left in Halim's refuge. Rânia put the light on, gave one look at the mess, and changed her mind: she took it into her head to sort the whole shop, and wanted to begin with the storeroom. Her face, neck, and shoulders were shiny with sweat. I came down with the boxes, and then she decided to throw out old metal, rotten bits of wood, rusted hooks, rolls of tobacco, measuring tapes, gourds, and bottles. She got rid of all her father's old junk, even throwing things from the previous century into the bin, like the miniature hookah that had belonged to Halim's uncle. It didn't bother her throwing all these things out. She operated with a fierce determination, quite aware she was burying a past. It was already late at night when we began to clean up the storeroom. We swept the floor with the big brush, took the old shelving down, and cleaned the walls. She was exhausted, dripping with sweat, but all the same decided to check the stock. When she bent over to open a box of sheets, I saw her breasts, tanned and sweaty, loose in her white sleeveless blouse. Rânia stayed in this position, and I was paralyzed seeing her like this, bowed down, with bare shoulders, breasts, and arms. When she got up, she looked at me for a few seconds. Her lips moved, and her insinuating voice whispered, slowly: "Should we stop?"

She was panting. And she didn't shy away from my body or avoid my embrace, my caresses, and the kisses I'd been wanting to give for so long. She asked me to put the light out, and we spent hours in that sauna. I'd longed for this night for years. Later she talked a little, quite easily, just looking at me, with her large, almond-shaped eyes. About her fifteenth birthday, and the party that didn't happen: it was to be in the Benemous' mansion, Talib was going to play the lute, and Estelita was going to lend crystal wine glasses. But Zana canceled the party at the last minute. "Nobody understood why, only my mother and I knew," said Rânia. "Zana knew my boyfriend, the man I loved . . . I wanted to live with him. My mother kicked up a fuss, got angry, saying her daughter wasn't going to live with a man like that . . . she wasn't going to let him come to our party. She threatened me; she'd create a scandal if she saw me with him. 'With so many lawyers and doctors interested in you, and you pick a pauper like him . . .' My father tried to help me, did everything he could, implored Zana to give way and accept him, but it was no good. She was stronger, and had my father spellbound to the end. I ignored all those suitors . . . some of them come around here to this day, pretend they want to buy something, and end up buying old stock . . . the leftovers . . . everything I haven't sold in the past year. Now this is my world . . . I'm the mistress of all this," she said, looking at the walls of the shop. We stayed silent, in the semidarkness; in the feeble light of the storeroom, I could hardly see her face. She asked me to go away, she wanted to be alone; she might even sleep in the shop. It was past two in the morning, and I knew I wouldn't sleep that night. All I could think of was Rânia, her voice, her beauty that I'd seen so close, closer perhaps than anyone else. I never found out who the man was she'd fallen in love with. I would have liked to spend many Saturdays helping her in the shop, but she never asked me again.

Zana must have thought it strange to see me in my room, reading and studying, while her son slaved in the garden. On one occasion, I saw Halim observing his son digging and moving earth, carrying bags of dead leaves, tiring himself out. He felt no pity for him. Bitterly, he commented: "It's curious to see how he sweats and struggles just to stay close to his mother."

One day, his mother did feel shame at one particular scene. Talib's two daughters, Zahia and Nahda, unexpectedly came into

the house and straightaway began laughing. Nervously, they covered their faces with their hands. We heard the laughter and the
clinking of the gold bracelets shaking on the girls' arms. Zana
appeared in the room, and before she asked what they were laughing
about, looked into the garden: her son, naked, was wound around
the trunk of the rubber tree, and slowly, artistically scratching its
trunk. Was he trying to extract milk from the ancient tree? When he
saw his mother observing him, he moved away from the tree, put his
hands between his legs, and felt his groin. He began to groan, making a terrible face. Zahia and Nahda stopped laughing, staring in
amazement. They retreated. He was howling, roaring like a madman, pressing his hands to his thighs. Zana shouted for Domingas,
and the two of them went to the trunk; my mother immediately
knew what the reason for the howls was. Omar was suffering. He
gritted his teeth to piss, bit his lips, and began scratching the tree
trunk again. "His *ramêmi* is full of pus," said Domingas. Zana was
shocked: "What did you say? Are you mad?" My mother shook her
head: "You don't know . . . It's not the first time he's caught that ill-
ness." Zana didn't believe it. At night, the artful gardener escaped
over the back fence . . . This time it was really serious, galloping
gonorrhea as we called it. The two of them took Omar to the bathroom, gave him medicine, and wrapped his *ramêmi* in gauze. He had
to go to the doctor, and put up with a couple of injections in his but-
tock. He came back from the pharmacy walking with a limp, like a
parrot. At home, the treatment was no more pleasant. Zana waited
for Halim to go out, Domingas boiled water with *crajiru* leaves, and
Omar crouched down beside the basin to get his mother's treatment.
He gripped his groin, twisted and turned, gnashed his teeth, spilled
the infusion, and tried to run away. Zana picked up a clean towel and
began the application again. In the end, he began to get some relief.
We knew when he pissed because of the howls he let out during the
night. It was terrible. "Who did this to you?" Zana wanted to know.

He didn't answer. He begged silence from his mother with a suffering look. He was an angel. He wasn't going to spit on the whores.
He stayed there weeding and gathering dead leaves. When he woke
everyone with his shouts, Halim was frightened: "What's happened
this time?" Zana calmed him with her lies: "Our son's got a
headache, leave him be, the pain'll pass."

"A headache? Snarling like a mad dog?"

He couldn't put up with the son's howls, much less his wife's
lies. He went out in the middle of the night; he knew where to find
nocturnal friends in the bars in the Educandos. In the daytime, he
slipped out more often, and didn't even wait for the siesta to get out
into the street. Zana wouldn't leave me in peace, knocking on my
door, berating me: I had all my life to study, and I was to go out after
Halim this minute.

Alone, he got out of the house, and went all over the place, hob-
bling with his stick under the hot sun. He hadn't lost his sense of
direction; he could still point at a shack and tell you which of his
cronies lived there, and walk aimlessly through distant places: the
Boulevard Amazonas, the Praça Chile, the cemetery, the English
reservoir. When I didn't find him sitting on the wicker chair in the
room above the shop, I followed his trail from bar to bar, all the way
along the edge of the river. My search took hours; in fact, he wasn't
hiding, just walking, on the loose, wandering, disenchanted, like a
balloon losing air before it reaches the clouds. Sometimes, when he
got home, Halim sat on the gray sofa and muttered: "Issa Azmar's
died . . . that man who lived by the shop, that Portuguese from the
Rua Barão de São Domingos, he's died . . . what was his name?
Balma, that's it . . . They never even waited for mass to be said . . .
they're knocking the big house down . . . We played billiards in
Balma's house . . . remember?"

He talked to himself, tapping his stick on the floor, nodding his
head. Zana tried to correct him: "Issa died a long time ago and

Balma sold the shop and went to live in Rio." He went on: "Tannus was crazy for that girl of Balma's . . . He'd leave us playing billiards and snuggle up with her in the sacks of sugar in the basement . . . She was lovely, that girl . . . large eyes, a little round face . . . really lovely! Balma's house . . . now there's just a hole in the street . . . a big hole with no shadows."

Zana kept an eye on him, but he sloped off, lying: "Just going around to the shop, Rânia needs me." Off he went, nowhere in particular, sometimes for a drink on one of the pontoons in the middle of the river. When it rained, he came back soaked, coughing, spitting, making a mess all over the house. He avoided seeing his son in the garden. He wanted the other one: "Where's Yaqub? Why doesn't he come with his wife?" The old man liked Lívia. He provoked his wife, eating the goodies Lívia sent from São Paulo, ignoring our own food. It was an insult to Zana, but he no longer cared. He stuffed himself with his daughter-in-law's almonds and dates. He no longer gorged himself hungrily, with real pleasure, he ate out of spite, with a sad expression, chewing mechanically, staring into the distance.

One afternoon when he'd escaped right after the siesta I found him on the bank of the river Negro. Beside him was his old friend Pocu, surrounded by fishermen, fishmongers, boatmen, and peddlers. Dumbfounded, they were watching the destruction of the Floating City. The inhabitants were swearing at the demolition men: they didn't want to live far away from the little harbor, far from the river. Halim was shaking his head, disgusted, watching all those little houses being knocked down. He lifted his stick, spitting swearwords, and shouting, "Why are they doing that? We're not going to let them," but the police prevented people getting into the neighborhood. He was choking, and began to cry when he saw the bars, and his favorite, the Siren of the River, being chopped down with axes. He wept while they ripped the partitions and cut the ropes tying the logs, smashing the thin wooden pillars. The roofs slumped inwards; beams and joints fell into the water and floated away from the edge of the river Negro. It was all finished in a day; the whole neighborhood disappeared. The logs floated on, till they were swallowed by the night.

Only once was my search fruitless. On Christmas Eve morning 1968, he went out, and we all expected him to come back at nightfall, carrying boxes of presents, ready to eat rice and lentils, roast leg of lamb, and other delicacies that Zana and Domingas were preparing. At the end of the afternoon, when the neighbors came by and asked after him, Zana said: "Don't you know Halim? He pretends to disappear and then comes back . . ." Before night came, Talib rang to say that his friend hadn't come for his Christmas game of backgammon. Talib and I looked for him all over, from the gullies of the Educandos to the bars of São Raimundo, until Talib, exhausted, realized that Halim wouldn't be back for a while. "When someone wants to hide, the night gives them shelter," he said.

Zana wanted to avoid a scandal, and didn't tell the police. Sooner or later he'd be back, she said. "His place is here near me, it always was," she said over and over. At other moments, she'd never been upset by Halim's wanderings; he preferred to seek comfort for his sorrows far from home. But now Christmas dinner was nearly ready, and at midnight we ate in silence. The dinner was gloomy, hardly anyone spoke, without Halim's voice and the chatter of the friends he invited. Zana didn't touch the food: she'd wait a little longer. "He knows this night's important to me . . . He never failed to come, never . . ." She sat alone at the table, looking at the chair at the head, his place.

We waited for him until far into the night. My mother and I in our room at the back; Rânia and Zana upstairs, lying down, with the door open, listening for any noise. Two struck, and no sign of Halim. At around three, I heard my mother snore, a sound like a deep whistle or breathing. A tinamou hooted somewhere near; I looked out into the garden, on the ground—there was no sign of the bird. Then I recognized the sound of an ani, and felt melancholy, and a bit dizzy. The thick tops of the trees covered the back of the house. A strange little noise came through the night; it might be a hungry opossum looking for a hen coop or bats eating sweet rose apples. I remember that the words in the book I was reading gradually faded and disappeared. The book, too, was swallowed by the darkness. I nodded over my worktable. About five in the morning (or a little later, because the slum at the back showed signs of waking and the night was beginning to lose its blackness) a noise woke me up. I saw a light in the kitchen, and then a figure. It was a woman. Zana's right hand appeared, lit by a candle. She came out slowly, holding a bowl, with the lighted candle in her other hand. She crossed the living room, and before she went up, stopped near the stairs. She stopped, turned her head, and gave a dreadful cry. The bowl smashed on the floor, and the candle trembled in her hand. Domingas woke out of her dream and seemed to plunge into a nightmare: her sleepy face turned into a terrified mask. The two of us went towards the room: Halim was there, his arms crossed, sitting on the gray sofa. Zana gave a step towards him, and asked him why he'd gone to sleep on the sofa. Then, shaking less, she managed to illuminate his body and found the courage to ask one more question: why had he come back so late? Then, in an Arabic accent, on her knees, she shouted his name, touching his face now with her two hands. Halim didn't reply.

He was quiet, as never before.

Silent, forever.

8

One October afternoon, some two months before Halim's death, Omar disappeared. It was hot as hell, and the October sun makes everyone feel lethargic; it produces a morbid, paralyzing sleepiness, like a powerful anesthetic.

He kept on working in this dense heat: Omar of all people, who hadn't the strength to put up with so much sun. He changed complexion several times, turning into a kind of hard-skinned human animal; he went red, yellow, and finally copper-colored. How long was he going to play at being a gardener, or a janitor? When would this self-flagellation stop? It had already gone on too long, and I was hoping he would go back to his endless nocturnal existence; why couldn't he get drunk once and for all, and stay in the red hammock for good? But no: he kept on at his drudgery. Not even on the hottest days of the year would he seek out shade to work in. He was mortifying himself. His body became swollen, and his fingers and toes were full of impetigo blisters. All he needed to do was exchange his arms for wings; the angel, the patron saint of the household.

When Domingas missed Omar in the middle of that October afternoon, Zana didn't get upset. In the garden, she lifted her head and shouted her son's name. Up there, where he was ensconced, he gave signs of life: he opened his arms, swung his body from a thick branch, and let out a shriek like a bird.

"He always liked that kind of tomfoolery," Zana remembered. "When he was a kid, he defied everyone and climbed up to the highest branch. Yaqub was terrified, poor thing . . ."

It seems he'd climbed into the rubber tree to rest and meditate, or, who knows, to look at the world from up there, like a god, a bird, or a monkey. Here on the ground, things were less comfortable, infested with ants' nests, pests, and tree parasites; anthills appeared overnight, creating hard, dark mounds in the wooden fence and the tree trunks. Omar always forgot to destroy these anthills, and I knew that task would be left over for me. Sooner or later, I would have to pour kerosene on these huge brown lumps and set them on fire. I really enjoyed watching a whole community of insects writhing and burning to a crisp, devoured by the flames. That was not all that was destroyed. I cut the bushes and dead plants down, and then pulled everything out, the stalk, the roots, everything. The holes in the ground turned into subterranean bonfires; the grasshoppers and the umbrella ants with their queen were incinerated as well. It was quite a spectacle seeing these organized families, like ordered, disciplined armies, going up in flames. What pleasure I got from witnessing a whole hierarchy of insects turn to ash. For some time at any rate, the ground was free of these pests. It was a relief to see our square bit of the garden smoking here and there. Omar avoided contact with fire: he was afraid. He couldn't bear the presence of ashes, carbonized matter that nourished the remaining vegetation in the garden.

He couldn't bear to see his father dead in the house, sitting on the gray sofa, where he used to see his son drunk or befuddled with sleep in the red hammock; the same sofa where Halim had sat for some minutes, panting, exhausted, after he'd slapped his son and chained him down. Omar must have remembered this, on the night when he was woken by the convulsive weeping of the women of the household. When he came downstairs, Omar didn't understand, didn't want to understand what had happened. On the gray sofa he saw the only man who had dishonored him with a slap. He began shouting, like a child burning with hatred, or some feeling like hatred. Beside himself, he shouted: "Isn't he going to chain his son up? Aren't you going to wipe the sweat off his forehead? Why doesn't he budge and talk to me? Is he going to stay there, with that look on his face like a dead fish?"

Shouts in the dawn: Omar shouting, Rânia and Domingas weeping. Zana covered her face with her hands; she was sitting on the floor surrounded by fragments of the bowl, near Halim, perhaps unaware of how it had happened. No one, that night, saw the old man come into the living room. He must have come in the very early morning, treading imperceptibly, a wounded old man fleeing from everything and everybody, to die. Omar surprised us with his angry gesture, his finger pointing at Halim's face, at the nearly closed, lifeless eyes in his father's lowered head. Rânia was paralyzed: she didn't know what to do; she couldn't stop her brother shouting, grabbing his father's chin and lifting his head. The widower Talib came in time to prevent a confrontation between the live son and the dead father. It was already dawn when Talib and his two daughters burst into the room and separated Omar from his father. Omar reacted, kicking out, shouting, and I couldn't bear seeing him so full of courage in the face of the dead Halim. I made a gesture to Talib and his daughters, pushed Omar out of the room and dragged him out into the garden. He was furious, grabbed a machete and threatened me. I shouted louder than him: let him face me once and for all and cut me in pieces, coward that he was. The machete trembled in his right hand, while I said over and over: "Coward . . ." He went quiet, gripping the big knife he used for playing at being a gardener. He did have the courage to look at me, and his look only inflamed my anger. He backed off, and stayed squatting under the old rubber tree, his shocked face turned towards the living-room door, from where Domingas was looking at us. She called me, hugged me, and begged me to come back into the room.

Talib's daughters were unfolding a sheet to cover the gray sofa, where the dead Halim was laid out.

"Don't touch his body, and don't weep near here," Talib said, three times over.

So, lying down, rolled in a white sheet, the father of the twins was ready to leave the house. Zahia and Nahda lifted the corner of the sheet and looked at the dead man, who had so often applauded them. The dancing girls knew it too: Halim would have preferred to die in the bedroom or dancing with Zana, as he himself said at her birthday parties.

Talib muttered a prayer in Arabic, and my mother kneeled down before the little altar. She couldn't pray. She went to her room; she wanted to be alone. When Talib and his daughters left, Zana locked the front door, and bent over Halim, weeping, then took off the sheet covering him and put his hands on her face, around her back, as if embracing him. "You can't go away from this house . . . or from my side," she murmured. Rânia tried to console her, but she wouldn't leave him, and during the wake she went on talking about Halim, remembering his love poetry, the ecstatic look in his eyes, his body with its smell of wine, the pauses he took to get the right tone of voice back. Surrounded by her women friends, the widow spoke painfully, sobbing, silencing the buzz of the wake, her voice describing the young Halim in some cheap room in lodgings frequented by immigrants and peddlers. "There, in nineteen twenty-odd, there lived that skinny little man, a beanpole that filled out until he got quite brawny," said Zana. From wandering around selling his trinkets, he got to know just about everybody. He and his friend Toninho, Cid Tannus, a poor devil who put on airs: he wore a red waistcoat and a silk tie, smoked cigars and cigarillos given him by the rubber barons. The two of them, as innocent as you like, turned up in Galib's restaurant. He was a sly one, that Tannus! As if everyone didn't know he was a regular in the foreign girls' house, right next to the law courts. He dragged Halim off to the little house where the Polish girls were. Everyone knew about that, all her friends knew about Zana's suitor, and his philandering. "A Christian, you've got to marry a rich Christian," they told her. That's when Halim stopped going around with Cid Tannus. Tannus never stopped partying. He dressed up for Carnival, got groups together and pulled floats along, and was within a hair's breadth of taking Halim along with him to the bachelor existence.

His eyes followed the girl who went around the tables, until one day she saw the envelope under a plate. Zana never said that she had read the *gazals*, and Galib never knew she had. She read the verses and gave the envelope to her father, saying: "That peddler's forgotten this piece of paper at his table." Then she laughed and cried at the wake. She laughed, sobbing, choking, and saying she'd thought of throwing the sheet of paper away, but her curiosity got the better of her disdain and indifference. A good thing she did read it: what would her life have been like without those words? The sounds, the rhythm, the rhymes of the *gazals*, and everything born of that mixture: their images, the visions they conjured up, their spell. "How wonderful the day / when wine flowed our way." She pressed her lips together and recited this refrain, bending over her dead husband. No, she couldn't resist reading the poems, alone in her room, after meals. And one day, in the restaurant, she shivered when she saw the young man ready to recite all the couplets by heart, ecstatically, confidently, like an actor with a good memory. She said this, over again, at her husband's wake and funeral, and yet again at home, talking to herself as she picked up the pods from the *jatobá* tree scattered about the garden.

After Halim's death, the house began to fall apart. Omar went to the funeral, but kept distant, so much so that his brother, who didn't come, seemed closer to his father's final departure. Yaqub ordered a wreath to be delivered at the cemetery and an epitaph, which Talib translated and read out: *Fond memories of my father, who was present even when he was far off.*

Halim's friends were touched. Omar, when he saw his mother crying, moved away from his father's grave.

A few weeks after the funeral, she reprimanded her son pointblank. He was caught off guard, and forced to hear words that shocked and frightened him. He had gone too far in the way he had treated his dead father; what he'd said would make your hair stand on end. Having her dead husband insulted: Zana wouldn't put up with that. On the morning Halim died, she'd heard Omar's absurd monologue in silence, and she'd not forgotten the raised finger in the dead man's face, nor his insolent voice, the disgraceful words addressed to someone who couldn't reply with a gesture, not even a look.

She found him squatting, half-hidden, gripping a machete, and about to cut caladiums and philodendrons scorched by the sun; mounds of leaves, here and there, were waiting to be put in sacks at the end of the afternoon. Between the cracks in the back fence, the children from the slum watched Omar's movements. He only had his underpants on, covered with scars, disguised as a slave. The children began to whistle; then they threw mango pits at him, which banged into his body. Omar ran to the fence, jumping over piles of leaves and branches. "Little bastards!" he yelled, lifting his middle finger at the children. He stopped swearing when the shadow of his mother's body fell across the fence.

"That's enough of playing the martyr, getting your hands and arms scratched with all this useless gardening," she said in a harsh voice. "Now you've got no father . . . you'd better get a job and stop this idle lunacy."

He turned around to his mother, disbelief in his eyes. Zana took the machete out of his hand and stuck it in the ground. "Go and look at yourself in the mirror . . . Your father couldn't face looking at you like that . . . He couldn't bear seeing a life thrown away . . . He didn't deserve to hear those vile things . . . A dead man . . ." She stopped chiding him and went into the living room, sobbing. She refused to speak to her son when he came to her and tried to caress her. She turned her head away and left him with his hands in the air. He moved away, and in the mirror saw his body full of pustules and scratches. Then he went upstairs looking at his mother, still trying to gain her attention on the afternoon when she'd surprised him with her harsh words and avoided his caress.

Omar never returned to the garden. He abandoned the dead leaves, the wormy fruit, and rotten branches. He gave up chasing the opossums and beating them to death, like a child possessed by some evil demon. Never again did I see him sitting alone in the middle of the garden, gazing at the blue honeycreepers jumping around in the leaves of the assai palms, or delighted by the *saurás* pecking at the ripe little fruits. Before he began his gardening, he used to sit and enjoy these things. He spent a good deal of time this way. Sometimes he smiled, almost happy, when the intense light of the equatorial sun blazed in the garden. He refused to use the new clothes Zana had given him. Rânia invited him to work in the shop, and pressed him often on the subject, until he opened his mouth, revealing yellow, pointed teeth, and let out a belly laugh, deepened by the echoes of chronic bronchitis.

"Work with you? You can't do a thing without asking your brother's advice," he said.

Rânia knew that Omar's aversion to routine and regular hours was radical and sincere; she knew he was clever enough to lay his hands on the fruit others had worked for, as naturally as could be. It was no effort for him to be sly, and he felt no shame at all living off the sweat of the three women of the household. And so, shamelessly, he returned to Manaus's nocturnal world. When he came back in the early morning, he didn't find his mother waiting for him. He saw Zana in mourning, sitting on the gray sofa where so often Halim had embraced her with passion. He couldn't bear his mother's stillness, her deep mourning since Halim's death, the afternoons she began to spend in the bedroom, avoiding visitors, brooding over something. I would see her next to the trunk of the *jatobá*, sitting on a stool, with the sun on half her body. She seldom went out, and on Sundays took flowers for Halim, coming back in a state of grief: nobody could get a smile out of her. But she asked after Omar, and never failed to find out when her son had come home, and if he was well. She asked Rânia to give him money, and at midday, when Omar awoke, she listened to the stories he had to tell. The Café Mocambo had shut, the Praça das Acácias was turning into a bazaar. Alone at the table, he sat recounting his wanderings around the city. The saddest news of all was that the Verônica, the lilac brothel, had been shut too. "Manaus is full of foreigners, Mama. Indians, Koreans, Chinese . . . The center's turned into an anthill of people from the interior of the state . . . Everything's changing in Manaus."

"That's true . . . there's only you doesn't change, Omar. You're still a mess, look at your clothes, your hair . . . When you come back home in the morning . . ."

She spoke calmly, a little reticent, and then looked slowly into her son's face, with a silent sadness. He certainly tried to draw her to him. He left little gifts in her hammock, things he'd picked up here and there, or bought in the kiosks in Remédios Square: a gourd cup with a little red heart painted on it, a necklace of black and red seeds; trifles. He carved his mother's name on the blade of the oar he kept; big letters, covering the names of other women. On the night of Zana's birthday, he gave her a bouquet of heliconias.

"Let's go out and eat a fish stew, just the two of us, in a restaurant in the middle of the river."

"What I most want to see is peace between my two sons. I want to see you together, here at home, near me . . . If it's only for a day."

They didn't go out for dinner. She left the bouquet on the table, went upstairs, and shut herself in her room; she refused to talk to anyone. Days went by like this; she only spoke with her eyes, leaving Omar cornered by her silence. He didn't want to hear talk of Yaqub; his brother's name infuriated him. Early in the day, when it was just growing light, before I opened my bedroom window, Omar was grumbling, leaning on the rubber tree: "What does she want? Peace between her sons? Never! There's no such thing as peace in this world . . ." He talked to himself, and I don't know who he was thinking about when he said: "You should have run away . . . pride, honor, hope, Brazil . . . all buried . . ." He didn't budge or look at me when I came out of my room. He stayed there, as if he'd fallen on the ground, his gaze on the places where his mother had always waited for him. I thought Omar was going to lose heart once and for all, and spend the rest of his life there, leaning on the old tree trunk. He began to come back earlier, didn't exchange banter with Rânia, or call Domingas in that easygoing, half-cynical tone of voice we always heard in the middle of the day.

Then, one Saturday, a little after nightfall, Omar came in accompanied by a man. Everyone heard Omar's voice. Zana was drawn by a foreign accent. Her son, coming back so soon, and with a stranger! The conversation between the two went on, until Zana came down, said hello to the visitor, and went into the garden: she wanted my mother to help her get a light meal together. Domingas wasn't feeling well, and took against the guest when she saw him sitting on the gray sofa, an eager look in his placid face. She wasn't pleased to see an intruder sitting in Halim's place. Domingas's aversion to him seemed like a premonition to me.

Rochiram, the visitor, was an Indian who spoke slowly, whispering in English and Spanish the words he thought he was saying in Portuguese. When he opened his mouth, he gave the impression he was going to tell a great secret. Omar had met him in the Hotel Amazonas bar, where the trio Uirapuru played boleros and mambos on Saturdays. With curiosity, I looked at this little dark-skinned man, with a nose like a toucan chick, and cheap trousers, shirt, and shoes. But the gold-and-ruby ring on his right hand would have cost an ordinary workingman more than a year's toil. On his face was a calculated, mechanical smile, and almost everything in his body was the opposite of spontaneous. This man of studied gestures observed every corner of the house; he could see he was charming Zana, and that some kind of mutual trust was possible. He began to frequent the house, always accompanied by Omar. He brought presents for Zana: Chinese vases, silver trays, Indian statuettes. My mother sullenly served *guaraná* and then distanced herself from the intruder. Gradually, Zana came out of reclusion, loosened her tongue, and took an interest in her son's friend. When Omar wasn't around, she mentioned the other son's name, showed photographs of Yaqub: "He's a great engineer, one of the best mathematicians in Brazil." She always lowered her voice when she heard Omar on the stairs: "My son's less untidy . . . Just look at what a friendship can do." Then she asked Rochiram to tell her a little about his life. The Indian didn't talk much, but he satisfied Zana's curiosity. He lived on the move, building hotels on several continents. It was as if he lived in provisional homelands, spoke provisional languages, and made provisional friendships. What kept him in each place were his business interests. He had heard that Manaus was growing fast, with its industry and commerce. He could see the city was lively, with its neon signs in English, Chinese, and Japanese. He saw he'd been right in his intuition. When Zana didn't understand Rochiram's gibberish, she asked her son: "What's this foreigner trying to say?" Omar translated into Portuguese, and ended the conversation; he was in a hurry to leave with Rochiram. Zana pressed them to stay a little longer, but Omar refused; they had various places to go to. Where? He wouldn't say. He went pale on the morning Rânia invited Rochiram to have lunch. During lunch, he rubbed his hands together nervously, afraid his mother might mention Yaqub's name. Rânia tried to divert his attention, and he was sharp with his sister, and reticent towards Rochiram. He only spoke, to disguise his ill humor, at the end of the meal, when the guest mentioned he wanted to build a hotel in Manaus. "I'm helping Rochiram to find some land near the river," said Omar sharply, before he got up from the table.

Domingas didn't feel at ease with this foreigner, stranger than all of us put together. She said to me: "Omar doesn't seem like himself. He's in a state, he doesn't know where to put himself . . ."

I found a strange look in his eye, and was surprised he had noticed Domingas's absence during lunch. He asked her if she suspected anything. My mother gave nothing away. She said: "I don't like your friend. The first night he came here, I dreamed of Halim."

Omar didn't want to hear; he ran away from his father's shadow, avoiding him even in other people's dreams. He never brought Rochiram inside the house: he waited for him on the sidewalk and left in a hurry. He hid with the Indian, always mistrustful, looking sideways at his mother, following her footsteps, concealing himself to hear any secrets.

Later, I found out what Omar suspected. Zana asked me to type a letter to Yaqub. She brought a typewriter into my room and began to dictate what was on her mind. She spoke of Omar's friend, an Indian tycoon who wanted to build a hotel in Manaus. The two sons could work together: Yaqub could do the calculations, and Omar help the Indian in Manaus. She had already talked to Rochiram, and asked him not to mention the matter. Her great dream was to have her two sons reconciled. That was all she thought about, and since Halim's death she had been waking up in the middle of the night, frightened. Who could know how much she missed Halim: the pain he left behind him. She didn't want to die with the twins hating one another like sworn enemies. She wasn't the mother of Cain and Abel. Nothing had managed to bring peace between them, neither Halim nor her prayers, not even God. It was up to Yaqub, learned and wise as he was, to think about this. She begged forgiveness for having sent him to Lebanon on his own. She didn't let Omar go; she thought that he'd die far from her side.

Zana came back again and again to this topic, with circumlocutions and euphemisms. I listened to the remorseful voice of a guilty mother, and kept writing. Sometimes she asked me if her words weren't betraying her. In a trance of self-reproach, she looked at me as if she was in Yaqub's presence. When she paused, she seemed to be waiting for a reply, afraid her son would say nothing.

She signed her name in Arabic, sent the letter, and spent the next few days thinking over every line she'd written. She doubted her own words, not knowing if she was showing disregard, or overstating things; or if her son would understand what she was most asking him for: forgiveness. I gave her the rough copy, and she read it out under her breath. One afternoon, I saw her reading the letter out to an imaginary Halim. After the reading, she asked: will Yaqub understand? Will he forgive his mother?

Then, almost a month later, Rânia gave her mother an envelope Yaqub had sent to the shop. It was short. He neither accepted nor refused forgiveness. He wrote that the clash between him and Omar was a matter for them, and added: "Let's hope it's resolved in a civil manner; if there's violence, there'll be a biblical scene." But he showed interest in the construction of the hotel, not knowing his brother had a part in it. He ended the letter with an embrace and no more, no extra adjectives. His mother read the word out loud and murmured: "I ask for forgiveness and he signs off with just an embrace."

However, the mention of the Bible worried her more. She realized that Omar had kept Rochiram away from the house, and that her son was suspicious, always on the lookout, prowling around his mother and sister. She asked Rânia to tell Omar everything. Rânia showed Yaqub's letter: it wasn't a plot on his mother's part, but an attempt to reconcile her sons. Omar read the letter and began to laugh as if he were making fun of everybody. But then the joking tone vanished: "What does the smart aleck mean by a *biblical scene*, eh, Rânia? What does your brother know about civility?"

Rânia wasn't cowed, and didn't get angry. "I don't know," she said. "I know you could work together in a construction firm . . ."

"Construction firm?" Omar interrupted, annoyed, shouting that *he* had gotten to know Rochiram, *he* had brought the Indian to the house, and had gone looking for a plot of land for the hotel. He seemed irritated by his sister's insistence, by her being so stuck on the idea that she could pacify the twins. Rânia wanted her brothers close to her; she wanted to be intimate with both. This intimacy, along with her compulsion for work, would give much more meaning to her life. All her efforts to calm Omar down were in vain. She thought that sooner or later he was going to fall into her plump, tanned arms; that the two of them would curl up in the hammock like lovers after a quarrel. He didn't give in to her blandishments. We watched him squandering the money from the commission on the sale of the land for the hotel. The expensive bottles of drink he emptied and then threw into the garden, or on the floor of the veranda! The gifts he bought for girlfriends and then left around anywhere, forgotten, as if they were useless, or all this had no importance any longer. The linen dress and two Chinese silk blouses he gave to Domingas, saying: "Now you throw the rags they sent you from São Paulo into the trash." He didn't address the other women; with no warning, he would burst out furiously in his mother's presence: "A biblical scene, right? OK, let's see if the smart aleck really knows his Bible."

No one replied to the digs intended for his brother. Mother and daughter glanced at one another, and this powerful silence between accomplices prevailed over Omar's anger. They let him give vent to his feelings, pretended to be indifferent to Yaqub, and it was strange to see them so passive when Omar demanded that no photograph of his brother be seen in the room.

For some time he avoided everyone, alternating between hatred and dissipation.

I wasn't party to what had been going on in the last few weeks, and couldn't make out the whispering between Zana and Rânia or decipher the gestures and looks they exchanged, but I heard Yaqub's name, and the hotel he was in. I was surprised he was staying in such a modest place, nothing more than a rundown house in one of the oldest parts of Manaus. It was the same one I'd been to with Domingas, when she had taken me for a walk in the Praça Pedro II, where foreign sailors went with the whores who had their patches on São Vicente Island. The hotel, hidden at the end of a narrow street, seemed far away from the crowds and the buzz of the center, now full of shops open all day and all night. Yaqub was there, in that quiet, winding street, as anonymous as the rest of its inhabitants, afraid of the city's hubbub. I told Domingas, and asked her if he was going to leave without visiting us. My mother answered nervously: no, she doubted it, he'd come to see her, I could rely on him coming.

Everyone at home seemed ill at ease. Zana and Rânia only talked behind closed doors; near to me, they exchanged words in soft whispers, fluttering like butterflies. Five or six days went by like this, and I remember that one Thursday it rained all night, and in the morning the roof was leaking. Dirty water streamed from the living-room ceiling, and the garden was awash. In the slum at the back, misery and confusion; the shacks were flooded, and from early on Domingas and I helped to drain the water from the corridors, and remove furniture from the tiny mud-spattered rooms. We left them with the sound of crying children in our ears, thinking our neighbors had lost everything. In midmorning a weak sun appeared over the city, the foliage took on a greener sheen, and a warm breeze moved the huge leaves of the breadfruit trees. Inside the house, silence: Zana had gone to exchange confidences with her daughter in the shop. Domingas went to change her clothes. When she came out of her room, she had a new dress and perfume on, and red lipstick. Her look couldn't hide her apprehension. I saw her tense face turned towards the living room: Omar had just come down and was having a cup of coffee. It was unusual to see him down so early. He didn't touch the food prepared for him every morning. He walked around the room, then suddenly went up and banged on Zana's door. When he came down, he didn't even look at Domingas: he said he wouldn't be back for lunch. He went out unkempt, scruffy, looking grim. My mother gazed after his reeling figure, treading the ground as if he were kicking it. She stood between her room and the kitchen, till she lifted her head and said: "The weather's still vile."

I began digging channels to drain off the pools in the garden and stop them from getting infested with insects. The ground was covered with dead lizards and grasshoppers, fruit and leaves; from the ditch, by the side of the flooded henhouse, came the stink of rot. Little by little, the garden began to heat up with the humidity, and

the sun, still watery among the thick clouds, wasn't strong enough
to remove the marks of the night's rain.

Before eleven o'clock Yaqub appeared: he wouldn't stay long,
just a short visit to relive memories and see the house again before
he went back to São Paulo. He had ordinary clothes on. His black
hair was combed back; his upright body and healthy expression
made him look much less aged than Omar. He'd brought math
books for me, and clothes for Domingas. He didn't ask after Zana.
He said: "I went to the cemetery, went to see the grave . . ." He
didn't end the sentence. He hid his feelings, looked at the table laden
with fruit and delicacies for breakfast, and asked, with an ironic edge
to his voice: "All this for me?" He sat down, opened a briefcase, and
spread out sheets of paper with sketches of metal girders, columns,
and reinforced concrete. He saw my body, dirty from the digging,
and took a long look at my hands. I wasn't intimidated, but I don't
know if it was a father's look. He never responded to my gaze.
Maybe his ambition made me doubt my connection with him; or that
same ambition didn't allow him to look at me honestly. He said he
had done the basic calculations for a huge building to be put up in
Manaus: "You can't spend your life cleaning the garden and writing
Rânia's business letters."

My mother heard the phrase and looked at me with a proud
expression, which lasted for a few short seconds. When she took her
eyes off me, her face took on its old look, half mistrustful, half fearful. The two of them went into the garden and, while they were
talking, he fingered a breadfruit. His hand went from the round fruit
to Domingas's chin; he laughed contentedly, with a triumphant air,
and at that moment I saw his intimacy with my mother. When he
put his arm around her, Domingas showed her apprehension: she
said he should go. Yaqub frowned: "I'm in my own house, I'm not
going to run away . . ." My mother begged him: they could go out

together, have a walk. He sat on the hammock, and asked her to come over, but she wouldn't. Now she was really anxious, couldn't keep her eyes off the living room, and the corridor. They said nothing more. The shouts and laments from the slum punctured the stuffy silence of the late morning.

Then I saw him: taller than the fence, his body looming larger, enormous, with his right hand clenched like a hammer, a crazed look in his indignant face. He was panting, in a furious hurry. When I cried out, Omar jumped in, lifted the hammock, and began to punch Yaqub on his face, his back, all over his body. I rushed to get on top of Omar, trying to hold him down. He was kicking and pummeling his brother, calling him a traitor, a coward. Some of the people from the slum came into the garden and came close to the veranda. In a sudden move, I grabbed Omar's hand. He managed to get loose. I saw he was surrounded by several men, and went away slowly, still eyeing the red hammock. I caught sight of him running to the living room and furiously ripping up the plans of the project; he tore all the sketches up, threw the plates on the floor, and ran headlong down the corridor.

Yaqub twisted and turned in the hammock, and couldn't get up. His face swelled up, his mouth wouldn't stop bleeding, and his lips were full of scratches and bruises. He groaned, feeling his head, back, and shoulders with his right hand. Two people from the slums helped get him out of the hammock; he could hardly walk. Two of the fingers of his left hand looked like hooks, and his body was bent over and shaking. Domingas went with him to a hospital, and before she went out asked me to clear the table, throw the broken china in the rubbish, and put the hammock to soak in the washtub. I hid the torn sheets of Yaqub's project in my room.

When my mother came back, she quickly dried the hammock and spread it out in her room. She abandoned the kitchen, and refused to get lunch ready. She said Yaqub's condition wasn't serious, though his left hand was in a mess, with two fractured fingers. He was going to lose some three teeth, his face was unrecognizable, and he had terrible pain in his back and shoulders. He had asked Domingas to keep her mouth shut, invent a story, and say to Zana: "Your son had to leave for São Paulo in a hurry."

Zana didn't swallow Domingas's story. She went into Omar's room, rummaged around, and found Yaqub's passport, which he'd stolen. She stopped, looking thoughtfully at the photograph of the engineer: his serious face, thick eyebrows, the stars on the epaulettes of his reserve officer's uniform. I could see the mother's vanity, and a gleam of remorse in her eye. It's the guilt torturing her conscience, I thought. She didn't know what to do with the passport, wandering aimlessly as if it might lead her somewhere. She sat down on the gray sofa, slipped the passport into her blouse, and when she lifted her head, she was crying, her hands crossed on her chest. The reddened eyes looked at the little altar and turned away towards the veranda, now empty.

Had he had to go in a hurry? Why? Zana repeated the question, as if she would get an answer by sheer repetition. She asked after Yaqub, but she was looking for Omar. She hardly spoke to Rânia, kicked the air for no reason, and sat thinking about Omar's fate. It was no longer the devil in the shape of a woman: it would have been easier to say to the neighbors: "These madwomen take our children from us, and our money." Words she'd used at other times, when Dália, the Silver Woman, danced for us all; when the other one, the Pau-Mulato, lived with Omar in an old boat, thinking she was going to spend her life sailing up and down the river, reading the palms of the people on its banks, forecasting bright futures for ruined lives. Both of them, Omar and Pau-Mulato, living it up onboard their boat or on deserted beaches, but watched over by a dense, powerful shadow.

Zana's dream of seeing her sons together, in an impossible harmony, was gone. She went back over her detailed and ingenious
plan. "My sons were going to start a construction firm, Omar was
going to have a job, work to do; I was sure . . ." She called my
mother over to her, and said: "Omar lost his head; he was betrayed
by his brother. I know all about it, Domingas . . . Yaqub got together
with that Indian, did everything in secret, ignored my Omar, ruined
everything . . ." Domingas listened and went away, leaving Zana
alone, cursing Yaqub's plot.

A few days after the fight, Rochiram went to the shop to talk to
Rânia. He looked like a stranger, Rânia said after the encounter. He
was short, sharp, never even pronouncing the twins' names. He said
in Spanish: "I've brought a proposal to close the matter." He gave
her a sealed envelope and said goodbye. She guessed the tone of the
document; even so, when she read the letter in front of me, she went
pale. Rochiram demanded a fortune in exchange for what he'd paid
Yaqub for drawing up the plans and to Omar for the commission on
the land. Apart from that, he'd wasted a lot of time on this business.
He threatened her with the law, and wrote that he already knew
influential people, "the most powerful in the city." Rânia asked for a
delay, "Some months for us to straighten our lives out."

She told her mother of Rochiram's demand. She said she'd do
everything to avoid Yaqub taking Omar to court.

"That Indian is a crook," said Zana. "Bloodsucker! The food
I cooked for the ungrateful wretch . . . I practically spoon-fed the
pale-faced parasite! He's ruined my son's future!"

She no longer dyed her hair, and the white curls made her look
older than her face, still almost unwrinkled. My mother wouldn't
pray with her, or tell her about Omar's attack. "Yaqub couldn't
react, he hadn't time," she said. Zana looked at her askance: her eyes
were really strange. But Domingas was not intimidated. She smiled

as if she were abreast of everything, and left her mistress perplexed, next to the oratory.

Domingas was worried about Yaqub, and was waiting for news of him, but he only came in a nightmare, one night when my mother heard Omar's steps and saw his tall body rise up from behind the fence and brutally hit his brother. The image of his disfigured face terrified her. But she seemed to suffer from Omar's woes. Leaning on the trunk of the rubber tree where he had once climbed so high, she said: "The two of them were born to fail."

9

I watched Domingas losing heart, less and less attentive now to the daily rhythm of the house, indifferent to the orchids she had always sprayed with such care, and the birds she used to watch in the tops of the trees and the palm fronds, later making carvings of them. Her hands could hardly manage to remove strips from the hard wood, and she couldn't even find the energy to plait palm fibers. The last animals she had carved were like little unfinished beings, fossils from other epochs. She didn't look as old as other housemaids, already done for in their early fifties. I asked her to rest, but she only lay down at night; she would slump into her hammock, and only wanted me to be there. She no longer opened the old book Halim had given her, thick, with a loose cover and illustrations of animals and plants whose names she knew by heart: Tupi words she had repeated for Yaqub in the nights when the two of them stayed alone in her damp room.

Our conversations became less frequent, and when she had time off, she sat on the ground or lay in her hammock, motionless. Only once, at nightfall, she began to hum one of the songs she'd heard in her childhood, there on the river Jurubaxi, before she lived in the Manaus orphanage. I'd thought her mouth was sealed, but no: she loosened her tongue and sang, in *nheengatu*, the short refrains of a monotonous melody. When I was a child, I went to sleep to the sound of that voice, a lullaby echoing through my nights.

One Sunday afternoon, my mother asked me to go for a walk with her to the Praça da Matriz. Nearby, berthed in the Manaus Harbor, the big freighters dwarfed the boats and canoes, hiding the forest on the horizon. In the center of the square, the multitude of birds that used to delight the children were no longer there. The aviary that had fascinated me so much was silent. Sitting on the steps of the church, Indians and migrants from the interior of the state were begging. Domingas exchanged some words with an Indian woman, and I didn't understand the conversation; the two of them crossed themselves when the bells struck six. My mother said goodbye to the woman, went alone into the church, and prayed. Then we went into the Manaus Harbor, and to the end of the walkway. The floating harbor was busy, with its stevedores, cranes, and forklift trucks. Someone recognized us and waved. It was Calisto, one of the people from the slum. Barefoot, wearing only shorts, he was waiting for orders to unload boxes of electronic goods. I didn't know he worked at the harbor on Sundays. Calisto had escaped from Estelita Reinoso's claws, but now he had another burden to bear.

Domingas wanted to go. "It's too hectic, too noisy," she complained, turning her back on our neighbor. The area surrounding the harbor was quiet. I saw the shop, now closed, and pointed out the storeroom where Halim, leaning against the window, had recounted parts of his life. My mother decided to sit on the low wall over the dark river. She said nothing for a few minutes, until the light had finally gone. "When you were born," she said, "Halim helped me, didn't want me thrown out of the house . . . He promised me you would go to school. You were his grandson; he wasn't going to throw you into the street. He came to your christening, he was the only one who came with me. He even asked to choose your name. Nael, he said, his father's name. I thought it was a strange name, but he really wanted it, so I let him . . . I felt the old man liked you a lot. I think he even liked his sons. But he complained about Omar; he said his son had stifled Zana." I felt her hands on my arm; they were sweaty and cold. She hugged me, kissed my face, and bowed her head. She murmured that she was so fond of Yaqub . . . since the time they played together, and went for walks. Omar got jealous when he saw the two of them together, in her room, soon after his brother came back from Lebanon. "With Omar I didn't want . . . One night he came into my room, making that racket, drunk, obscene . . . He forced me, with his man's strength. He never asked me to forgive him."

She was sobbing, and couldn't say any more.

Worried, I began to keep watch on the hammock my mother slept in. She didn't let herself be affected by Zana's agitation, as she swung between promises of vengeance and moments of melancholy, trying to reconcile her conflicting feelings. For weeks, Zana mixed up the past and the present, memories of her father and Halim with Omar's absence. "My father . . ." she said, putting her hands on Galib's photograph, her mind on the vast distance between the Amazon and Lebanon. Abbas's *gazals*, which she used to read in her room, she now recited out loud, and these words provided a lull in her madness. But the image of the absent Omar wouldn't leave her. She blamed herself for having written the letter to Yaqub. She called him impossible, and the victim became the aggressor. Rânia said her brothers would never be able to live in the same house, but that time might calm them down; time and distance.

"Nothing in this world can pacify a man betrayed," said Zana.

"Yaqub might regret what he's done," said Rânia. "He's not going to persecute anyone."

Her mother looked at her sadly, and said in a voice that was hoarse but unfaltering:

"You've never lived with a man, much less a son."

Rânia said no more.

Now Zana had no husband to help her, and Domingas's withdrawal left her even more abandoned. Talib's daughters came to see her; Nahda held Zana's hands and Zahia chatted, trying to distract her. Zana's wandering gaze disconcerted visitors. On the morning when Cid Tannus and Talib appeared, she said, with no warning, that it wasn't right, it wasn't right that one brother should steer clear of the other. "You must find my son; you must bring Omar back to my house. Do it for Halim's sake."

Talib, who was more intimate with the family, took a long look at the only plate on the table set for lunch. Omar's plate, glass, and cutlery hadn't been removed from the head of the table. As he went out, the widower said: "God shuts one door and opens another."

One day, when she woke up weeping, Zana ordered Rânia to take everything out of the safe, everything, all the old papers Halim had kept. She called a carter and four men to lift it; they were to take the steel box away, and throw the accursed safe into the jungle. It was the memory of her son in chains.

I went with the carter and the men to the shop, where Rânia was waiting for us. When I got back home, Zana, immersed in bad memories, had shut herself in her room. It was almost midday, and my mother wasn't in the kitchen. I found her curled up in Omar's hammock, which she'd hung in her own little room. The hammock had lost its original color, and the red, its vibrancy gone, was only in the memory of our eyes. I saw her dry lips, her right eye shut, the other covered by a lock of gray hair. I drew it to one side, and saw the other eye was shut. I rocked the hammock; my mother didn't move. She wasn't asleep. I saw her body slowly swaying, and began to cry. I sat on the ground beside her and stayed there, stunned, suffocated. While I looked at her, as the hammock swung back and forth, I relived the nights we had slept in each other's arms in the same little room that stank of cockroaches. Now, another smell, of wood and *copaiba* resin, was stronger. The little animals carved in brazilwood were arranged on the shelf. There, the polished birds and the snakes shone. My mother's menagerie: miniatures her hands had molded, night after night, by the light of an oil lamp. The slender wings of a *saracuá*, the loveliest bird of all, perched on a real branch, fixed into a brass bowl. Its wings wide open, narrow breast, beak pointing upwards: a bird about to take off. All my mother's strength and energy had gone into serving others. She kept those words to the end, but she didn't die with the secret that so irked me. I looked at my mother's face and remembered Omar's brutality.

Birds were singing outside and through the open window I could see bowed branches and ripe fruit scattered on the soil. I stopped rocking the hammock and stroked my mother's callused hands. Then came Zana's voice calling Domingas, three or four shouts coming from the first floor, then a noise on the staircase, the steps coming closer and closer, in the living room, the kitchen, the noise of leaves in the garden, and Zana's frightened eyes on the face with its eyes shut. She shook the hammock and, on her knees, she embraced Domingas.

I couldn't tear myself away from Domingas. A boy from the slum went to hand Rânia a note. I wrote: "My mother has just died."

At that time, I tried to write other things too. But words seem to wait for death and forgetting; they seem to be buried, petrified, in abeyance; later, they slowly regain heat, and kindle in us the desire to recount events time has dispersed. "Only time turns our feelings into truer words," Halim said to me during one conversation, using his handkerchief over and over to wipe the sweat brought on by the heat and his anger at his wife's entanglement with her younger son.

I asked Rânia for my mother to be buried in the family grave, next to Halim. She agreed, and paid for everything without protest, and I never knew how much complicity there was in such a generous act. My mother and my grandfather, side by side, under the earth, had found a common destiny; the two of them, who had come from so far away to die here. Now, so long after, I still visit their tomb. One Sunday, I even saw Adamor, Toad-Leg, in the cemetery. We glanced at one another; all I could see was his face, the rest of his body was hidden in a hole. But he soon lifted his arms up and went on working. He was one of the gravediggers.

10

The house gradually emptied, and aged in a short time. Rânia had bought a bungalow in one of the districts built on in the deforested areas north of Manaus. She told her mother the move was inevitable. She didn't explain why, but Zana reproached her: she'd never leave her house—she'd rather die than leave her plants, her living room with the altar and the saint, her morning walk around the garden. She didn't want to abandon the neighborhood, the street, the familiar things she looked at from the bedroom window. How could she live without the cries of the fishmongers, coal heavers, peddlers, and fruit sellers? The voices of people who already in the early morning had stories to tell: so-and-so was sick, such-and-such a politician, a nonentity only yesterday, had gotten rich overnight, a high-up had pinched bronze statues from the Praça da Saudade, the son of that bigwig in the law had raped an Indian girl—news that never got into the paper and that these morning voices retailed from door to door, until the whole city knew about them. When Rânia came in from the shop, her mother lost no time in saying: "You can go to your bungalow, I'm not budging from here."

It was at this time that Zana had her first fall and had to have her left arm and collarbone in a cast. Even so, she put Halim's clothes out on the line, placed his shoes on the floor of the veranda, his braces and stick on the gray sofa. She did this on sunny days, and in the evening took it all in again, and sat at the table, at the right of the head, where her son had his lunch. At night, she would call Domingas; I took fright and went running to the living room, to find her standing near to the oratory, her chaplet in her right hand.

Rânia could no longer bear seeing her mother living in the company of ghosts. She felt cornered at the mere thought of Rochiram's threat, and suspected that sooner or later she would have to sell the house to pay the debt. She wanted to live far away from there, and from the racket of the center of Manaus. When there was heavy rain, there was total chaos at the Escadaria harbor and in the Rua dos Barés. While I got up onto the roof to cover it with a tarpaulin, Rânia tried to save the goods in the storeroom. On the pavement, people who had just come in from upriver ate the leftovers from the Adolpho Lisboa Market. She gave them a few coins to keep away from the shop, but others came back and slept nearby. Sometimes, in the middle of a downpour, one of her old suitors came in, left his wet footmarks on the floor, and went out again, humiliated by Rânia's disdain. At night he would again knock at the front door, ask for her to come down, start up a serenade in a drunken voice, then come back next day to the store, sober, on a false errand, asking to buy the most expensive cloth, spellbound by Rânia's large eyes. Other men saw her working alone and thought it would be easy to seduce her. She let them buy, spend their money, and then smiled at the next customer. When I was in the shop, these undesirables disappeared.

Then she went, leaving the house and her room. Every morning, on her way to the Rua dos Barés, she came to visit her mother.

She said to her: "The bungalow's really pretty, mama. Yours is the most spacious room, there's a little garden for the animals, the plants, and a little veranda to put up your hammock . . ."

Now Zana and I were alone, I in the room at the back, she in the upstairs bedroom. I could read and study more at my leisure, because she had given up keeping the house in order. Visitors were few and far between, and didn't stay long, put off by sudden gestures, or by her silence. When Estelita Reinoso came into the room to crow, Zana didn't wait for her neighbor to sit down, she immediately started up: "That pushy niece of yours was always prowling around my house after my sons."

Estelita backed away with a start.

"You know who, Lívia, your sister's daughter . . . You know very well who she married . . . She hooked my son in one of those movie sessions in your basement. When he married, Yaqub was as pure as the driven snow. He married in São Paulo, in secret, far from his family, like a wild animal . . . Look what the two of them did to Omar."

Estelita's bossy voice. I opened the door for her to go, and laughed in her face, a laugh that had been waiting a long time, and as brazen as I could make it, for I knew that the Reinosos were being excluded from high society in the new order of things.

"I don't want to see anyone else," Zana said when someone knocked at the door. She only had patience with one visitor: the old matriarch Emilie, who rarely came by. When she came, Emilie listened to everything, all the complaints, and then spoke in Arabic, in a loud but calm, unassertive voice. I heard that voice: its engaging, strangely lilting sound; and I saw that woman, still strong at the end of her life: her attention focused, her words full of feeling, the proverbs that came from centuries back. I remembered Halim, and the considered words he tried to win Zana back with, right to the end, to free her from her younger son.

Little by little, Zana told me things perhaps few people knew: the name she was baptized with in Biblos was Zeina. In Brazil, when she was still a child, she learned Portuguese and changed her name. I found out more about Galib and Halim, and about my mother. Domingas changed a lot after she got pregnant. She spent hours lost in thought. "You had to see it . . . alone by herself, until Halim gently opened the door of her room and asked, 'What are you thinking about?' 'What? Me?' Your mother answered like that, startled . . . She sharpened a little knife and got hold of a piece of wood to make those animals. Halim said to me: 'That girl . . . For goodness' sake, something's happened to her . . .' What a struggle your mother was in the orphanage! She was rebellious; she wanted to go back to that village, on her river . . . How was she to grow up alone, in the back of beyond? Then Sister Damasceno offered me the little girl, and I accepted. Poor Halim! He didn't want anyone here, no one at all. Over and over he said: 'It must be tough, bringing up someone else's child, nobody's child.' When you were born, I asked: 'Now what? Are we going to put up with another nobody's child?' Halim got angry, he said that you were somebody, a son of the house . . ."

She spoke in fits and starts, and asked her own questions: "On the carpet? Did we make love on the carpet where he prayed? Thousands of times . . . Didn't you watch us, my boy?"

I shuddered when she said this. Did they see me, did they realize I was there? Perhaps it didn't bother them; perhaps they weren't ashamed. They must have laughed at me. Nobody's child! Zana forgot the rebellious Domingas and evoked the other one, maid and cook for so many years, who accompanied her at her prayers, my mother the woman.

When she went silent, I saw that the will to live into old age without her beloved son was fading. "Omar, won't he come back?" she asked as if she were begging, as if I were able to give life to her dream, before the end. She spent whole afternoons lying in her son's hammock. She grilled fish by the brazier, and kissed Omar's photograph, saying: "Why are you taking so long, my love? Why? The others have gone, now there's only us at home, only the two of us . . ." She took the hammock to his room, and in the nighttime a stifled voice filled the house with suffering. She cried so much, with her hands on her head, her face wet, and I held my breath, thinking she might die at any moment. She didn't open the windows, tell me to tidy the garden or sweep the veranda. Geckos and dead beetles covered the dusty little altar, the tiles on the front of the house were grimy, and the patron saint's image was yellowed. Five weeks like this was enough time to take the shine off the house, and give it an air of neglect.

Then, one afternoon in March (it had rained a lot and Rânia had called me to unblock a drain), a man in a cape stopped in front of the shop window, looked inside the lighted store, and came in slowly, leaving a trail of mud on the floor. It was Rochiram. His hair, plastered down and combed back, gave his face a more serious look; now he had gold-rimmed glasses on. The greenish lenses hid his eyes, and this above all made his face look different. Rânia heard the words she'd been expecting: the two brothers' debts in exchange for Zana's house. However, she was surprised when he added: "Your brother, the engineer, is in complete agreement."

A few days later, a truck parked in front of the house and its contents were loaded and moved to Rânia's bungalow. Zana put the key in the bedroom door, and from the balcony she saw the green tarpaulin covering her old familiar furniture. She saw the altar and the saint she had prayed to so often, and all the objects that had been hers, before and after her marriage to Halim. Nothing was left of the kitchen or the living room. When she came down, the house was like an abyss. She walked through the empty living room and hung Galib's photograph on the wall where the altar had left its mark. On the bare walls, lighter patches marked the place where things had once hung.

I did the shopping and Zana cooked by the brazier, as she had done when her father had the restaurant. She wandered around in a daze, and hesitated in front of the door of Domingas's room. She spent some minutes like this, and sometimes went in, lay down on the stained hammock where Omar had sprawled after his nocturnal sprees. She was waiting for a visit that never came.

Zana left before the final act. She took the hammock and all Omar's possessions, the photograph of her father and the furniture from her room. She left only Halim's clothes hanging on a rusty metal rack.

I stayed on in the house alone, with the shades of those who had lived here. Ironic, to be the absolute ruler, even for a short time, of a handsome house in the vicinity of Manaus Harbor. I was the master of the walls, the roof, the garden, and even the toilets. I thought of Yaqub, and remembered the portrait of the young officer, his proud face with its smile full of hope for the future.

She was away for more than a week: she reappeared very early one Sunday, with her left arm in a cast again. Rânia asked me to look after her mother while she went to the market. "Call one of the girls from the slum to do the cleaning and don't leave Zana on her own," she said.

I didn't call anyone; Zana didn't want strangers in the house. She went up, aired her room, got Halim's trousers and hung them on her sling. I saw her kneeling down, in the middle of Omar's room, begging God for her son to come back—praying, in a fervent ecstasy, for Omar not to die. I saw the dark edges of her lusterless eyes, lengthening into her eyebrows. Her suffering, missing Halim and Omar so much, dulled the beauty of her face. I never heard her pronounce Yaqub's name. The distant son, who had embraced a glorious destiny, had been banned from her vocabulary. Then she refused my help to come down, and said she wanted to stay on her own on the veranda, I wasn't to worry about her. I went into my room, and my attention was taken up reading a book. When I saw Rânia's face at the window, I realized Zana had disappeared. I searched the whole house, pushed the door of her room open, and finally found her in a forgotten part of the garden: the old hen coop, where Galib had fattened the birds on the menu at the Biblos. Zana was lying down on dead leaves, her body covered by Halim's clothes; the hand of the arm in the cast was already purple. I asked the neighbors' help to carry her in my hammock. She kicked, screaming: "I don't want to leave this place, Rânia . . . It's no good; I'm not going to sell my house, you ungrateful wretch . . . My son will come back." She never stopped yelling, irritated by her daughter's silence, furious at the only sentence Rânia uttered, calmly: "You'll get used to my house, Mother."

That made it worse. She tried to get away from me, almost fell from the hammock, and there was a real ruckus until we managed to get her into the car. She cried, as if she were feeling terrible pain. She never came back. She lay down in another room, far from the harbor, in a home that hadn't been built for her.

Then I heard about the internal hemorrhaging, and went to visit her one more time in a clinic near Rânia's house. She recognized me, and stared at me. Then she whispered names and words in Arabic that I knew: life, Halim, my sons, Omar. On her face, I saw the struggle, the effort to murmur a phrase in Portuguese, as if from that moment on only her maternal language would survive. But when Zana felt for my hands, she managed to stammer out: "Nael . . . dear boy . . ."

11

She died when her younger son was at large. She never saw the changes to the house; death spared her that shock, among others. The Portuguese tiles with the image of the patron saint were removed. And the dignified design of the facade, a harmony of curves and straight lines, was covered by an overblown farrago of styles. The front of the house, which had been perfectly presentable, turned into a horrific mask, and my mental image of the house was soon destroyed.

On the night of the opening of Rochiram House, a display of gadgets imported from Miami and Panama filled the windows. There was a huge party, and in the street a line of black cars disgorged politicians and military chiefs. They say that important people came from Brasília and other cities, intimates of Rochiram. I didn't see anyone from our street, not even the Reinosos. Outside, the crowd, openmouthed, watched the silhouettes lifting their glasses to each other in the shining reception rooms. Many of them stayed out in the damp night air, waiting for dawn, and grabbed the leftovers. Manaus was growing fast, and that night was one of the landmarks in the coming jamboree.

In the plans for the remodeling, the architect left a side passage, a little corridor leading to the back of the house. The area left to me, small and backing onto the slum, is this square patch in the garden.

"Your inheritance," Rânia muttered.

"Good will win out," we say: is it really true? I later found out that that was the way Yaqub wanted it; he wanted to make my life easier, just as he wanted to ruin his brother's. He'd written a letter to Zana, revealing that he had been very upset by Domingas's death; she was the only person to whom he'd confided certain secrets, the only one who'd never left his side during his childhood. There were things the two of them had in common that Zana was determined not to know. He didn't explain why the plans for the hotel had fallen through; he simply wrote that the best thing would be to sell the house and a good part of the land with it to Rochiram. If this weren't done, Omar would suffer the consequences.

The letter was addressed to the shop, and Rânia never showed it to her mother. She didn't know, and never found out if there was an agreement between Yaqub and Rochiram. She did realize that selling the house would save Omar trouble. I witnessed Rânia pressing her mother to sign the letter of sale.

"Are you mad? My house . . . to a crook? Look what he did to Omar."

"Sign it, Mama, for the good of your children . . . to avoid worse things happening. There might be worse still around the corner if you don't."

But Zana only signed in the clinic, and it must have been her last attempt to reconcile her sons.

Later Rânia found out that, on the day he'd been beaten, Yaqub was going to spend a night in the hospital in Manaus. He did go

there, but had to move his return to São Paulo up. He left for the airport at nightfall, in secret, accompanied by a doctor. This, because
in the middle of the afternoon of that same day, Omar burst into the
hospital and very nearly attacked his brother again. Yaqub shouted
when he saw Omar in the ward. He was expelled from the hospital,
dragged forcibly into the street, and was left staggering off into
the heat. He was seen going in the Cabacense bar for a swig. He
recounted his recent feats to a group of men, in a mocking, boorish
fashion. Then he disappeared. They say he went to look for Pau-
Mulato at the Escadaria harbor, and only Rânia's action saved him
from being caught. She bribed the policemen and officers, giving
them banknotes in sealed envelopes, asking them to leave Omar in
peace, free; let him escape. Cid Tannus and Talib sent letters to
Yaqub, asking him to forgive Omar, or at least forget it all. Yaqub
didn't reply to anybody. Rânia soon realized that her brother, in São
Paulo, had engaged lawyers and was coordinating Omar's persecution. There were witnesses galore; the doctors and nurses who had
prevented the aggression in the hospital; and an examination of the
corpus delicti that Yaqub underwent before his return to São Paulo.

Little by little, she discovered that her distant brother had calculated the right moment to act. Yaqub waited for his mother to die.
Then, like a panther, he pounced. It was worse for Omar when he
tried to run away. Now it wasn't his mother's claws he was trying to
escape from, but the hounding of an officer of the law. He jumped
from perch to perch, spending the night in safe houses belonging to
his drinking cronies. He knew he was in for it; there was no way out.
What had entered his head? He just abandoned his hiding place and
wandered around anywhere. Cid Tannus saw him in a bar on the top
of the Colina, where he'd often gone with Pau-Mulato. Then he
found out he'd stayed at the Pensão dos Navegantes, throwing parties for girls from upstate. Rânia began to get visits from the owners
of lodging houses and pensions; visits and threats—they badgered

her about Omar's debts, the shindigs they said he gave. He'd come back in the small hours, with a girl in tow, then the two of them raised the roof till morning and stopped the guests from sleeping. Next time, they'd call the police. He vanished from the Pensão dos Navegantes, and all his other hideouts. Rânia lost track of her brother, and thought he might be on some beach or by some lake, lying low and waiting for her to clear his name. Now he was wanted for various crimes; there were all kinds of complaints against him, because Rânia couldn't settle all her brother's debts. She knew: she had to save money for what would happen later.

Sooner or later, time and chance catch up with us all. Time had not effaced one of Laval's lines, painted on the floor of the gazebo in the Praça das Acácias. Some years later, one day early in April, a stroke of fortune linked Laval's destiny to Omar's.

I had promised to hand in to Rânia a tedious task she'd given me to do. I found the shop shut, and no one could tell me where she was. Lately, she'd been shutting at lunchtime and going out in search of her brother. That April afternoon, it was already spitting rain when Rânia caught sight of him in the Praça das Acácias. She froze. He was thin, his skin yellowish, a week's growth of beard, and his hair was frizzled, almost like a mane. His arms were full of scratches, his head swollen, full of lumps. His deep, glinting eyes gave the impression of someone adrift, even though he'd not totally lost the will or the energy to get back something he'd lost. Rânia had no time to get close to him. She heard bangs, saw people running, dropping umbrellas that bounced on the paths in the square. There were three policemen, then five, then a lot more. It was a hunt. She saw Omar crouching down behind the trunk of a *mulateiro*. The police were sniffing around, guns in hand. The shots stopped. Did they want to kill him or just give him a fright? Now it was gusty, with bursts of rain, and the Praça das Acácias was open, like a stage. They knew that Omar might react. And he did, in his own way: he laughed in the cops' face. The rifle butt he got in the face was the beginning of his entry into hell. He fell back and was pulled, dragged to the van. Rânia ran towards her brother, and saw a thick red streak running down his face, which the water couldn't erase. She argued with the police, demanded to know where they were taking him, and was brutally repulsed. In the prison, he spent some weeks incommunicado. Rânia and a lawyer tried to speak to Omar, but the violence didn't stop. She sent carrier bags of presents to the jailers, asked for news of her brother, and begged them not to torture him. Then she found out that her brother had spent some days in the military headquarters, and I guessed that his friendship with Laval was a kind of political damnation.

The morning he came into court, escorted by plainclothes police, Rânia saw she was alone. She couldn't embrace him in court, but she heard him recount a sudden descent into hell. The days were the same as the nights, and every day a darker prolongation of the night. When it rained a lot, the cells flooded, Omar dozed off on his feet; the dirty water was up to his knees, and the eels, as they rubbed against his legs, didn't frighten him, but felt loathsome. He was disgusted by the viscous skin of these freshwater fish, brown and covered in mud, wriggling on the floor of the cells when the water drained off. Just as well he couldn't see anything on dark days. Sometimes, in the small window in the wall, the frond of an assai palm moved, and he imagined the sky and its colors, the river Negro, the vast horizon, freedom, life. He put his hands over his ears; it was unbearable hearing the buzzing of the insects, the prisoners' screams—everything seemed to have no beginning or end. She couldn't imagine how her brother lived in a sordid cell of the prison she used to look at, almost without thinking, when she was crossing the metal bridges to sell sandals and clothes to the wholesalers in Manaus's most populous neighborhoods.

Omar was condemned to two years and seven months imprisonment. He couldn't leave; he had no right to conditional freedom. "Just skin and bone . . . My brother doesn't look human," Rânia said, in tears. Angrily, she said to me that she was going to write a letter to Yaqub. "He betrayed my mother, planned everything, and tricked us." She was courageous: in the solitude so essential to her, in her old maid's permanent seclusion, she wrote to Yaqub what no one had dared to say. She reminded him that vengeance is more contemptible than forgiveness. Hadn't he already had his revenge when he buried his mother's dream? He hadn't seen her die, he didn't know, he'd never know. Zana had died with her dream buried, in a nightmare of guilt. She wrote that he, Yaqub, rejected and resentful, was also the more brutish and violent of the two, and would be judged for that. She threatened to despise him forever, burn his photographs, and return the jewelry and clothes she'd been given if he didn't give up his persecution of Omar. She carried out her threats to the letter, because Yaqub calculated that silence would be more effective than a written reply.

It was at this time that I distanced myself from Rânia. I didn't want to. I liked her, I was attracted by the contrasts in a woman like her, so human and so unworldly, so ethereal and so ambitious at the same time. The memories of the night we'd spent together, the intensity of that encounter, still made me shudder. But she resented me, and was offended by my lack of concern, my contempt for her imprisoned brother. At bottom, she knew what I was brooding over, what was eating me inside. She must have known what Omar had done to my mother, and all the wrongs he had done us. I stopped working for her, I never wrote any more business letters, or rushed out to clear out the drains, pile boxes, or sell things from door to door. I moved away from the world of buying and selling, which wasn't mine and never had been.

Omar left the prison a little before the end of his sentence. He came out thanks to the small change Rânia had accumulated. Talib met him once, and said all he talked about was his mother. He cried in desperation when the widower offered to go with him to the cemetery to visit Zana's grave.

Rânia did everything to get close to him, but Omar fought shy of his sister, avoiding her and all the neighbors. For some months he could still be seen here and there, wandering around the city at night. Rânia resorted to all kinds of ruses to send him money, trying to attract him, to win him back. She dreamed of having her brother in the house; the room where her mother slept would be his.

In the letters Yaqub sent me, he never mentioned his brother or Rânia; he didn't even touch on the subject. They were short, infrequent letters, in which he always asked me to cover Halim's grave and my mother's with flowers. He asked if I needed anything, and when was I going to visit him in São Paulo? I put the visit off for more than twenty years. I had no urge to see the sea. I had already thrown away the sheets with Yaqub's architectural plans that Omar had ripped up in his fury. I was never interested in structural designs with their reinforced concrete, or in the math books Yaqub had so proudly given me. I wanted to keep my distance from all those calculations, from the engineering and the progress Yaqub aspired to. In his last letters all he talked about was the future, and even demanded to know my opinion—the future, that never-ending fallacy. I only kept one of the letters. Not even that, in fact: the photograph in which he and my mother are together, laughing, in a canoe moored near the Bar da Margem. She's nearly adolescent, he almost a child. I cut my mother's face out, and kept that precious piece of paper, the only image of Domingas's face left. I can recognize her laughter on the few occasions she laughed, and imagine her large, full eyes, lost in some place in the past.

I remembered—I still remember—the few moments when Yaqub and I were alone, and him being there in my room, when I was ill. But long before he died, five or six years ago, my desire to distance myself from the two brothers was much stronger than those memories.

The madness of Omar's passion, his excessive hostility to everything and everyone in this world, were no less harmful than Yaqub's plans: the danger and the sordid underside of his calculating ambition. My feelings of loss are only for the dead: Halim, my mother. Now I think: I am and am not Yaqub's son, and maybe he shared that doubt with me. What Halim had so fervently wanted, the two sons realized: neither of them had children. Some of our desires are only fulfilled by others, but our nightmares belong to us.

At that time, when Omar came out of prison, I saw him one more time, late one afternoon. It was our last encounter.

The downpour was so intense that the city shut its doors and windows well before nightfall. I remember I was nervous on that afternoon; the sky could hardly be seen. I had taken my first lesson in the school where I had studied, and come back here on foot, in the rain, looking at the waste being dragged down the gutters, the lepers piled on top of one another, hunched up under the *oitizeiros*. I looked, shocked and sad, at the city which was maiming itself as it grew, distancing itself from the port and the river, refusing to come to terms with its past.

A flash of lightning had caused a short circuit in Rochiram House. The Indian bazaar was pitch-black in the afternoon, darkened by heavy, low clouds. I went into my room, the same one, at the back of the old house. I'd brought with me the menagerie my mother had carved. It was all that was left of her, and of the work that had given her pleasure: the only gestures that at night gave her back the dignity she surrendered in the daytime. That's what I thought as I looked at and held these little animals and birds made of *pau-rainha*, which before only seemed to me like miniatures imitated from nature. Now I look at them and see them as strange beings.

I had begun to put Antenor Laval's writings together, for the first time, and to take notes about my conversations with Halim. I spent part of the afternoon with the words of the unpublished poet, and the voice of Zana's lover. I went back and forth between them, and alternating in this way—remembering and forgetting, like a game—gave me pleasure.

The deluge covering Manaus, a respite from the equatorial heat, brought me relief. Fruits and leaves floated in the pools surrounding the door of my room. At the back, the grass had grown, and the fence with its rotten wood, full of gaps, no longer separated me from the slum. Since Zana's departure, I had left the little that remained of the trees and climbers to the fury of the sun and the rain. Looking after all this meant submitting myself to the past, a time that was dying inside me.

It was still raining, with thunder, when Omar invaded my haven. He came slowly up to the room, just an indistinct figure. He came a little farther forward and stopped right close to the old rubber tree; the size of the tree made him look small. I couldn't see his face clearly. He lifted up his head to the crown of the tree, which covered the whole garden. Then he turned his body around, and looked back: the veranda was no longer there, and the red hammock no longer awaited him. A high, solid wall separated my little corner from Rochiram House. He ventured forward, his bare feet in the puddles; Omar, a middle-aged man—already almost old. He looked straight at me. I waited. I wanted him to admit to the dishonor, the humiliation. One word was enough, only one. Forgiveness.

Omar faltered. He looked at me, silent. He stayed that way for a time, his look piercing the rain and the window, beyond any angle or fixed point. It was the look of a man cut adrift. Then he slowly backed away, turned around, and left.

GLOSSARY

ANI (Portuguese ANUM): a bird of the cuckoo family (*Crotophaga ani*), and of similar shape to a cuckoo, with uniformly black plumage. In many parts of Brazil it is thought to be a friend and intimate of death, and thus a bad omen.

ARRACK: distilled liquor, from the Eastern Mediterranean.

ASSAI PALM: a palm tree (*Euterpe oleracea*) that grows on riverbanks, whose fruits are used to make a soft drink.

ATURIÁ: an Amazonian tree (*Machaerium lunatum*) of the Leguminosae, with long twisted branches.

BATUÍRA: common name for various species of wading birds, such as plovers and oystercatchers.

CAÇULA: a term, of African origin, for the youngest child in a family, or the younger of twins.

CACHAÇA: cheap and very strong liquor distilled from sugarcane juice.

CHORINHO: a musical ensemble consisting predominantly of wind instruments in which the flute takes the lead, popular throughout Brazil; by extension, the music they play, which is often sentimental, sometimes lively.

COPAIBA: a plant (*Copaifera officianalis*) common in the Amazon, which produces a clear oil used for medicinal purposes.

CRAJIRU: one of the most popular medicinal herbs in the Amazon area. The infusion made with its leaves is used to cure colic and stomachache. The liquid from its boiled leaves is used to treat muscle pain, swelling, and to speed the healing of wounds.

CUPUAÇU: Amazonian tree (*Theobroma grandiflorum*) whose fruit is a large velvety capsule like a cocoa bean, with a white pulp and large number of seeds. The seeds make a kind of chocolate; the pulp is used for drinks and sweets.

CURIMATÃ: the name of several species of fish of the *Prochilodus* genus, which feed in the muddy bottoms of rivers.

DARBUK: a small drum, made with single skin, common in the Middle East. In Lebanon it is also known as *durbaka*.

DOLPHIN: the white river dolphin, common in the Amazon, which has a rich existence in local folklore. It is supposed to seduce girls and carry them off to the bottom of the river. Illegitimate children are called "dolphin's children." Its eye is infallible as a love charm.

FAROFA: a dish made of manioc flour fried with pieces of egg, meat, etc. It is often used as a stuffing.

GAZAL: a kind of amorous and erotic poetry, common in Persian and Arabic, and structured in couplets. The Arabic word means a seductive dance, or swaying of the hips.

GUARANÁ: a climbing plant (*Paullinia cupana*) native to the Amazon, whose fruit is used to make a fizzy drink very popular throughout Brazil.

HELICONIA: a plant (*Heliconia rostrata*) that can be more than nine feet high, native to Amazonia, with slender stalks and long red leaves with yellow edges; much used for decoration.

INGÁ: a fruit tree (*Inga edulis*) much cultivated in Amazonia and other parts of Latin America and the Caribbean. The fruit has white, sweetish flesh and is eaten raw. It is known in the West Indies as the ice cream bean.

JACAMIM: name given to various birds of the *Psophia* family, native to the Amazon, which are large, with long legs and necks, and have a loud cry; known in English as agami or trumpeter.

JAÇANÃ: a water bird (*Jacana spinosa*) similar to rails and moorhens, with long toes that allow it to walk on floating plants.

JAMBO: a tree of Asian origin (*Eugenia jambos*) with pink fruit, known in English as rose apple.

JAMBU: a herb of the Compositae family (*Wulffia stenoglossa*) with yellow flowers. Its leaves are eaten boiled, and used to flavor rice. It is an essential ingredient of *tacacá*.

JARAQUI: a fish (*Prochilodus toeniatus*), common in the Amazon, that lives in shoals.

JATOBÁ: a tree of the Leguminosae (*Hymenaea courbaril*) found throughout much of Brazil, and exploited for its wood.

KING OF THE BELGIANS: Albert I (1875–1934), who visited Brazil in 1922, during the celebrations of the centenary of the country's independence.

MANAUS HARBOR: originally the name of the (British) company that administered the Port of Manaus; the name came to signify the whole port area of the city, with its warehouses, docks, etc.

MATRINXÃ: a medium-sized fish of the freshwater genus *Characinidae*.

MULATEIRO: another name for pau-mulato (q.v.).

MURUPI: a small, yellow pepper.

NHEENGATU: a language of indigenous, Tupi origin, though with European influence, also known as *língua geral* (general language), and much used as a lingua franca in the Brazilian past and in the Amazonian region.

OITIZEIRO: a tropical tree (*Licanea tomentosa*) of the Rosaceae family, much used in streets, parks, etc., with pale yellow flowers.

PACOVÃ: a type of banana, also called *banana comprida* (long banana) in the Amazon. It is eaten fried or roasted.

PACU: a fish of the freshwater genus *Characinidae*, similar to the piranha, but a herbivore.

PARÁ (ESSENCE OF): PATCHOULI: a herb native to India, from which an oil much used for perfume is extracted. In Amazonia, the powder made from this herb is used to fill sachets for perfuming clothes.

PAULISTA: name given to people from the state, and the city, of São Paulo, the largest in Brazil, and the center of the country's wealth and industry.

PAU-MULATO: as is said in the novel, the pau-mulato (*Calcophylum spruceanum*) is a large, handsome tree of the Rubiaceae, which also contains the coffee bush. The name also has an obscene connotation, however: *pau* is a common word for "cock."

PAU-RAINHA: a tree of the rain forest (*Centrolobium paraense*), a member of the Leguminosae, with valuable wood, streaked yellow and brownish-red.

PIASSAVA: a palm tree (*Leopoldina piassaba*) that produces a coarse fiber used for making brushes.

PIRARUCU: the largest freshwater fish (*Arapaima gigas*), which grows up to eight feet long. Its meat is highly prized, and it has a rough tongue used as a grater.

PITOMBA: the fruit of a bush of the Sapindaceae family (*Talisia esculenta*), which is small and red.

QUIBE: an Arab dish, made of raw lamb and whole wheat, seasoned with mint, etc.

RUI BARBOSA: a famous Brazilian politician (1849–1923), the first finance minister in the Republic (1889), later candidate for president (1910), who is particularly famous for representing Brazil at the peace conference at The Hague in 1907. He is known as *A águia da Haia* ("The Eagle of The Hague"), but has another reputation, for pomposity, vanity, and exaggeratedly "fine" writing.

SAPOTI: a tree (*Achras sapota*) native to the Caribbean, but cultivated all over the tropics. It produces chicle, the main ingredient in chewing gum, and a small round edible fruit, which does not keep well, known in English as sapodilla.

SAURÁ: a bird (*Phoenicircus carnifex*) of the Contingidae, found in northern Brazil, with bright red and brown plumage.

SURUBIM: a scaleless fish (*Pseudoplatystoma fasciatum*) native to the Amazon and prized for its meat.

TABULE: an Arab dish, sometimes known in English as tabbouleh. It is a salad made of roughly ground wheat, coriander, and chopped onions and tomatoes, mixed with olive oil and lemon juice.

TACACÁ: a porridge made with tapioca, flavored with *tucupi*, *jambu* (q.v.), prawns, and pepper. It is sold hot, in small gourds, in the streets of towns and cities of the Amazon region.

TAMBAQUI: a scaly fish (*Colossum bidens*) prized for its meat, which also produces an oil used for cooking and lighting.

TIPITI: a native dance, performed at the June festivals popular throughout Brazil, in honor of St. John, St. Anthony, and St. Peter.

TUCUM: a palm tree of the *Astrocaryum* family that produces fiber used for making nets and hammocks.

TUCUMA NUTS: the fruit of a palm tree (*Astrocaryum tucuma*).

TUCUNARÉ: a brownish-green scaly fish (*Cichla temensis*), much appreciated for its meat.

TUCUPI: a condiment made of pepper and manioc juice reduced over a fire to the consistency of molasses.

ZATAR: a herb (*Thymus vulgaris*) similar to oregano, much used in the Mediterranean, and known in English as garden thyme.